Swallow

Swallow

SAM SCHILL

wattpad books

wattpad books **W**

Published in Canada by Wattpad Books, a division of Wattpad Corp.
36 Wellington Street E., Toronto, ON M5E 1C7

www.wattpad.com

First Wattpad Books edition: July 2021

ISBN 978-1-98936-534-2 (Trade Paper original)
ISBN 978-1-98936-542-7 (eBook edition)

Library and Archives Canada Cataloguing in Publication information is available upon request.

Printed and bound in Canada.
1 3 5 7 9 10 8 6 4 2

Cover design by Jay Flores-Holz
Typesetting by Sarah Salomon

For my mom, Brenda

Frumpy, greasy, chubby Mildred. Zitty, dorky, ugly Mildred. Weak, slow, stupid Mildred.

Those were Mildred's foremost thoughts on a typical early morning, an entire school day ahead of her. She glared at her reflection in her floor-to-ceiling bathroom mirror. Mirror Mildred stared back at her out of sad, mud-brown eyes, the kind of brown found in swamps and backed-up toilets. The kind of brown people ignore or immediately turn away from should they realize they've looked too deeply into them. There she stood, surrounded by cold, expensive seafoam-green marble flooring and semiglossed matching walls. A troubled girl.

A broken girl.

Her day began with her mind racing through all the jabs at her appearance she'd heard throughout the years. *Unibrow.* Her eyebrows were too close together. She hadn't even known until the other students at Roanoke High told her so. They were both thick and thin in patches and met on the bridge of her nose—

two friendly neighbors not really shaking hands but reaching out. *Mouth breather*. She hadn't realized she breathed loudly and through her mouth until her classmates teased her about it. They teased her about her clothes, her hair, her shoes, her backpack, her bad gym skills, her breath—any little thing that Mildred did wrong, they let her know. Often. Once the taunts were spoken out loud, Mildred kept hearing them in her mind as they replayed on a loop—all the ugly judgments, mockery, and cruelty. All the nasty insults she was accustomed to hearing swished through her mind like a vicious tornado, leaving a relentless trail of self-loathing behind. She felt the sharp pain of each hurtful word as it pierced her ears and stung her eyes. Felt her heart break from the cruel jabs. Felt less than human—like some alien creature pretending to be human but not doing a very good job of it at all.

Pictures cluttered the edges of her mirror. She'd taped them there herself with clear tape. These were photos of girls she admired. Girls who weren't her friends—they'd *never* be her friends. Some of them she'd taken from school yearbooks, others she'd lifted from her classmates' social media, and some were famous girls from magazines. The photos were supposed to be there for motivation—a suggestion she'd read in a magazine—but the photos of beautiful people had the opposite effect on Mildred.

She stared blankly into the mirror, hating it the same way she hated those classmates—which is to say deeply, but with a desperate, nagging need to be accepted by them. For nine years, since the second grade, she'd been the outsider, the unaccepted. With the rest of junior year and senior year to go, she'd give anything for that to change. She wanted the mirror to show her someone she would be proud to be. Someone like Michelle "Chelle"

Martin, the pretty girl at school, or even Selena Gomez, who always smiled with a confidence that Mildred wished she had.

But no matter how much Mildred wished, Mirror Mildred remained that girl everybody hated, even though she couldn't exactly pinpoint why. She had never hurt *them*, but hurting *her* seemed to be their favorite hobby. Mildred hadn't teased Chelle when she'd gotten a bad haircut in sixth grade. Mildred hadn't made fun of Chelle's best friend, Yvette, when she was caught stuffing her bra in seventh grade. Mildred didn't lash out at any of them when they said horrible things to her. She felt angry at herself instead for not finding the courage to stand up to them, for feeling that somehow—deep down—it was all her fault. When she got so frustrated that she cried, it made them laugh harder. Every little thing they teased her about stuck to her as if she was the world's biggest insult magnet.

Raggedy Ann. Her dull, dark hair hung thin and stringy down to her round shoulders. Lifeless as yarn. She'd washed it the day before but it was already oily. *Crater face.* Her pockmarked cheeks poked out like those of a puffer fish, giving her eyes a slightly squinty look. She used various creams for her skin but nothing seemed to work. *Piggy.* Her round belly stretched her shirt and spilled over her pajama pants. If only she had more willpower, she told herself. Dieting had never been easy for her.

She knew if they had never told her most of these things she wouldn't see them in herself. Her hair would just be hair. Her skin would just be skin. She knew that she was bigger than most girls—she had been struggling with that issue since childhood. The other students at Roanoke High seemed to have so much more of a problem with her faults than she'd ever had. With their constant insults, she hyperfocused on their opinions about her.

All she could see in the mirror was the person they'd coaxed her into believing she was.

She decided there wasn't a single thing about herself that she liked. Not one.

She looked down at her silver bathroom scale. The digital numbers glowed back at her accusingly. Last week, the scale showed two fewer pounds, but then she ate the chocolate pie. And the cupcakes. She'd worked out extra those days. She'd worked out with her mother's old exercise videos every day this week—a task that she found extremely tiring and lame. All that work made her so hungry. There was only so much jumping around and sweating a person could take, yet she did her best. Still no improvement. All her efforts had been useless. Tears welled up in her murky brown eyes and slid down her pink cheeks. They fell *plop* onto her unicorns-and-rainbows pajama top, leaving a wet circle that grew on the fabric, getting bigger and bigger—just like her.

She stepped off the scale and kicked it across the room. It banged into the marble bathtub, then stayed still. Her toes throbbed.

"Stupid scale," she said, as if it were personally insulting her the way everyone did at school.

School or hell: it was all the same to her. She would be late if she didn't get a move-on. Mildred wondered why she even bothered to go to school sometimes. The classes were hard. The teachers didn't notice her. She had no friends. Everyone hated her. She was too quiet, too weird, too dumb—and, as if that wasn't enough, there was also the way she looked. Everything about her repelled others. The ones she didn't repel only wanted to tease her. She wouldn't even bother going to school except she knew it would be worse for her at home if she didn't go. Even on days when her parents were away on some work-related trip—which was often—they could still call with their lectures and their threats.

"If you don't want to go to school," her father would say, "maybe you'd prefer to get a job and get your own home."

"School is the most important part of your early life," her mother would say. "You'll never find success without it."

Easy for them to say, Mildred thought. *They aren't me.*

Her mother—Barbara, a slim woman who'd inherited the silky, dark hair of her great-grandmother from Japan—was a marine biologist. Mildred's father—Ben, a serious man who grew up in Texas—was an ecologist. Science was their life. Her habit of zoning out when they talked work prevented Mildred from knowing exactly what they did at their jobs, but she did know they loved them. Their jobs had brought them together: they had met while studying polar bears in the Arctic.

I just want you to find an interest in science, Mildred, Barbara often said. *It's something that's essential in life. Something solid. Scientists are important.*

Her parents just didn't understand. Mildred wasn't an important kind of person. Science was easy for them. Life was easy for them. They were smart, athletic, and attractive—everything she was not. People actually *liked* them. Sometimes, she suspected that she'd been adopted. They couldn't possibly share genetics.

How could two gifted people like them have a loser daughter like me? she wondered.

Sometimes she hated them, because she'd convinced herself that her misfortune had to be their fault somehow. They hadn't donated to enough charities or helped enough old ladies cross the street. Maybe they'd refused to sacrifice a virgin to a volcano god.

Mildred didn't know how they'd failed, but they must have done something wrong.

Today, her parents were both gracing the kitchen with their cheerful presence. Barbara stood at the stove, a white apron protecting her ironed blouse and khaki slacks. Pops and sizzles came from the pan—bacon and eggs by the smell of it. Ben sat at the head of the table, browsing the newspapers on his tablet. He wore an outfit similar to Barbara's: a white top with buttons and tan khakis, minus the apron. They both liked to dress in plain, solid colors, and everything they ever wore looked new. They greeted Mildred with smiles as she shuffled into the room wearing a faded purple sweater and old jeans that looked as if they'd been through a few hundred wringers. Mildred didn't like to smile—she hated her crooked teeth. She tried to focus on the floor tiles, counting the small gray flecks scattered on the white background as she pulled out a chair at the table and parked herself in it. Her father was to her right.

Barbara's smile faded.

"Are your clothes all dirty, dear?" she asked as she took in Mildred's outfit. "Has Naomi been skipping on your laundry?"

"No, Mom," Mildred said. "Naomi does a good job. I just like these clothes. They're comfy."

"*Comfortable*," Barbara corrected. "The word you're looking for is *comfortable*. That reminds me, Millie, did you hear about Richard?" Richard was the son of Barbara's best friend from college. "He got accepted to Yale."

Mildred couldn't see any connection between being *comfortable* and Richard going to Yale at all.

"You told me last night," Mildred said, slightly annoyed.

"You know, you can still get into a good college if you just apply yourself," her dad said, looking up from his tablet long enough to give her a quick, stern look. "You don't want to end up like Tyler Vaughn, do you?"

The Vaughns were their neighbors, and Tyler was their son. He was two years older than Mildred, and just as bad as the others who teased her, even though he was on her parents' payroll as their lawn boy. Every time he passed her he had a name for her that wasn't on her birth certificate. *Lardass. Tubby. Weirdo. Dingbat.*

"He had to settle for *community college*," Barbara said, and she cringed as if that was the worst thing a person should have to do. "Could you imagine?"

Mildred watched the wave of disgust wash over her father. He put the tablet aside as Barbara set a plate before him.

"One thing is for sure," he said. "No daughter of mine is going to be a flunky."

Mildred had known something like this was coming. She'd been through these talks before with her father. If she said anything in her own defense, he would bring up her grades. He'd bring up her extracurriculars. Her overall "lack of effort," as he saw it. She grumbled, ignoring the comment, and stared sulkily at the plate her mother placed in front of her. A small portion of eggs—all whites—a slice of bread—wheat—and a grapefruit filled only the center part of the dish. No regular eggs or bacon, like on her father's plate. No regular toast, the way she preferred, like on her mother's. Just a bit of egg whites, wheat bread, and one silly grapefruit. In fact, Mildred would bet it was the smallest grapefruit in the bunch. It wasn't a meal. Not even a proper snack, really. How was *that* supposed to hold her over until lunch hour?

"Can I have some regular eggs, toast, and bacon?" she asked.

Barbara clicked her tongue on the roof of her mouth in her disapproving way. "Millie, honey, you've got to stick to a strict diet if you ever hope to drop the weight. You'd be so pretty if you'd just—"

Mildred rolled her eyes thinking, *Here she goes again.* "I just want some normal eggs, Mom, not a chocolate-filled doughnut."

Her mother pursed her lips while she considered the request. "I don't think you should. You have the protein you need in those egg whites, and—"

"Thanks, *Mom*," Mildred said hatefully. "But I don't have time for breakfast this morning. I'm going to be late." Her chair's legs *screeeeched* heavily across the tile floor as she scooted back from the table. She could see she wouldn't get a decent breakfast here. Not under the watchful eye of Miss Perfect.

"Okay, honey," her mom called after her as Mildred slipped on her shoes and headed for the garage door off the side of the living room. "Do your best!"

Instead of walking to school, like she'd vowed to do every day since last week, Mildred got on her light-pink moped. She thought she'd save some time exercising by walking, but that was before she realized how long getting results took. There didn't seem to be much reason to waste time and energy walking if she was still going to be overweight at the end of the day, she decided. She strapped on her helmet, started the motor, and sped out of the driveway. On her way to Roanoke High School, Mildred took a short detour to Debbie's Doughnuts.

The little bakery was just opening for the day. She walked up to the brightly lit display counter and let her eyes roam over the delectable sweets inside. Debbie was talented and took pride in her displays. She baked fluffy doughnuts and coated the tops with frosting in sports team colors, flowers, hearts, emojis, and she also took requests. Round cinnamon buns glistened, stacked neatly in a pyramid. Beside them were cupcakes covered with edible glitter and rainbow icing, cookie sandwiches, and then Mildred's favorite: chocolate-filled doughnuts. Everything looked neat and smelled fresh enough to taste in the air. From experience, she knew they would taste as delicious as they looked and smelled. There wasn't a bakery around that could beat Debbie's Doughnuts.

Debbie, a cheerful woman with bright-yellow hair, was behind the counter kneading dough. When she saw Mildred, she stopped and gave the girl her full attention. "What can I get'cha today, Millie?"

Mildred ordered a chocolate-filled doughnut. It was heavenly, as always. Soft, sweet dough and fluffy chocolate filling that caressed her taste buds with bursting flavor. She chased it with rich chocolate milk. It was bad for her, she knew that, but the taste made her feel less sad inside. It made her feel like life was worth living to enjoy the flavors. As far as she was concerned, every single bite of her doughnut was worth the extra pounds and the trouble of being a little late. It was so tasty, she bought another one for the road.

2

The unrelenting screech of Patsy Porter's alarm clock flooded her ears and reverberated in her head, snapping her out of a deep sleep. Instinctively, she stretched toward the sound, but found a barrier holding her back from its shut-off button. An end to the racket was hidden somewhere beneath a strange cover of fabric.

"What the—"

Leaving things on top of her alarm clock was something Patsy would never do. It was, in fact, something she hated very much. She worked through her sleep hangover and tried to think clearly. Where did it come from? Her bedroom was so small and filled with so much that everything had a specific place to be in her room. If she couldn't file it away, it didn't belong. This thing had been left in the one place where she would be sure to notice it as soon as she woke up, which meant that someone had been in her room while she slept—a concept that gave her a twinge of the creeps. Not only because she was out cold and vulnerable but also because their presence threatened her organized personal space. There was only one person she knew who had an annoying habit of invading her personal space.

Mom.

Patsy reached beneath the barrier to stop the blaring noise, then went back to the fabric, allowing herself a moment to enjoy its smooth silkiness. It was as soft as powder in her hands—expensive material for sure. She unfolded it as she stood up. A cashmere and silk Burberry scarf spread open and her jaw dropped as she thought about the value. Those scarves didn't come cheap; they cost big bucks. There was no way anyone in the Porter house had that much money to spend on an accessory. Of course, she knew instantly that nobody had spent anything on it. Coming from Kathy Porter, it was most likely stolen.

Patsy did a once-over to check if anything needed tidying after the invasion. Nothing else in her room appeared to have been touched. Not her neat makeup vanity. Not her dresser or her closet—contents sorted neatly by size and type—and not her school things lying on the small chair by her door. Not the special little wooden box hidden behind the old photo on her top shelf. Everything, aside from the new scarf, was exactly how Patsy had left it when she had shut her eyes the night before. She clutched the delicate fabric in her hand, careful not to scrunch it.

"Mom!" Patsy shouted as she left her room.

She found her mother lying on the living room couch, wrapped tightly in a blanket. There was only one bedroom in their apartment, so the couch doubled as her mom's bed. Her thick strawberry-blond mane covered most of her finely lined, freckled face—a face that looked a lot like Patsy probably would in twenty years.

"Mom. Where did you get this?" Patsy demanded, although she already had a strong idea.

Kathy snorted as she opened her eyes. "Gift," she said. "Happy birthday."

"It's not my birthday, Mom. My birthday was in April."

"I know." Kathy sighed and sat up. "So then happy whatever. Can't you just be grateful?"

"I asked you to not bring me stuff from your employers. What happens when someone notices it missing and sees me wearing it somewhere? What then?"

"Relax. Mrs. Harding gave it to me."

"Did she really?" Patsy asked suspiciously. It still smelled of whatever perfume Mrs. Harding had doused it with. Something exotic, most likely. She had several bottles from Paris, even without counting the two that her mother's sticky fingers had slipped away undetected. Patsy studied her mother, willing a truthful answer she knew she would probably not get.

"Yep," said Kathy, who didn't seem to care she was being scrutinized. She yawned and finger combed her untamable hair away from her eyes. "I'm going to go shower. Make me an omelet?"

Patsy deflated. "Sure," she said, knowing further scolding would do no good. Her mother was set in her ways. And how had Patsy become the mother figure instead of the other way around anyway?

As she prepared ingredients for an omelet breakfast for two, Patsy couldn't help but stare at the back of the dining chair, where she'd draped the scarf, as if it were sending her messages from across the room that distracted her from the task at hand. *Look at me!* There weren't many eggs, but four was enough. Two each. The scarf was so pretty. Eggs sizzled in the pan and she rinsed the shells out so they wouldn't smell in the trash can. The way the fabric had felt: delicately soft, like a bunny. There were no fresh veggies to add to the omelet, as she would have liked—they just hadn't had enough money over the past few weeks to get fresh food. She rummaged in the cabinet and didn't find much. Some canned spinach would work. She added it to the eggs.

That scarf was luxurious. Something as upscale as that could really give her an upper hand at school. She wasn't envied there, but she wasn't invisible either. She was known to the popular group, even if she did feel out of place at times. Dating Seth, a popular football player, had put her on the map. She had tried out and made the cheerleading squad this year. Other students knew her but didn't adore her. Not like they adored head cheerleader Chelle or her best friend, Yvette, the star of the swim team.

At least they *knew* Patsy. Just the previous day, she could have sworn that Chelle had almost called her by her real name instead of Patty. The point was that Patsy—which *definitely* had an *S*— had her foot in the popular door. A ridiculously upscale article of clothing could tip her over, actually make her one of the It girls. They'd see her wearing it and think, "I need to know her." It could make Chelle—who always looked like she'd just stepped out of a runway show—want to be her friend rather than basically tolerating her because she was Seth's girl.

Patsy put the omelets on plates and set them on the table where her freshly showered mother joined her. Patsy took small bites and chewed slowly while her mother took large bites and barely chewed at all. Patsy grimaced as she watched how her mom still ate as if she was stealing food from a trash can. She had confessed to Patsy that she had been forced to eat this way often as a teenager, but that had stopped when she'd met Patsy's father.

He had taken her out of that life and then showed Kathy how to make her own way when he wasn't around anymore.

She hadn't had to steal from garbage cans in a long time. Patsy would have thought her mom would have dropped the habit by now. It mortified Patsy. While eating at school, she worried she might look like she was starving—even if she kind of was sometimes. She did her best to maintain polite control, but would it look that way to others? The worst thing anyone could do at school was eat with abandon, to eat like her mom or . . . no, Patsy wouldn't think about *her*. It bothered her to think about *her*. Mildred. When she thought about Mildred, it made Patsy feel ill and sad at the same time. And guilty.

She pictured Mildred in the cafeteria, watched and judged by everyone while she shoved food into her mouth and dropped bits on herself. It wasn't that Patsy had a problem with Mildred. She thought Mildred was nice and they'd had so much fun together when they were younger. But everyone else at school hated Mildred. They found her weird and ugly and who was Patsy to tell them to stop feeling that way? What if she tried, only to make them start feeling the same way about her?

Kathy stood up and took her empty plate to the sink.

"Better shake a leg, chickadee," she said, "if you want to get down to the Nortons' house before Seth shows up."

Last year, when Patsy started dating Seth and had expressed embarrassment at their tiny, run-down apartment, it was her mom's idea that Patsy pretend she lived in one of the upscale houses Kathy cleaned. She knew what it was like to try to fit in. Patsy thought it was a great idea and it became a routine. When Seth pulled up in his nice new truck, Patsy would be standing over there as if she'd just seen him through her window and had rushed out, but it would be a total lie. Just like letting them all believe she was rich enough to afford half the clothes she wore. The clothes were just things her mother had given her. Her eyes wandered back to the dining chair.

"Hey, if you don't want it, I'll give it back to her," Kathy teased, obviously referring to the scarf Patsy was eyeing.

A rock sank in Patsy's gut. She hated that she wanted it, but she did.

"Maybe I'll wear it to school just once," Patsy said.

For a brief moment, she wondered what would happen if Mildred dressed nicer at school. Her family had money, they could buy her the newest trends…but would it make a difference? Hadn't people already decided to not like her? If she didn't do things like pulling down group projects with her C average work. Maybe Patsy could secretly tutor her? No, they would find out. Seth would think she was cheating and she would have to confess her true whereabouts.

What am I thinking? Helping Mildred should not be one of my priorities. If Mildred doesn't help herself, it can't be my responsibility… at least that's what Patsy told herself.

She put her leftover omelet in the fridge then went back to her room to put on makeup. She changed into clean clothes and slipped on the scarf. Guilt washed through her but quickly dissipated. The scarf felt nice wrapped around her shoulders and she looked good in it. The brown and red colors matched the tones in her hair in a complementary way.

Such a sad world we live in, she thought, *where it takes beauty to get people to accept you and it takes money to make you beautiful. Where it's your wallet that makes you stand out and not your kindness.* She was looking at herself and liking everything she saw but hating it at the same time. She hated how she couldn't just be liked for being her. She had tried, and her popularity never took off before she pretended to be someone else. Patsy's only friend back then had been Mildred, and she was kind. If only other people could know the real her. She had been a good friend, but now they weren't friends anymore. Patsy watched her matte red lips draw slightly downward in the mirror.

"That was a long time ago," Patsy told her mirror self.

She shouldn't think about those days. She always felt sad when she thought about Mildred. Or saw Mildred. Or heard anyone talk about Mildred—which they liked to do often. Mildred was a joke to the very people Patsy tried so hard to impress. Maybe she tried so hard because Mildred tried so little. If Patsy could do anything in the world to save herself from the treatment Mildred suffered, she would do it. If that meant wearing stolen stuff, so be it. If that meant rushing off to a house that wasn't really hers to get picked up by her boyfriend, then so be it. If it meant skipping cheese in her omelets and counting calories, or if it meant covering her real face with makeup, she would do it. So long as they never called her the horrible things they called Mildred. Patsy didn't think she would be able to stand it if they set their cruel targets on her, so she tried her hardest to make sure they never did.

Kathy drove Patsy to the Nortons' in her old dented and scratched Camaro, which might've been cool back when Kathy was a teenager and Patsy's dad was driving her around town in it. Moments after Patsy stepped out and her mom had driven up the driveway and out of sight, Seth pulled up.

"Hey, babe," he said brightly, and then he looked at her chest and frowned. "What's that?"

"It's a scarf," she said. "Don't you like it?"

"It's covering your . . . you know."

"Well, yeah." She knew what he meant. He had a one-track mind when it came to her *you knows*. "But isn't it nice?"

He gave her a confused look and she took it to mean that he had no idea what he was looking at or what it was worth. *Others will know,* she told herself.

"I spent a lot of money on it."

"Really? Cool."

That's all it took for him to accept the strange article of clothing. He would probably wear a hot-dog suit if Patsy gave it to him and told him it was made by Gucci. She fought the urge to roll her eyes and instead smiled at the thought of him running down the football field in a hot-dog suit.

"Come on."

She climbed into the passenger seat and kissed him lightly on the cheek, leaving a cute red lip print. Smiling, she flipped down the visor to look in the mirror as usual, to make sure her lipstick wasn't smudged. As the visor came down, something fell out. It flittered toward her lap and had barely landed when he snatched it quickly and tossed it out the window before he pulled away. Patsy looked after it. For just a split second, she had seen it.

"What was that?" she asked.

"Just some trash," he said.

She didn't like the way he'd shrugged when he said it, as though he was trying to be nonchalant.

"What kind of trash?"

"I don't know, just some coupons or something that Mom gave me."

He was lying. She didn't know why exactly, but she could hear the stress behind his voice. Her first thought was that it had something to do with another girl, and if she knew anything, it was to trust your first instincts. That left her with a decision: cause a fight, maybe break up, and possibly lose the status she'd worked so hard to reach so far . . . or she could say nothing and pretend like everything was fine.

She worked up a playful tone. "You're such a litterbug," she said.

She settled with the knowledge that it was suspicion, not proof. Before truly making such a decision, she should be sure that there was proof. Though the thing she'd seen that one second looked an awful lot like the red kiss mark she'd left behind on his cheek . . . except it was in a deep maroon. She'd never cared for dark lipstick.

3

Roanoke High's parking lot was full of vehicles. Nice convertibles, sensible sedans, beaten hand-me-downs, handy trucks, sporty SUVs . . . and then there was Mildred's moped. Mildred glided past all the vehicles and took up a whole car space at the back of the lot. The one time she'd parked closer to the school, she'd come out to find her moped buried in a litter of paper scraps, candy wrappers, and other garbage. To top it off, there were even a couple of soda cans mixed in, the contents of which had been used to coat the moped beforehand. Sticky residue had lingered on the handlebars and seat for weeks before finally wearing away—she hadn't bothered to clean it, assuming they'd just do it again. She discovered that if she parked far in the back, her moped would be left alone. Most people wouldn't bother walking past their own vehicles in order to litter hers before they left the lot.

Mildred stuffed her helmet and keys into her backpack, careful not to drop her remaining doughnut. She scarfed down the rest of her unhealthy breakfast without feeling any guilt at all;

in fact, consuming the sweet treat somehow made her day a little brighter. Once she was finished, she slowly made her way up the steps and into the school, breathing heavily. A pair of girls walked by her, giggling to themselves as if she wasn't there. Most students had already rushed off to their first class, leaving behind an echoing silence that made Mildred painfully aware of how late she was.

Rows of lockers lined the hallways of Roanoke High, but Mildred's was the easiest to find. It was the one covered in words like *dumb bitch*, *fat ass*, and *loser*. Permanent marker, ink, scrapes made with keys, lipstick—anything her peers could find for their spiteful scrawls—all joined to form a collaboration of broken words that spoke one clear message: Nobody likes you, Mildred.

Her hand shook slightly as she dialed the combination on her lock. She messed up on the second number, passing it just a little too far, and had to start over. Staring at the locker made her even more depressed than she felt when she woke up this morning, so she tried hard to concentrate on opening the lock. The words were hidden from her as she retrieved her books and deposited her bag but met her again head-on after she closed the door. They stung her anew, those unkind slurs. Twisting black ink or harsh grooves in the paint, they all packed the same punch. At some point in the day she knew the janitor would scrub her locker and repaint it. She rarely saw it in its freshened state, however. By the time she returned, it would already bear at least one or two new graffitied insults. She expected it, so it was never a surprise, but it always hurt.

Ø

The door to the biology classroom was open when Mildred got there. It always remained wide open until Mrs. Kline entered and shut it. Class hadn't started yet. Mildred let out a sigh at her good fortune. Promptly, one of her books slipped out of her arms, reminding her that any luck wouldn't stick around long for anyone named Mildred Waco. She retrieved the tenth edition of *Biological Science for the Classroom* with sticky doughnut fingers, hating having to bend over because her tummy got in the way and pressure squeezed at her lungs.

As soon as she stepped inside biology class, she was met with collective groans. It was as though she'd ruined everyone's fun simply by being present. Suddenly, Mrs. Kline's absence made Mildred nervous. The last time she'd been in a teacherless class, some jerk had thrown his textbook square into her back. With nobody in charge to see, he had claimed it was an accident and nothing was done about it. The memory gave her half a mind to turn back and wait in the hall for the teacher, but then she'd look very silly having to come back in when Mrs. Kline returned. It would only give them more ammo. They'd call her a coward and a suck-up.

She put her head down and scurried to the only empty desk in the room, which happened to be a special seat for Mildred. Since she was too wide to fit in the regular seats, where the chair was connected to the desktop, the school had arranged for an alternative in all her classes. These desks were as old as the school and reeked of aged wood and the school basement, where they'd carted them up from once they realized she wouldn't fit in the nicer, new desks like everyone else.

"Ugh," someone grumbled as she passed. "That smell!"

She passed quickly but wondered, *Do I really smell?*

A few others rode on the coattails of that first comment as she moved along by saying things like "Eww," and "It smells like garbage."

She tried to pick up anything unpleasant in the air around her and only detected fresh paper, and something that could've either been someone's soap or a lemon-scented cleaning product.

Mildred took the seat at her special desk, right in front of Chelle Martin—one of the very faces that lined Mildred's mirror. Chelle was too beautiful for her own good—the kind of beautiful that allowed a person to breeze through life. A girl so pretty that if she sat very still, one might mistake her for a mannequin in a high-fashion shop. Arched eyebrows, skin as smooth as silk, and a voice like wind chimes tinkling in a light breeze. That was Chelle. Perpetually having a good hair and makeup day and looking as though a group of stylists was always at her beck and call. Today she was wearing a powder-pink top that hugged her bosom and waist.

Mildred didn't know anything at all about high fashion, but sometimes she heard Chelle bragging about her clothes. Mildred had seen this shirt before. The shirt was a new design, sent to Chelle from her uncle in New York, who was a celebrated fashion designer. It wasn't even due to be released to the general public for another month. Mildred looked down at her own faded purple top. Old. Worn-out. Why hadn't she worn something better? Because it was the first thing she saw on her shelf and it was comfortable. Besides, she didn't know what was in and what was out. When she tried wearing something her mother bought, she always felt gawdy in it. It made her feel out of place, like seeing a clown without their makeup.

If I could do makeup, maybe nicer clothes wouldn't look so awkward on me, Mildred reflected.

As she stole a sheepish glimpse at Chelle, Mildred became painfully aware of how large she was in comparison. Suddenly, she regretted the doughnut, as if that one treat had instantly added twenty pounds to her.

"Gross, Moldred. Did you even brush your hair?" Chelle teased, her narrow nose scrunched up in disgust. Her own neat waves touched her shoulders in shiny shades ranging from sepia to copper, with the slightest hint of wheat.

Mildred stared at Chelle's waves and didn't reply. Even if Mildred had wanted to, the words would have refused to slip through her timid lips. Her face heated beneath the harsh scrutiny of the students in the class, who were now all staring at her. She *had* brushed her hair at home, but not after she had taken off her helmet. Her hair was probably tangled and sticking up everywhere now—maybe even a little sweaty from being cushioned tight to her scalp for the entire ride to school.

I really ought to bring a brush and leave it in my locker like the other girls, she thought sadly. *Why can't I even remember a stupid brush?*

"Of course she didn't, Chelle," Aaron Renfro said loudly from the seat beside the small-town fashion model. "Disgusting pigs don't brush their hair or take showers, they just laze around, getting fatter and dumber. Do you even know how to use a hairbrush, Piggy?"

The rest of the class howled. Laughing with Aaron was habitual for all of them. Even on the rare occasion that he said something dull, his audience would still erupt in a loud roar. Aaron was a funny, cool guy according to everyone else at Roanoke High. Mildred would also like to think he was entertaining, but most of the time, her self-esteem was battered at the expense of his jokes. For the others, laughing with him was better than becoming part of his material. Mildred had no reason to put on a facade, because she was already the star subject of his comedy routine. Once he named her Piggy, that was it. And when he suggested she was obsessed with him because of the way he made her skin flush, there was no going back. Never mind that Mildred flushed because she was embarrassed rather than flattered. Forget that. What he said was comedy gold to everyone else—no reason to let facts get in the way of a great joke.

The class chortled around Mildred while she shrank as small as she could at her desk, which only created an awkward effect in her mind. She pictured herself looking the way an elephant might look cowering away from a classroom of mice. Mortified, she kept her head down to hide her beet-red face.

"You forgot uglier," added Chelle, taking the opportunity to ride on Aaron's coattails.

Why do they do it? Mildred wondered. They'd already made her see how ugly and frumpy and fat she was, but she couldn't understand why they felt the need to laugh and poke fun at her because of it. She had tried working on those things, but their never-ceasing insults had made her feel like there was no point. Surely whatever she did wouldn't end the torment, they'd just find different things to tease her about. Her chest tightened as the laughter stung her eardrums.

"Did you see the lazy way she slouched in here?" Aaron asked. He got up and did a slumped, sloth-like impression of her.

Mrs. Kline walked in then, catching everyone in the swing of another round of laughter. She clapped the door shut with a loud snap and their voices caught.

"Enough, class," she said in a frustrated voice.

The class straightened in their seats obediently. *Nothing happening here,* their faces said, but Mrs. Kline knew different. She zeroed in on Mildred knowingly.

"Please see me after class, Ms. Waco," she said.

Hunched down in her chair, face pink and sweaty, Mildred nodded. She wished she could just *poof* out of existence, but of course she couldn't. The kids spitting soggy wads of paper in her hair kept reminding her she was visible. She was there, and she was an easy target. All through class, Mildred felt the soggy little pellets showering her but she didn't react to them. Reacting, she'd figured out early on, made the abuse worse.

✺

Mildred read the long-faced look her teacher gave her once the class had cleared. Mrs. Kline was disappointed, a sad kind of angry look. The kind you give puppies when they've done something bad. Mildred suddenly started to panic. She had been so worried about seeing Mrs. Kline after class, she couldn't remember a single thing about the lesson. What if Mrs. Kline quizzed her? Mildred swallowed hard and her chin began to tremble.

"Oh, Mildred," Mrs. Kline said, then she stopped a few seconds to gather her words. "Mildred, I worry about you." She snatched a tissue from her desk and trotted over to Mildred, extending it to her. Mildred stared at it.

"Are you . . . going to make me cry?" she asked suspiciously, without taking it.

"No, I'm going to tell you that you should stand up to them. Don't sit there and let them make a joke out of you."

"But how? There are so many of them . . . and only one of me."

"It doesn't matter how many there are, don't worry about that. When you stand up, most of them will back down. They'll get bored of it when they can't get a rise out of you."

Mildred had heard it all before and knew it just wasn't true. When she'd seen that advice on television two years ago and tried it, she wound up getting beat up by a group of girls during gym class. The ghosts of the bruises still haunted her. The one on her cheek hadn't gone away for weeks. The one on her knee went so deep the doctors called it a bruised bone. She couldn't remember who dealt the blows—her eyes had been shut for most of it—but she recalled the pain vividly. She wondered if Mrs. Kline was trying to get her to make a mistake. Did she *want* to see Mildred get beat up? All broken and bruised?

"Also, you have chocolate right there." Mrs. Kline pointed to the side of Mildred's mouth. "You may want to take care of that before going to your next class."

Mildred snatched the tissue and first wiped, then scrubbed like she was trying her best to erase her face. The chocolate was gone, replaced with red, irritated skin. She felt embarrassment and hatred bubble up. Mrs. Kline watched them pick on Mildred every day and never punished them. Now Mrs. Kline was trying to push it further. She wanted Mildred to fight back. Put herself in more danger. Even worse, she had let Mildred sit through an entire class knowing chocolate was on her face. *Mrs. Kline is no different than they are: cruel and always ready to make a joke out of me,* Mildred thought.

"Did you wash your face this morning?" Mrs. Kline asked. "Are you able to? Is everything okay at home?"

Mildred wasn't listening properly. The first part of Mrs. Kline's sentence was so similar to something Chelle or Aaron might say that it was all Mildred could hear. *Piggy,* her mind taunted in Aaron's voice. *You like chocolate, don't you, Piggy?* His voice morphed into Mrs. Kline's. *Mildred the piggy. Look at her fat, chocolate-covered face, everyone!*

Mildred dropped the tissue and took off out of the room, almost knocking the bulky desk over with her haste.

"Mildred! Please," Mrs. Kline said, but Mildred didn't listen.

She was already down the hallway, running in a slow and awkward wobble. Students roared with laughter in the hallway at the sight of her. Her awkward run to escape them actually brought more attention to her, and of course they jumped on her, the way a hungry mountain lion attacks the helpless antelope calf that is too slow to keep up with its herd.

"Hey shitface, did you eat shit for breakfast this morning?" said Seth Montgomery, a burly jock.

His much smaller girlfriend, Patsy, stood beside him.

Mildred knew Patsy. Once upon a time, in grade school, they'd been inseparable. Patsy's mother worked for Mildred's family as a housekeeper then. Patsy used to come along while Mrs. Porter completed her twice-weekly cleaning routine, much like Naomi currently did. The girls had become fast friends.

Ø

"Let's play pretend," young Patsy said. "I'll be Hello Kitty, you be Mimmy."

Patsy was covered in freckles and had bushy dark-red hair.

"Hello Kitty's best friend?" said young Mildred, a chubby child whose shirt was always rolling up to show her belly.

"Yeah, silly, because you're my best friend." Patsy hugged her and Mildred felt loved. Happy.

"You're my best friend too!"

Patsy had always been willing to overlook a lot of things that held other kids at bay: Mildred's awkwardness, her slowness, her overall undesirableness. She would play dress-up with Mildred and not care about sharing the same lipstick. It was a true friendship.

Mildred's mom was so relieved that Mildred had made a friend, any friend, that she had been willing to overlook the disappearance of expensive items in their home. She had ignored the fact that it always happened when Patsy's mother was on the clock. Until she couldn't ignore it anymore.

"I'm sorry, but the loss is just too great," Mrs. Waco said.

"But, Mommy, Patsy wouldn't ever," young Mildred protested.

"I know she's your friend, Millie, but . . ." She sighed. "It was great-grandma's pearl and diamond necklace. It was the only thing she brought with her from Japan and it was very expensive."

"But maybe if we just tell them how important it is, they'll give it back."

Mrs. Waco tsked and dialed Mrs. Porter on the phone.

"They only borrowed it, I'm sure. Just ask, Mommy."

Ø

Mrs. Waco had not asked. She fired Patsy's mother and, for good measure, banned Patsy from the property as well, not knowing whose sticky fingers had taken the necklace.

Losing Mildred's friendship didn't seem to stifle Patsy. Before Mildred's eyes, Patsy opened like a butterfly fresh from its cocoon. By the time they reached high school, her features that were once out of style—her thick eyebrows and face scattered with freckles—became trendy and even desirable, while Mildred stayed her same old self. Patsy gained more friends while Mildred still had none. Patsy's weekend schedules were, in Mildred's assumption, no doubt full of exciting and fun high school things that Mildred would never experience. Maybe if she had stayed friends with Patsy, Mildred often thought, she would have grown popular with her by association. She would have gone to the cool parties. She would have talked to people who didn't judge her for how she looked but gave her a chance because she was Patsy's friend.

But she wasn't Patsy's friend.

∅

"Mrs. Porter?" Mrs. Waco said into the phone. "Yes, I'm sorry, but we won't be needing your services anymore."

"Mommy, no!" Mildred wailed.

"We know about the necklace. And . . . I'm afraid Mildred can't be friends with Patsy anymore either."

Hearing the words left Mildred hollow. Alone. She felt the cold surface of the table as she buried her head in her arms on top of it, wanting to melt into it and become an object, incapable of feeling this new horrible feeling of loneliness.

At school, Mildred hoped that they could still be friends, but when she tried to talk to Patsy, Patsy said, "My mommy and your mommy said we can't be friends anymore."

And that was that.

∅

Back in the halls of Roanoke High, freckled and popular Patsy smacked Seth's bulky arm and said, "Stop it."

Mildred wobbled along, trying to ignore her, and almost tripped over her own feet but caught herself on the wall and kept going.

"Run all the way home, loser, nobody wants you here," said a girl named Sarah. She wasn't *that* popular, but some people giggled anyway, because they hated Mildred.

"Ogre!" Aaron shouted excitedly when he saw Mildred dashing down the hallway. "Quick! Everybody hide! It's on a rampage. It could crush anyone it catches in its path!" Everyone nearby burst into hysterics, as though it was the most hilarious thing they'd ever heard. Aaron had hit a new high with them, but Mildred's eyes stung.

Inside the bathroom, Mildred was alone. Lockers opened and shut outside as the last of the students scampered here or there, shouted at friends, and laughed, while Mildred sat on the toilet and sobbed loudly into a generous wad of toilet paper. Her sobs were so violent she didn't hear the restroom door swing open.

"What the hell?" Yvette Darling said. "Who's blubbering in there?"

"Moldy Mildred," Chelle replied, saying her name as though it tasted bad. "She ran in here earlier—oh my God, she's so loud!"

"What a loser. Can't even make it to second period without pulling this crap. Shut up already!" Yvette shouted, then she grumbled. "How's a girl supposed to touch up her makeup with this racket going on?"

"I know, right?" Chelle agreed. "It's like she thinks she'll get sympathy or something."

"Yeah, like that'll happen," Yvette said. "Why should we care about Moldred's fat ass, she obviously doesn't care about it."

The girls banged on the side of the stall Mildred was in. It startled her but she didn't dare say anything back to them. She sat on the toilet seat with her pants on and tried to muffle her sobs, but found it difficult.

"Oh, I see the problem," said Yvette.

To Mildred's surprise, Yvette's hands shot out from beneath the stall next to hers and came straight at her. She snatched one of Mildred's shoes in each of her hands and easily slipped them off her feet before Mildred even knew what was happening.

"She's wearing these old things," Yvette said.

"*So* five seasons ago," Chelle said. "And so . . . what's the word? Dry?"

Mildred heard a heavy splash and her heart dropped as surely as the shoe that had just hit the inside of the toilet bowl.

"That should do it," Chelle said in a happy voice that made Mildred's stomach sick.

"Gotta make them match."

Plop. Mildred groaned.

"Seriously, like, go home and cry, you're just making us hate you more by sticking around," Chelle said.

The bell rang.

Mildred felt something large and sloppy smack her head, then heard it splat to the floor, followed by another. The girls giggled while they washed their hands. Their good cheer at Mildred's expense followed them all the way out of the restroom, leaving Mildred in silence.

They're so mean, she thought. *They're all so cruel.*

She leaned against the cold restroom wall and wished she could be anyone else. Two more classes, then lunch, and three more. It felt like an eternity of torture laid out before her.

Wouldn't it be nice if she could melt away and mold what was left into a new person? One they wouldn't recognize? They wouldn't know they hated her. Her mind was compressed with the pain of rejection from her peers. She wondered why her, but then she realized why not? Wasn't she fat? Wasn't she ugly? Her skin wasn't clear, her mind wasn't sharp. She couldn't think of comebacks or stand up for herself at all. She was so pathetic she was sitting in the nasty bathroom crying her heart out instead of doing something to improve her situation. Then it struck her: she *should* do something.

Mildred had had enough. She wiped the tears from her round face. No more crying. It was time for her to take a stand. Time to take control of her life. Time to change things.

4

Mr. Turner had certificates and degrees hanging on the baby-blue wall behind his desk. They all pertained to psychology and counseling and looked very official to Mildred. Beside them hung a poster displaying a big, cartoonish turkey, who was Tom, the school's mascot. Mr. Turner's office was neat, except for his desk, which was littered with books, notes, school flyers, and even a small red and brown flag that said Go Turkeys!

"What brings you by, Mildred?" Mr. Turner asked. "Have you thought more about the extra credit we talked about, to bring your grades up?"

He liked to follow trends. Up until a few weeks ago, he'd worn thick-rimmed black glasses, but he'd recently traded them in for a brand-new beard—an inch-long and neatly trimmed fluff of chestnut brown, like the hair on his arms, which showed because he'd rolled up the sleeves of his seersucker shirt. Paired with his bald head, the beard balanced him out.

"I—well, no," she said.

Now that she was ready to talk to someone about what was going on, she found it hard to form into words exactly what the problem was. Opening with something like "They all hate me," might sound a little too dramatic, but on the other hand, something like "I feel a little unliked," was seriously understating the situation. She hadn't thoroughly thought this through before coming and now she was starting to lose her nerve.

"Shall we start with why your shoes are wet?" he asked.

Mildred looked down at her soggy feet and wiggled her toes, feeling the swampy cushioning inside.

"I want you to know that it's nothing to be ashamed of," he said. "Many kids need items from the charity bin. There's no need to come up with elaborate plans, like spilling drinks on yourself or conveniently losing a jacket so you can dive into the bin to get a new one."

Mildred gave Mr. Turner a blank stare. It took a moment to grasp the meaning behind his words, but she followed his hand gesture to the corner of the room where a big plastic bin sat. On the wall above it were the words CHARITY BIN. Jacket sleeves and jean legs hung over the top.

"No, I didn't do this myself," she said. "I'm here because I'm being bullied."

Mr. Turner studied Mildred. She couldn't read his expression. Sometimes, that sort of thing was difficult for her. Kind faces could seem judgmental, and resting faces could seem displeased. Some faces were more difficult to read than others. Mr. Turner had the sort of face that showed more expressions than one at the same time, and Mildred was at a loss.

"That is disappointing to hear," he said.

He shoved some papers around on his desk, revealing a candy dish full of candies wrapped in shiny yellow plastic.

"Care for a caramel?" he asked. "They're soft and chewy, my favorite."

The offer took Mildred by surprise, but she reached forward and grabbed four. She liked soft caramels. She popped one in her mouth and chewed, savoring the creamy sweetness.

"I know bullying is a huge problem, Mildred," he said. "The worst part is that it's almost impossible to control what others do when we aren't looking, and we can't always look. Are you following?"

Mildred nodded. The caramel was very sticky. She worked her jaw and her tongue to get it out of a back molar where it had buried itself.

"Because of that, it may seem that bullies have all the power," he continued. "But they really don't have the power, Mildred."

"They don't?" Mildred asked as she opened another caramel and stuffed it in.

"Nope. Because we can control ourselves and that's something they can't take away."

Yes, they can take it away. They have. That's what Mildred wanted to say, but the fresh caramel seemed even chewier than the last and by the time she readied herself to speak up, Mr. Turner was continuing.

"Take an egg, for instance. Its existence is all about what's on the inside. If I drop an egg, it will break and spill all the contents, because they're liquid. But if the egg is hard boiled before I drop it, it will only crack. Do you follow me?"

Mildred did not follow, but she was trying.

"What I'm saying is, if you don't let them get to you, they can't hurt you. When they figure out that they can't break you, they will give up."

"I don't think they will."

"They will. The fun of it for them is seeing someone feel bad, but when you show them that it's not easy, they get tired of it. It becomes work. Trust me, Mildred, they'll stop. I've been through this many times before, with many students."

But those students weren't me, and they weren't as ugly or slow or fat or disliked. Again, Mildred didn't say any of that, because she was chewing a new caramel. They were very tasty, and she just couldn't seem to stop. She worked on swallowing, then she started to speak, but the door burst inward before the first syllable of her rebuttal passed her sticky lips.

The art teacher, Miss Morgan, poked her blond head through the doorway.

"Sorry to interrupt, Michael—erm . . . Mr. Turner—but Effie Hinkle is having *another of her episodes*. Please, come quick."

"Right away," he said.

She dashed away without shutting the door behind her.

"I've got to run, Mildred, I'm sure you understand. Please feel free to come see me anytime. Take as many caramels as you'd like before you leave."

He hightailed it out of there as fast as Miss Morgan had. Mildred didn't know exactly what sort of *episodes* Effie Hinkle had, but she guessed they were serious. More serious than her bullying problem, or so they assumed. They didn't know what it was like to be Mildred. If they did, maybe they would think her case was more urgent.

Mildred sighed and took another handful of caramels from the dish before she left his office. There were other people that could help in this school. The posters in the hallways said to tell a teacher, counselor, or your principal.

Ø

The bench in the school lobby was hard, bare wood. Mildred, having finished all her caramels, was sitting quietly near the wall, in clear view of the school secretary, Mr. Lawrence. She wiggled, trying to even out her weight so the seat wouldn't be so uncomfortable. The bench groaned beneath her. Mr. Lawrence was glancing awkwardly between Mildred and the intercom on his desk. At any moment, Miss Spade, the principal, would beep through to let him know if Mildred could come in for a private conference.

Mr. Lawrence wore a collared, button-up shirt and thick glasses. His hair was short and already receding, even though he couldn't have been older than his early thirties. He was much younger than Roanoke's last secretary—a nice old woman who had retired the previous year. Awkward Mr. Lawrence was a nervous wreck most days and didn't know what he was doing behind the desk half the time. He seemed afraid of his own shadow in this environment—as afraid as Mildred felt in this school. She thought of her future self as she watched him wrestle with a stapler he was trying unsuccessfully to reload. Would she ever learn to not be afraid or was she doomed to be this frightened version of herself her whole life?

"These things can be very tricky," he said.

Mildred nodded shyly, then reminded herself of her goal. She straightened up on the stiff bench. She wouldn't be afraid anymore after today. She was sure of it. This was it. After years of bullying, she was finally going to tell the principal and demand that some sort of action be taken. She hadn't done a great job of trying to convey everything to Mr. Turner, but she had been distracted. This time, she meant business. Adrenaline pumped through her, making knots twist and turn in her stomach. This was a big step. Would they give the bullies detention? No, that was too good for them. Suspension?

The speaker crackled. "Send her in," Miss Spade's voice said.

Mr. Lawrence sprang nearly a foot out of his chair at the sound of Miss Spade's disembodied voice. The stapler flew out of his hands and smacked him in the face. His glasses bounced on his long, pointed nose. When they came back down, one of the lenses rested on his cheek and the other on his eyebrow. Adjusting his glasses, he waved Mildred along.

Middle aged and slightly pudgy, Miss Spade grinned as Mildred stepped timidly into her doorway. A smile from Miss Spade always seemed devoid of warmth, even with the fiery color she'd painted on her lips. Somehow, she had managed to find a red lipstick the exact shade of her bottle-red hair, which was short and curled close to her head. She held a bulky black desk phone to her ear and nodded Mildred toward a soft, cushioned chair, much different than the bench out in the lobby area. Perhaps it meant that Mildred should feel more at ease in the room, but she didn't. She plopped her bottom in it all the same, her heart pounding in her ears.

"Yes, yes. I'll be sure to look into it," Miss Spade said into the receiver. "Yes, I will get back to you."

She hung up the phone on her desk and crossed her hands, letting them rest on top of some papers in front of her. Her lips remained in a tight scarlet line, her eyes boring into Mildred as she held an expression full of faux patience. Mildred could read the frustration simmering below the surface of the principal's weak facade.

Maybe she's having a bad day, thought Mildred. There were a million things that phone call could have been about. She was picturing a hateful voice on the other line, demanding that Miss Spade get to the bottom of something serious within the school like a sex scandal, or whatever kind of mischief the popular group got up to. Things that had the potential to be much more important than Mildred's issues. Her resolve faltered a bit, fizzling at the sight of Miss Spade's surly expression. Mildred suddenly felt very much like an intruder. She began to wonder if now was a good time.

"What's this problem I hear about, Mildred?" she said in the kind of voice that said, I'm much too busy to tackle extra things right now.

Mildred took a deep breath. Now was as good a time as any.

"Well, things are getting bad with . . . with some of the other students. They . . . they pick on me," Mildred worked out. Expectantly, she stared at the principal.

Miss Spade studied Mildred. "I see," she said cautiously. "You know, high school can be a difficult place for kids your age. Not everyone will be nice. Not everyone out there in the world is nice, Mildred. I wish they were, but that's just not how the world works. High school gets you ready for that world, you see?"

Mildred was silent, her mouth hanging open. This was not going how she'd hoped. This was starting off even worse than it had in Mr. Turner's office. Where was the outrage? Where was the support? These students were making her life a living hell, and it felt like nobody cared.

Miss Spade continued. "When I was in high school, do you know what they called me?"

Mildred shook her head.

"Well, that's not important," Miss Spade said quickly with a slight shake of her head, as if shaking out a bad memory that she wanted to forget. "What's important is I overcame it. Those kids, they can't hurt you forever. In the meantime, try something new. Shower more. Ask your parents for some new clothes. Apply the effort to fit in, Mildred. It could change your entire high school experience."

Mildred was confused. "But all those posters out there in the hallways, they don't say to fit in, they say to tell someone, to . . . to do something about it—"

Miss Spade waved her hand through the air as if she was swatting Mildred's statement away. "The school board makes us hang those." Clearly, from her light tone and carelessness, she thought the posters were silly and useless. "Bullies are the backbone of high school. They teach us to be stronger, better people. You've got to learn how to stand tall and deal with them. You've got to be tougher, Mildred. One of these days, you'll learn how to handle all of this and will be stronger because of it. You may even thank them."

Mildred couldn't think of a single reason to ever thank the people who put her in this situation. This was so wrong. She expected support. She expected the adults to be on her side, but it seemed like they were going to allow this to continue.

"Why can't you just force them to leave me alone? Tell them they will be suspended or . . . or I don't know. Tell them something that will make them stop," Mildred pleaded.

"And then?" asked Miss Spade, her eyebrows raised high into her bangs. "Should I follow you around your whole life, threatening anybody you feel is being mean to you?"

"No," Mildred sputtered. "Just do it here, where you're in charge."

"That's right, I'm in charge, and the only student I've seen complaining about bullies is you, Mildred. You expect me to threaten my students because of one complaint from one student?"

"I expect you to do *something*!" Mildred shouted, then she caught herself and snapped her lips shut tight.

"That's it. This discussion is over. One more outburst from you and it will be *you* who is suspended. You may return to class now."

The very idea that she should be the one in trouble rather than those who were hurting her was so absurd, she couldn't think of a retort to Miss Spade. One thing was clear to Mildred: Miss Spade did not understand and was not willing to help. Dumbfounded and downtrodden, Mildred burst out of the office. Tears came back, but these were of anger rather than embarrassment. How could the principal say those things? It was the biggest crock of bull that Mildred had ever heard. Something needed to be done, but the counselor and principal were both completely useless. She would have to find another approach.

The third-period bell rang. She had half a mind to leave without finishing out the day, but that would only cause her difficulties at home. She went to her locker, which now had some new scribbles. Someone had drawn a figure with a big, round circle for the body, short sticks for the arms and legs, and a pig nose on its round face. This figure—no doubt meant to be her—was hanging from a noose.

"Do you like my artwork, Piggy?" Aaron said, so close to her that she jumped. He ignored her and kept on. "I thought you might appreciate it."

"Wow, Aaron," said Chelle. "The resemblance is uncanny."

"Stop it!" Mildred shouted. All chatter and clatter around them stopped. "Why do you treat me this way? What have I done to any of you?" She looked now, not only at Aaron and Chelle, but at the students all around, like a pack of wolves closing in on prey.

"You're sickening," someone shouted.

Then they all started shouting and the words ran together. *StupidloseryousmelllikeshitIhateyougodie.*

Words like knives, sending stab after stab into her soft exterior. The only thing she could do to protect herself was run, while they chortled and shouted behind her.

5

Patsy felt guilty. She didn't say those harsh things to Mildred in the hall-way, but she stood there among all those laughing faces while Mildred ran away in tears. She had looked right at Patsy for a whole second and that memory now left a dull ache inside her chest.

"Patty!"

Patsy startled and focused on Chelle, who'd just called her by the wrong name. The gym bleachers spanned wall to wall behind Chelle, who was standing with her hands on her hips, elbows out, the Roanoke Turkey proudly displayed on her gym top. It was the same head cheerleader stance she used on the field as they performed in front of a crowd, except she wasn't smiling. She was glaring at Patsy with impatience.

"I've been calling you for forever!" Chelle complained—which wasn't true, because they'd only started third-period gym.

Well, if you used the right name . . . Patsy thought.

"What is wrong with you? You've been spacing out all day!" Chelle said.

"Totes spacey," Donna Anderson said as she came up to Chelle's side.

Being one of the shorter girls on the cheer squad, Donna's head came up to Chelle's shoulders. Her extremely long, dark hair was loose, trailing down her back like a grim reaper's robe.

This was Donna's first year on the squad, one of their freshman intakes. She was a horrible cheerleader. Loud but forgetful, she sometimes shouted the wrong words over all the other girls, but she came along with Joan Renfro. Joan stood at Chelle's other shoulder, her long hair as blond as Donna's was black. Patsy thought of them as the yin-yang twins, because they always stuck together, one dark as a raven, the other light as a dove.

As Aaron's younger sister, Joan had been an automatic addition to the squad, but besides that, she was exceptionally good. Good enough to probably earn scholarships—unlike Patsy, who didn't have any scholarship offers and couldn't afford to go to college. That thought plagued her daily. What would she do when the others started talking about college plans? Patsy could never tell the other girls the truth.

"Sorry, I was just . . ." Her mind stumbled around for something vapid to say. "Thinking about what I should wear on my date with Seth tonight."

"Oh! The blue skirt, you know the one, and the white long-sleeved crop top. Definitely not that cheap Burberry knock-off you wore earlier. That thing was so ugh," Chelle said, then she readopted captain cheerleader mode. "Donna, stay up here with me. Patty, you take Donna's place near the back until you decide you're ready to stop spacing out."

The insult followed by the idea of being replaced by Donna jolted Patsy.

"I'm sorry, Chelle, really," she said. "I can focus."

Chelle kept her eyes on Patsy, but held her palm up at Donna, stopping her in her tracks.

"You better, because I can't have this kind of thing happening at the game. You'll make us all look like losers."

"I would never," promised Patsy.

Chelle waved Donna back and they took position once more. This time, Patsy tried hard to focus on the cheer and do all the right moves. *High V, daggers, clasp, low V, daggers, clasp, broken T, T, hip swing, head nod, make sure you're smiling as if all of this isn't just a vexatious attempt to try to fit in with people you don't even really like.* Patsy went into a left lunge with a left bow and arrow position, but her left foot entangled with Paige Carpenter's. Paige tried to dodge Patsy's fist as it came close to her face in the bow and arrow. Both girls lost their footing and went down.

"Ouch, Patty," Paige said. "What the hell?"

"Sorry, sorry! Are you hurt?" Patsy stood up quickly and tried to help Paige to her feet.

"Stop, just don't touch me," Paige grumbled, cradling her ankle.

"I just . . . I'm sorry. I—"

"Are you good, Paige?" Chelle asked, but she didn't move forward to help the girl on the floor. The words were the right ones, but they were void of true sympathy. Purely factual. What Chelle meant was, are you okay to perform rather than are you okay as a fellow human being with emotions and nerve endings.

"My ankle hurts a little," Paige said.

"Crap. We need some ice quick, there's no way we'll find a replacement before the game. Patty, this is your fault, go get her some ice. Ten minutes, everyone!"

Patsy took off across the gym and up the steps into the first-floor hallway, determined to break the record for fastest run to the nurse's station. She'd been an idiot, letting ancient history seep in. Current social standings were on the line at the expense of her disinclination to put the past behind her. Mildred wasn't her friend anymore. She hadn't been for a long time, even though that fact saddened Patsy. The truth was, even if the falling-out hadn't happened between their parents, Patsy probably would have ditched Mildred by the end of junior high anyway, because Mildred was so unpopular.

The nurse's door was wide open when Patsy arrived, and Mrs. Weller, a young, slim, honey-blond woman, was sitting at her desk scribbling something Patsy couldn't see. The room was clean as a whistle, with everything in shades of white and gray. It gave off the same feeling as a waiting room in a doctor's office; something sterile, but more inviting than an actual medical room.

"Mrs. Weller?" Patsy asked.

The woman looked up and smiled.

"Hey, Patsy," Mrs. Weller said in a very deep Texas drawl. "How can I help ya?"

"We had a little fall in the gym. No big deal, I just need an ice pack."

"Sure can do," Mrs. Weller said.

She made her way over to a small cooler at the back of the room. Patsy got a glimpse of Gatorade bottles, some Lunchables, several ice packs, and a vial or two of some liquids. Mrs. Weller took an ice pack and handed it to Patsy.

"Have you been having any more stomachaches?"

"I've been doing better," Patsy said.

She hadn't been better, she had just gotten more used to the stomachaches. Since her mother had recently lost yet another job, food hadn't been as abundant as it should be around the Porter house. Patsy didn't work. She had cheer practice and a social life to keep up. There was no time, which was just as good, because even if there had been, she could never have let the others know that she had to work. She couldn't let them find out that her father was in jail and her single mother struggled to take care of her. That was the kind of thing she didn't think popular kids dealt with. None of the other girls had mentioned any similar situations, and the one girl they knew in school who worked in a restaurant often got called out for coming from a poor family. Patsy hated it. It wasn't fair, and at least the girl was trying to do something to change her life. But Patsy kept her mouth shut. Then when her mother lost one of her cleaning jobs, Patsy kept her mouth shut. She went to Mrs. Weller a few times for a snack near the end of the school day, because she knew there would be no snack waiting at home.

"That's good to hear, sugar," Mrs. Weller said. She said *sugar* a lot, and Patsy liked it a lot better than *Patty*.

"Thanks," she said as she backed out of the room.

Before she could get all the way out, she bumped into something.

"Oh, sorry, Patsy, dear," Miss Morgan said breathlessly.

"It's okay, it was my fault," Patsy said.

She took her leave by going around the winded art teacher and headed back to the gym. She passed Mildred's locker, still hanging open. Random garbage now spilled from it. Crumpled papers, something wet, and someone had opened a condom and thrown it in there.

"Assholes," Patsy mumbled.

She suddenly wanted to call and ask Mildred if she was okay, but on second thought, she felt that would be a stupid question. Of course Mildred wasn't okay. Patsy saw what Mildred dealt with day in and day out. How could anyone be okay? Embarrassment flooded Patsy. Part of that was her fault. If she had just said something—but Mildred rushed away without acknowledging Patsy at all, and the opportunity was missed.

∅

Chelle called off practice and let them play volleyball with the other students in gym class, but not before she threatened Paige's position on the squad, due to her new ankle injury. Chelle promised her that if she couldn't pick it up later in the day at practice, she'd be replaced.

Patsy didn't bother hitting the court with the others, where they'd set up a makeshift volleyball net. She wanted a break from the popular group and found solitude in the gym showers. Warm water beat down on her and splashed on the tiles while she let her mind roam. From somewhere inside, she longed for the days when she would just hang out with Mildred in front of the television, enjoying one of their fun '80s horror movie marathons. Mildred had the best collection, but she always got so frightened at the scary parts. Patsy wondered if Mildred still watched them even though Patsy wasn't there to tell her when it was okay to open her eyes again.

6

The school had failed Mildred, but there was one more place she could try. The moped motor hummed beneath her as she rode along, steadily calming her mind. Thinking through the fog of helplessness was possible, and she realized the best course of action now was to bring the situation to her mother.

It was still early in the day, so the most likely place for Barbara to be was in her home office. She might be upset with Mildred for leaving school early, but when Mildred explained why she left, she hoped her mom would understand. Ashamed that she hadn't taken after her mother, Mildred had never actually explained to Barbara why she hated school so much. It was now time to clue her in; there were no other choices. Despite her harsh attitude, Barbara still cared about her daughter's well being. Hearing that it had gotten this severe at school for Mildred would make Barbara rethink things. Mildred doubted her mom would allow something like this to go on even a moment longer. She probably would have already handled it if she had known what Mildred dealt with daily. Mildred knew that her mom was a very persuasive woman who liked to be on top of most situations. Mildred had no doubt that the taunts would soon be history. Mrs. Waco would visit Roanoke High and Mildred's life would change for the better. She would see to it that Miss Spade punished Mildred's bullies, and they might even get in trouble with their parents. They'd never mess with Mildred Waco again. The thought made her cackle out loud as she zoomed down the busy street.

Ø

Mildred walked into her house and saw the stuffed suitcase by the door, zipped up and ready to go. Immediately, her spirits fell. This sight was an all-too-common one for her.

"Oh, Millie, you're home," Barbara exclaimed. Her black hair was pulled into a ponytail. Her outfit was a Victoria's Secret Pink joggers and a jacket—what she referred to as her comfortable traveling clothes. "Why are you home so early?"

"There's something—"

"Just a moment, dear," she said as she checked the noise that was coming from her phone. "That's my office again. We really need to hurry."

"The reason I left school—"

"Don't, Millie," Barbara said. She busied herself going through her bag, making sure everything was accounted for. "Honey, I can't deal with your excuses today. Miss school, go to school, today it doesn't matter. We've got something huge going on and your father and I have to get to Hawaii."

"What? Now?"

"Yes, now." She stopped looking through the bag and went

into the kitchen, where Mildred watched her take a few packets of a special fitness powder she mixed in her drinks. "I was going to text you, but I'm kind of glad you're here to see us off instead. I do hate leaving while you're out."

"Mom, can you just stop rushing a minute so we can talk?" Mildred asked, not bothering to inquire what the urgent work was this time. She knew it would concern some type of animal in a place that was warm, exotic, and completely void of their oddball daughter. Her heart grew somehow heavier.

Barbara finally removed her attention from her luggage and her phone and looked at her daughter. She noticed Mildred's troubled, red eyes. "What is it, honey?"

Here was Mildred's chance, if only the lump in her throat would shrink enough so she could squeeze the words around it. "Um . . . there's these . . . these kids—"

"Barbara!" her dad yelled from their bedroom, his voice much more demanding than poor, timid Mildred's. "Where's my traveling razor?"

"It's in the bathroom drawer!" Barbara yelled back.

"Where? I don't see it!" he shouted.

Mildred's mom blew a frustrated breath and mumbled, "He does this every time." Then she patted Mildred's arm with her bony ring-clad hand. "Look, honey, whatever it is, do what makes you happy. Don't give in to peer pressure. Tomorrow is a new day. Things change."

"Barbara!" Ben called.

She ignored him and kept talking to Mildred. "If it's still a problem, we'll talk about it after we get back, okay? There have been strange reports about dolphins and we're going to get to the bottom of it."

"Oh . . . okay, Mom, but first—"

"Barbara!"

"I'm coming!" her mom cried sharply.

Mildred flinched. *So much for parental backup.*

Ø

Ben found his travel razor. He and his wife left after giving Mildred some cash for "healthy food and not pizza" and reminding Mildred about her emergency credit card. It was where it always sat: on top of the desk next to the stack of books that Mildred barely ever cracked open. It was a books-all-high-schoolers-should-read collection compiled by Barbara, and it included a stack of science books that didn't interest Mildred in the least.

They were gone and she was alone with her pain, as she often was. Those ugly words shouted at her in the hallway bounced around in her head for the next few hours, without restraint. There were no outside voices to tell her to ignore them or that those voices were wrong, so she started adding to them herself.

Not good enough, not smart enough.

The voices seemed stronger than ever now that she was alone, thinking that not even the people she thought she trusted were willing to help her.

Not pretty enough, not talented enough.

The pain ripped through her, and it began to hurt so much Mildred felt angry. How could the teachers dismiss her the way they did? How could her own parents just ignore her suffering like that? Anger fueled her to act despite the carelessness of the teachers and her parents. She would find a way to make the bullies stop. There had to be some technique to use. Something that would make them sorry.

The problem was, she didn't know how. She had no knowledge of ways to handle these situations, and not a single person was willing to help her.

Mildred lay on her neatly made bed. "A clean bed is the first step to a good day," Barbara liked to say. She must have made Mildred's bed after Mildred had left for school. But the tidy bed didn't do a thing to make her day better. It had been just as full of despair as the day before and the day before that. Tomorrow and the next day and then the day after that would be the same unless she took some sort of action.

Mildred knew she couldn't just sit around and do *nothing* about this. Not anymore. It was killing her. Smothering her. She felt like she'd just been letting them pull her deeper and deeper underwater, and she had reached the point where she could either kick off the bottom and break the surface or succumb to the heaviness in her chest. She wanted to break free. She didn't want to be a victim her whole life. She refused to be their victim any longer. Those people had had a good nine years to pick on her, but that was all about to end as far as she was concerned. As soon as she could figure out *how* to stop it.

In a fit of frustration, she took her laptop off her nightstand, plopped it in front of her on the bed, and turned it on. The screen filled with a starry background and a plethora of game shortcuts. Ignoring them, she pulled up the browser and typed *get back at bullies* into the search engine. Results flooded the page. So many came up that she felt nervous. Where should she start? What if none of them worked? She needed something to distract her worries and decided she needed a snack while she tackled the long list.

Several restaurants she frequented were listed as saved

numbers in her phone, but she looked for one specifically: Dominico's, her favorite local pizza place. She preferred them because they weren't ever stingy with the toppings, like the other places in town.

"Thank you for choosing Dominico's, will this be delivery or pickup?" Dominico's familiar voice floated into Mildred's ear.

"It'll be delivery today."

"Hi, Mildred! You want the usual?"

"Yes, a large supreme."

"Sure thing. Hey, sure you don't want to come down? Some kid beat your score on the pinball a few days ago."

Mildred felt a tiny flash of jealousy; it had taken her a long time to make that score.

"Maybe tomorrow. I'm working on something else right now," she said.

"Okay, okay. We'll have it out to you in about thirty minutes."

Mildred ended the call, feeling like thirty minutes was ages away, but her stomach was queasy now. She pulled a bag of barbeque-flavored chips from her hidden stash under the bed. From the first taste of flavor, she began to calm down and found that it was easier to concentrate on her mission. She crunched away, momentarily mollified, while she scrolled, clicked, and waited for her pizza delivery.

The first article on the search suggested she tell someone. *Already did.*

The next handful were support groups. *No,* thought Mildred, who'd already been let down by her principal, counselor, teachers, and mother. In another life, she might have trusted these well-meaning, faceless people. But after what she'd been through, she wasn't ready to join a group of strangers who she felt might pretend to care so they could laugh behind her back. To her, it seemed very impersonal to get support from someone she couldn't see. An anonymous person could really be anyone. It even occurred to her that it could be her attackers hiding behind the screen, which was a terrifying notion.

Maybe there were support groups for victims of bullying being held in some building downtown. Unfortunately, she didn't see any times or addresses for any such meetings. Just as well, she decided, because she wasn't sure how she'd feel about opening up to a room full of people all staring at her either. She didn't want to be put on the spot when the leader said, "Now stand up and introduce yourself." Imagining herself standing in front of those people—people she had made up entirely in her head, with no faces or names, only eyes that stared, waiting—made her hot and nervous.

She clicked away with fervor.

The next couple of sites were mostly other people asking the same thing, on a website where others could submit answers to questions. *How can I stop my bullies?* A lot of people were confessing that they were also bullied, sympathizing with the questioner. Some people told them to get over it, which she thought was an ignorant reply, because she couldn't simply get over it. Especially not when she was bombarded by it every single day. How lucky for them, she thought, that they could be so oblivious to how painful it is to be bullied. That they couldn't fathom how she could be so crushed and broken that putting it out of her mind would be impossible. They didn't realize that the awful abuse played over and over and over, haunting her.

Ø

Mildred was nine and she was wearing a shirt that she'd fallen in love with in the store. It was white with black spots, as if ink had spilled on it, creating an array of interpretive shapes. In them, she could make out a rabbit, a bird, a heart, and there was one that looked like an angel from one angle and a dragon from another.

Her spirits were high that day, as she walked toward Mr. Pratt's second-grade class. The primary students were never in classrooms alone, and so they lined up in the hallway to wait for Mr. Pratt to come unlock the door to the classroom.

On this day, Mildred was hopeful when she saw Chelle outside the door, waiting in line with the look of sleep still on her face. Maybe she would notice Mildred's clothes and say, "I like your shirt, Mildred," the same way she had to Yvette the day before, when she wore a rainbow-colored shirt with white leopard prints. Upon seeing Mildred, Chelle brightened and sucked in a huge breath. Mildred grinned, expecting to be praised for having a cool shirt that stood out in a crowd.

"Cowgirl!" Chelle said. She made the words sound nasty, as though she was calling Mildred a girl who was a cow, rather than a girl who ranched cows, neither of which had been Mildred's goal. The words were venomous, spewing out in a sizzling spray that spread to the rest of the students lined up outside Mr. Pratt's classroom that day.

"Cowgirl. Cowgirl. Cowgirl!" And it surrounded her, closing in on her like quicksand.

How wrong she'd been.

How embarrassed she'd been.

Ø

And then she saw it, while sitting on her humdrum gray comforter, surfing the web on her laptop as regular sixteen-year-old Mildred, a far cry from her "cowgirl" days. On the screen, she saw the strangest answer, posted to some other unlucky soul who was being bullied and desperately seeking an end to it all. *Curse them,* it said. Simple, but powerful.

I can do that, Mildred thought as she crunched another salty chip between her teeth. A light sprinkle of crumbs landed on her keyboard. Curses had never occurred to her before, but the idea didn't sound ridiculous. She believed wholeheartedly that with enough intent and the right type of guide, a curse could be perfectly feasible. She'd seen it on television before, in some of the scary movies she used to watch with Patsy. There were reasons people wouldn't walk under ladders or open umbrellas in their houses. It was because those things brought bad luck. Curses seemed somewhat similar in nature: bad luck sent to an individual with intent, although there had to be more to it than that. One would have to know what they were doing. She wasn't a witch or anything, so she didn't have the skill to perform a curse on her own. She needed to find the right instructions . . . or someone who could perform the curse for her.

It might be a little odd, but it was the best suggestion she'd found. Nothing else had gripped her like this. Nothing else had felt right.

She typed *curse my enemies* into the search engine this time. Dozens of pages of results came up. Excitement lurched inside her, bringing with it the possibility of a tomorrow where she didn't have to be afraid to be seen by her peers. Where she didn't have to map out an escape route for every room she entered, just to feel safe. For the first time, she was hopeful that all the teasing would end. But beneath that hope was also fear: fear that it wouldn't work.

No, it would work. She was certain. She just had to find the real deal. Keep away from the fake stuff. She needed real dark magical hexes or curses.

The first few sites in the search results looked silly. Make Your Bully Love You, one was titled.

Gross, Mildred thought.

Give Your Bully Pimples, said another.

How weak, she thought.

She bumped into many amateur spells that sounded childish. Write the name of your bully on a piece of paper and burn it in a bonfire.

What good would that do? Mildred wondered. She clicked away from it angrily, feeling her hope slowly evaporate into the stuffy air of her bedroom, where her mother had sprayed some type of air freshener when she made the bed.

What Mildred needed was something advanced, something to give efficient results. As she searched, the screen suddenly began to fail. The image pixelated and blinked out to a black screen a few times. Her heart lurched.

"No, no," she said. She smacked the screen a few times, leaving greasy fingerprints with barbeque crumbs on it.

The screen came back clearly, with a website displayed as if she'd clicked it by accident. For a moment, Mildred feared the heavily sprayed air freshener in the closed room had gone to her head. When she blinked, it didn't go away: it was real. She couldn't believe her luck. It was the perfect website. There was no list of fake spells on it. Only a name and address: Crossroads Magicks, 6 Hollow Grove, Roanoke, Virginia. It was in her town, although she wasn't sure she knew exactly where Hollow Grove was. Crossroads Magicks sounded like exactly the kind of thing she needed. The design of the page alone made her think it was serious stuff. Skulls, dark colors, bones . . . it all gave off a spooky vibe.

The doorbell rang, jarring her out of the web. She checked the digital clock beside her bed. It had been only twenty minutes since she'd ordered her pizza. *Dominico's is really stepping up their service,* she thought, pleased. She rolled off her bed and went to the door. On the other side was her old friend Patsy Porter, who did not work for Dominico's. Mildred knew for a fact that Dominico's was a family-run business and Patsy wasn't one of them. Up until now, Mildred was certain Patsy had purposely forgotten the directions to Mildred's house, as though forgetting any other terrible childhood memory. As far as Mildred was aware, Patsy had absolutely zero reason to be standing at her door ever again. They were in two different worlds now, and Patsy made it clear at school that she wanted no part of Mildred's world.

"What do you want?" Mildred said suspiciously, and a little rudely. She checked behind Patsy to see if any of the popular kids were waiting to bomb her with water balloons, rotten eggs, or whatever awful things they had in mind. Nobody was in sight, but it didn't mean they weren't there.

"I just wanted to check on you," Patsy said sweetly.

She was wearing a school spirit shirt, yellow with Roanoke High Turkeys written in maroon across the front. The yellow made the golden undertones in her hair look bright. She was smiling. Patsy looked innocent enough, but the others couldn't be far behind her, Mildred knew. Her heart skipped. What if they knew what she was doing?

She was much too busy to find out what they had planned.

"I'm fine," Mildred said quickly, and shut the door in Patsy's face.

Just to make sure the girl left, she watched through a crack in the blinds. Patsy stared, moved as if intending to ring the bell again, seemed to think better of it, then finally turned and left.

Mildred was still watching out the window as the pizza delivery driver, Dominico's daughter, Ariel, arrived. Ariel, like her father, had thick, dark curls and a warm smile. She was in her late twenties and a little on the heavier side herself. Nothing like Mildred, but she did have an awkwardness about her that helped Mildred relax in her presence. The smell of the pizza filled her head even before Ariel opened up the box to show her the quality of the pie. The delectable cheesy mess was already paid for—Dominico had Mildred's emergency credit card in the system. She gave Ariel a five from her not-pizza money as a tip, and then something occurred to her.

"Hey, you drive around here a lot, right?" she asked. "Do you know where 6 Hollow Grove is?"

The young woman gave the question some thought. "Nah. Can't say I do. Sorry."

Weird, Mildred thought. If anyone knew their way around town, it should be a delivery driver. Ariel had delivered from the time she was a teenager.

"Why do you ask?"

"Just some place somebody told me about," Mildred said, not wanting to go into detail.

"Sorry, must have meant some other town maybe," Ariel said. "Enjoy!"

"Maybe," Mildred said. "Thanks!" She shut the door, then bit into a slice of pizza as she went down the hall toward her laptop.

The screen had changed. White lines now wound through a black background. Mildred recognized a map of her town, with a line labeled Hollow Grove leading off the familiar Norwich Drive. There never used to be a Hollow Grove there. As far back as she could remember, that place had been thick forest. Mildred shrugged. New roads were built all the time. She scribbled the address while she ate.

7

Many significant subjects plagued the hectic mind of a teenage boy. Aaron, for instance, stared at the cartoon turkey on the Go Turkeys! sign at the concession stand by the football field and thought, *What if we added a bra to the turkey? Wouldn't that be funny? Because, like, a bra, turkey breast . . . I mean, the jokes practically write themselves.*

"Aaron!" Coach's voice cut the thought short.

Aaron startled and the stupid smile on his face relaxed into something resembling seriousness. He worked his fingers through his shaggy blond tresses and cleared his throat. "Yeah?"

"You listening to me, boy? You got a look on your face like you just got asked what the square root of 256 is."

"Sixteen, sir," Herman—towel boy and the brain behind most of the homework assignments by members of the football team—called from nearby on the bench.

Herman was probably the dorkiest guy Aaron had ever seen. The polo-shirts-under-vests type, which made sense to Aaron;

after all, if Herman spent a lot of time learning useless stuff and doing homework for half the football team, he had less time for things that mattered, like fashion. A couple of the guys laughed at Herman's comment and Aaron thought, *Good one, dude,* but he didn't say it while Coach was on one of his rants.

"Shut your mouth, Bernstein," Coach said. The old guy had hairy arms, black slacks pulled up too far, and a black collared shirt tucked in neatly. He had been wearing out the grass in front of the bench with his pacing, shouting about weak defenses.

"Yes, sir," Herman replied.

He hadn't even cracked a smile, taken by surprise at the humor everyone else saw in his comment. He was merely answering a serious math problem as if Coach had meant it literally, and that was the thing that made it most hilarious to Aaron. He fought back howling laughter as Coach's intense gaze burned into him.

"I said, are you proud of that throw you made out there? You know, the crappy one?"

He knew exactly which throw Coach was talking about. As soon as the pigskin had left his fingers, he'd known it was a mistake. He'd let go a fraction too soon, sending the football sailing right out of Seth Montgomery's reach. If it was an actual game, that could have cost them the win.

But it wasn't his fault. Surely the mistake must have somehow been the fault of the ball and not his own. It could have even been the wind, for all he knew. He couldn't possibly take full responsibility for something so uncertain, so when his answer came out, it was an indecisive one.

"Yea-no, Coach!"

"Well, which is it, Renfro?" Coach asked impatiently. "Yes or no? Because I'll tell you how I feel about it. It was *bullshit*! You think we're going to win against Powell Valley with bullshit tosses like that?"

"No, sir!" Aaron said, because he knew that was what Coach wanted to hear and he was ready to get out of there. He wanted to go home and film himself playing Xbox so he could post it online. He had some new gamer jokes to try out. His fan base was still fairly small, but steadily growing, thanks to his wisecracks.

Coach Thorpe, on the other hand, was a down-to-earth sort of guy. Funny had never worked on him.

"You going to crush Powell Valley Saturday or what?" Coach shouted.

What he was looking for was competitiveness.

"Yes, sir!" Aaron said.

"What?"

Persistence.

"I said we're going to crush 'em, sir!"

"What?"

Viciousness.

"I said we're gonna *crush Powell Valley!*"

The rest of the team, all forty-two—forty-three if they counted Herman—pitched in, sounding like an angry, psychotic mob. "Crush Powell Valley! Crush Powell Valley!"

"That's what I like to hear!" Coach shouted, with a hint of a smile on his otherwise grumpy face. "You bring that attitude to the game, and we got this cat in the bag."

The boys cheered, smacking palms together and clapping each other on the shoulders and backs.

"Hit the showers!" Coach said.

The Turkeys dispersed from the field, through the gate in the chain-link fence, and into the school building. The boys' locker room contained a line of toilet stalls, two rows of lockers, and finally the showers. Some players hit the shower area right away, flinging their filthy uniforms at Herman along the way. The room quickly filled with steam as the showerheads spewed hot water onto the sweaty players. As the towel boy, Herman habitually cleaned up after the team and he already had a hamper at his side to hold all the soiled uniforms. Aaron tossed his shirt at Herman's face instead of at the hamper, because it was slightly more entertaining to see if Herman could catch it or if it would just whack him. Apparently, Seth wasn't in on Aaron's little game. Seth took off his uniform and tossed the articles toward the hamper. Aaron noticed a deep-red hickey on Seth's upper chest.

"Dude," Aaron said, pointing at the evidence. "So Patsy finally give it up?"

"Nah, dude," Seth said. "This didn't come from Patsy."

Aaron's eyebrows rose and Seth grinned at him sheepishly, then quickly changed the subject.

"You think we got a chance at winning against Powell Valley?" Seth asked Herman.

"Without Tyler? Not likely," Herman admitted. "Maybe a thirty percent chance, considering you beat West Jefferson and they beat Powell Valley three weeks ago. Although if you count the fact that their player Darrell Hall's knee isn't in the best of shape since that game, it could bring the odds up even higher." Someone's sock landed on Herman's shoulder. He plucked it off, dropped it in the hamper, and continued. "Then again, Aaron's shoulder is still on the fritz—"

"My shoulder is fine," Aaron said as he threw his jockstrap across the locker room straight at Herman. The cup hit him on the nose. "See? On the field . . . that was the wind."

Herman didn't blink. "The wind wasn't blowing."

"Neither is Patsy, apparently," Aaron said, shooting Seth a look. "So what's up with that?"

"Dude, I can't say."

"A hint, then?"

By the time Aaron left the locker room, he still hadn't found out who Seth was seeing on the sly. Naturally, he assumed whoever the mystery girl was, she was probably ugly. Why else would he keep it a secret? Wouldn't it be funny if it was Mildred? Aaron laughed out loud as he got in his Jeep Wrangler. Then he cringed. How could anyone really do that, though? There was no way around Mildred's gross factor. *Even if you turned out the lights, she'd still smell like a farm*, Aaron thought. But who knew—he pulled out of the parking lot—maybe Seth was into bad smells. Everyone had a kink.

All Aaron wanted to do was get inside, turn on the Xbox, turn on the camera, and get some good footage. But before even opening the door he could already hear his dad's raised voice inside. Aaron rushed to get the door open.

The smell of burned food assaulted his nose and his father's voice filled his ears. The living room was smoky. He saw the television playing *Family Feud*—appropriate—and saw all the beer cans his father had emptied while sitting on the couch. His father's and sister's voices pealed from the kitchen, and Aaron ran toward them.

"It was burning, I had to shut it off!" Joan cried.

"Mary! Mary, listen to me!" his father was yelling. "I had it under control! You don't trust me! That's your problem, Mary! Just because *you're* a liar doesn't mean everyone is!"

It's not even five o'clock and he's already acting like a sloshed asshat, thought Aaron. *No wonder Mom left.*

"Dad, what the hell?" Aaron said, bursting into the room.

His father—tall, graying, thick moustache, and a plaid shirt—was hovering over Joan, her small frame looking even smaller in contrast to the large man. She was no taller than his chest and rail thin, and Aaron didn't like the way his father was standing or the way he called her Mary. He was clearly so out of it that he didn't even know what decade he was currently standing in. He'd warped back to a time when Mary Renfro was his wife, back before he'd ruined it all with his drinking problem.

Aaron had been nine when he last saw this scenario. His mother had looked a lot like Joan did now, so much that the memory flashed vividly in his mind. Their clothes had been different. Joan currently wore a school spirit shirt; Mary had been wearing a Bon Jovi tee. Her hair was wavy instead of straight like Joan's. She was just as small and as equally afraid. Jason never hit Mary—not that Aaron ever saw—but his words stung her. They were reverberating and cruel.

How many times had he seen the same scenario as a young child before his mother had finally given up on his father?

Late that night, Mary snuck into Aaron's bedroom to tell him good-bye. "I'll come back for you after I find a job and a proper place to live," she said. "Until then, you'll be safe with him. He won't treat you this way."

Look how wrong you were, Mom, Aaron thought. *Wrong about coming back and wrong about our safety.*

"Dad, I'm Joan! I'm not her!" Joan cried. "I'm not Mom!"

Jason's angry face went slack, as if he'd just heard devastating news. His eyes filled with confusion. He swallowed hard. Again. Then he vomited down the front of Joan's Roanoke High Turkeys shirt. She squealed and ran to the bathroom, leaving a trail of beer barf along her path. Jason finished hurling on the floor, then looked at Aaron. Guilt. Shame. Anger.

"What are *you* lookin' at?" he said. "Don't judge me!"

"You gotta stop drinking, Dad."

"I make the money, so whenever I'm off work, I'll do whatever I want."

"Even if it means hurting your daughter?"

Jason lifted his brows as if he was trying to widen his eyes and see more clearly. "She's not hurt. She'll be fine."

"No, Dad, she won't. Neither will I."

"Aww, poor babies," he mocked. "Then go and kiss her cry-baby boo-boo. You guys make me sick."

"Yeah, you *are* sick."

They glared at each other, sky-blue eyes versus olive green. The olive eyes turned away first.

"I'm going to get another drink," Jason said.

His father's footsteps drifted away, and the front door slammed. *At least he was on foot,* Aaron thought. He would have chased him down and taken his keys had he been trying to drive like that, but he was glad he didn't have to. Aaron cleaned up the vomit with a couple of kitchen towels and threw them in the laundry-room hamper.

Water was running in the bathroom and Joan was sobbing over the rhythmic sound of the shower. Aaron knocked on the door.

"Go away!" Joan shouted.

"He's gone, Jo," Aaron said.

"Good! I hate him!"

Aaron knew the feeling. He wished he could leave like Mary had, but unlike her, he would take Joan with him. No false promises. There was no way he would make her stay and wait for him to come back, knowing he never would. His best shot at getting them out of there was football, he thought. The water cut off in the bathroom.

"Hey, I've got to go work on something," he said.

"You're leaving?" Joan said. "Fine! Leave just like him! I hope neither one of you comes home tonight!"

Aaron started to reply but thought better of it. Any reply would turn into an argument with her and he didn't want to argue right now. He just wanted to practice more. It was time to take football more seriously if he ever hoped to give Joan and himself a better life. She would understand one day.

Dust flew up behind Mildred's moped as she rode down the dirt road to her destination. A rusty old mailbox came up on her left side and she slowed. She had expected to come upon a new residential development, but this didn't look new at all. There were no tracks indicating any heavy equipment had been by to clear out any wood. The trees were thick, almost hiding the aged mailbox, dented and worn by the elements, and tall grass almost obstructed the little path beside it from view. At first impression, it didn't appear this shop got much business at all. Someone had used black paint and written 6 Hollow Grove on the weathered mailbox in a scraggly fashion. Mildred looked down at the pizza sauce–stained slip of paper in her hand: 6 Hollow Grove. Turning onto the little path, she carried on.

In only a few yards, she stopped and turned off the motor. Scrawny chickens ran around the yard, pecking at the ground. A goat stood next to an old porch, chewing grass contentedly. She looked up at a spooky dilapidated house. It seemed more like a large shack to Mildred. Mud caked some of the aged wood, as if it was holding the porch together. It struck her as some sort of hovel she might find hidden in a swampland. *Could anyone really be living in there?* Squinting her eyes, she searched for some sign of life through the grimy windows. There was some movement inside. A subtle swishing of a curtain. It could have been her imagination.

Or a ghost? *This looks like a house that might have a ghost or two,* thought Mildred.

With timid precision she approached the front door. As she came closer, faint music could be heard from within. The words were foreign to her, and the instruments were screechy. She didn't like it. The same skinny writing was on the door, spelling out the words *Crossroads Magicks*. Close up, she could see that the wood underneath the peeling paint on the siding and the door was cracked, as if the house was ready to crumble in upon itself. She felt a strange sensation rush over her, as though the place was radiating power. *Could the only thing keeping this house standing be some kind of ancient spell?* Mildred wondered. If it was, that was definitely the kind of magic she needed. Something solid enough to fix something terribly broken.

Nervously, she rapped her thick knuckles on the door. It felt rough as tree bark and dust trickled down from the impact, leaving dirty marks on her hands, which she tried wiping off on her pants. The god-awful screeching music stopped. The door swung open suddenly, and Mildred gasped. A beautiful woman stood in the doorway, willowy and unsmiling. She wore a long flimsy dress that was deep red, goldenrod, black, and brown. A similar fabric was wrapped around her hair. Mildred gawked at her lithe figure, until she saw the earrings. Metal and bone dangled from the woman's delicate ears and it made Mildred shudder.

"What would you be coming to my door for?" the woman asked in an accent that sounded unfamiliar to Mildred.

She didn't fully expect the pointy hat and flying broomsticks of lore, but she had expected maybe a hooked nose or a wart on the chin. She thought the woman would be old and ugly, like witches on Halloween decorations or in old cartoons. She didn't expect to find anything of beauty in this creepy, run-down dwelling. This woman could be a ballerina or a model. The last thing Mildred ever would have guessed, if she'd bumped into her while in a supermarket or a park, would be the word *witch*. The contrast of the stereotype versus the reality took Mildred by surprise and somehow made her feel uglier.

"It says magicks . . ." Mildred stammered.

The woman stared a moment, then a wide smile spread across her shapely lips. "Magicks are not for children. Something easy, maybe. A nice love potion? That's it. It will not make the boy you like see a movie star when he looks your way, but it will make him get warm feelings. Yeah?"

The boy she liked? The very idea was ridiculous. Mildred had never let herself like any boys. How could she, knowing they all hated her? They all made fun of her and, when she was in grade school, a few had even pushed her down and pinched her. She had a scar on her knee to remind her of the time Tyler had shoved her down the slide.

"Erm . . . it's not about a boy," Mildred said, taking off her helmet, providing an open view of her chubby face. "Well, not *one* in particular, anyway. Honestly, I . . . I need something more dangerous . . ."

The woman looked around outside, then stood back and let Mildred enter. Inside, the scent of incense was strong. Something earthy, like patchouli. The striped wallpaper and the floors showed just as much wear as the outside of the house, with tears and dark age spots. In places the wallpaper was dark green, and in others it was grayed or even blackened by the effects of time. The tall woman led Mildred through a furnished yet worn-down sitting room and straight to a wide room with rows and rows of jars lining the walls. They held things that looked to Mildred like alligator teeth, frog legs, and essential oils. Mildred set her helmet on a counter with an antique cash register on it and looked into a dingy jar of what appeared to be sharp nails, clipped from some sort of creature.

"Not a boy. What brings you here, then?" the woman asked, drawing Mildred's attention back to her. She stood behind the counter, where a small fire burned in a little metal bowl. Beyond the woman, a doorway was blocked by strings of bamboo beads hanging down, swaying to and fro. Most of the beads were dyed brown and tan, but a strange black symbol was painted on them as well.

Mildred took a deep breath and went for it. "I want my bullies to pay. I want people to regret everything they said about me. Everything they did to me, or . . . or every time they laughed at me or hurt me."

The woman's brows raised. "High school bullies? Not often I hear such a request," she said. "Most people try other methods."

Please help, please! The pain inside Mildred twisted her face. "I have nothing else."

"It's very dark, what you seek. Very black. It will turn your soul black, that kind of revenge," the woman said.

"I don't care," Mildred said, feeling as if this was her last chance. "My life is dark anyway. They're like shadows standing over me all the time, keeping out light. So why should I miss it?"

The woman gave some thought before she replied. "Be best if you would take a rebound potion and be done with it."

"What's a rebound potion?"

"Nothing too strong. It might stop the worst of them."

"Might? No. I need something strong."

"Strong is dangerous. No."

"But, please! I need help. Nobody will help me. Nobody," Mildred whined.

Mildred's thin lips pulled back and her forehead creased as her eyes filled with salty tears. She turned away before they spilled over her thin lashes. She didn't want the stranger to see her cry. Then she felt sharp nails dig into her shoulder, forcing her to turn around. The woman's lovely face loomed above, a dark look in her eyes.

"Swish. Spit," she said, handing Mildred a small glass of liquid and nodding at the tiny fire.

Mildred swished the glass's contents without asking what they were. She was so desperate for any kind of reaction. The tiny fire blew up ten sizes when she spit into it. Red-hot flames licked and danced. It meant nothing to Mildred, but the woman's eyes grew wide.

"Come on," the woman said in a hushed whisper that gave Mildred the chills. "I will give you what you seek, but you must do as I say. *All* I say."

The flame was still high and in its light a wicked grin distorted the woman's face. In that instant, she looked exactly like an ugly, scary witch. Mildred felt a flash of fear, but then the fire shrank down and the woman's face was as it had been before.

"Come," the woman said, without a hint of a whisper. "You'll do it?"

Mildred pushed that spark of fear down. This woman was going to help her when nobody else would. How bad could she be?

"Anything," Mildred said, desperately. "I'll do anything."

The woman curled her lip in a smile and waved Mildred in her direction, beckoning her to follow, then slipped through the beaded doorway behind the counter.

As soon as Mildred stepped through the beads, she felt different. There wasn't a single window anywhere. All light in the room came from torches that hung on the walls, giving off a fiery glow, and candles scattered across the floor. Flames crackling, wax melting. To the far right sat some sort of altar, and a shelf stood behind it with things unfamiliar to Mildred. The only recognizable thing was a dagger, whose handle was made to look like multiple faces of monsters. A plain wooden chair rested alone in the center of the room. Mildred gasped, seeing various-sized bones around the chair. Some even looked human—especially the skulls. She was no bone expert, but they looked pretty real. The floor was stained with dried blood and covered with odd markings drawn in a willowy scrawl—just like the door and the mailbox. These markings splashed all the way up the grimy walls.

What have I walked into? Mildred felt her eyes sting and her heart race, but she couldn't leave now. The exit wasn't where it had been. It wasn't anywhere.

Strings with feathers and bones wrapped up in them hung about the ceiling, sort of like morbid dream catchers. The strange room was as dark and cold as death. It felt like it was sucking all the goodness out of Mildred.

"Sit," the witch said, pushing Mildred into the wooden chair.

Mildred tried not to think of what had bled onto the surface beneath her. She tried not to think about where those skulls had come from. Had she not been so desperate for help, she never would have waited in this horrific room while a witch prepared some dark magic spell for her.

The woman went to her altar, put her hand down in the darkness where Mildred couldn't see it, and brought it back up seconds later holding a large rattlesnake. It slithered around in her hands, shaking its rattler, but then she kissed it and it fell motionless, as if in a trance. Mildred saw her lay it upon her altar and raise a sharp dagger. *Chop!* The snake's head rolled off the table and onto the floor. A clay bowl caught the blood that flowed from the snake. Once it was down to drips, she tossed it aside, then retrieved one of the many skulls. With old-fashioned pliers, she plucked out a human tooth, then crushed it with a pestle, grinding it to dust before adding it to the blood bowl.

Mildred didn't want to see these things. They were vile and gave her chills. *It must be done.* The words came to her as if from a whisper over her shoulder—she twisted to find its source but saw no one. A gust of air soothed her anxieties, and suddenly she knew the events before her were necessary. *It's all okay, because it's necessary,* she thought. *I'm here for help. I'm safe. Calm.*

"Nothing will stop you from giving them what they deserve?" the witch asked.

It took Mildred a few moments to realize something was expected of her: a reply. The room was making her feel as though she was in a dream. Weightless, as if she'd left Earth's orbit.

Finally, she replied. "N-no." She took a deep breath and tried again for a steadier voice. "No. Nothing."

Where was all the oxygen in the room? It was being replaced with a moldy smell. The stench of rot and primeval burial sites.

The witch took vials and jars from the shelf and expertly added ingredients to the bowl that weren't familiar to Mildred.

"Follow my instructions and you will steal all their beauty, their talent; whatever you desire from them. Beware, girl, they will pay the highest price. Their pain will be grand. You want it?"

What were those words again? Oh yes. Did she want to steal all their qualities? That would teach them a lesson. If they were stripped of what made them so much better than her, they would understand how it felt when they called her names. If Chelle wasn't so pretty, maybe she wouldn't feel so superior to ugly Mildred. If Aaron wasn't such a loudmouth, maybe he would stop embarrassing her. If. If. If.

But Mildred's subconscious shook her awake. What was the cost of all that? Living without those things was hard. Mildred had done it for years and it was eating her alive. Could she really hurt them that way? Even though they didn't care about hurting her, a small part of Mildred felt like it would be wrong. Could she take away all the good qualities that they had misused?

Their taunts and pranks came back to her. All the names they'd called her, the endless words and crude drawings on her locker, the time they'd snuck cat food into her sandwich, the time they'd beat her up in the girls' locker room for causing them to lose a game of dodgeball. Every time they elbowed her or pinched her as they passed her. Everything they'd done to her rushed into her mind, almost knocking her backward, even as she tried to fight back the wave of awful memories. Something about this place drowned her in those moments. All the pain and humiliation hit her like pinpricks of icy water.

"Yes!" she screamed, grasping for the surface. She wanted it to stop, but she also felt it. That moment, she really felt in her heart the desire to see the pain of all the people who had tortured her for so long. The need was overwhelming.

"Drink."

Mildred took a little shot glass of a clear liquid and drank quickly.

"Good. Give me your hand," the lady said, her eyes as red as a devil. Mildred's breath caught and her heart skipped a beat, but her hand shot out readily. She was afraid not to give it. The witch sliced Mildred's finger with the same jagged dagger she'd used to slice the snake, then squeezed Mildred's fingertip over the bowl. A bead of fresh blood was added to the other ingredients and smoke twirled up in acceptance. Next, she held a vial to Mildred's face, touching her cheek quickly, and added that to the bowl as well. *It was tears*, Mildred realized. She hadn't even registered them. Reliving those terrible memories had made her weep as it had often done before, only she had been so overwhelmed by her surroundings she hadn't taken stock of the tightness in her throat or the soppy state of her face.

With both hands, the witch mixed the bowl, then spread the contents on Mildred's face as she chanted in a language that Mildred didn't understand. She didn't know the words, but she could feel them, rising in her like a phoenix from ashes. Pain. Anger. Revenge. This burning anger-fueled vendetta was flaring, raging like something wild. The heavier and more urgent the chanting grew, so grew the rage. Mildred could almost burst with it.

And then, like a switch, it shut off and there was only darkness.

Ø

Mildred woke up back in the main area of the shop. Groggily, she tried to shake off the awkward feeling of a hangover. Not that she'd ever had one, but she knew the symptoms: queasy stomach, headache, thirst. She didn't think about the dark room where some very strange things had just taken place. The strange woman was busying herself with the jars on the wall. Mildred dug her phone out of her pocket and gasped: 7:30. It was so late. She hated driving the moped at night. It had always felt dangerous to her. Visibility was significantly down and a two-wheel vehicle could possibly be overlooked, she reasoned, so she avoided it for her safety.

"I've got to go," she said.

The woman continued straightening up her shelves, as though it was a very normal evening and having an unconscious girl in the shop wasn't abnormal in the least.

"How much do I owe you?" Mildred asked.

"Your debt is already paid," the woman said, without sparing a glance.

"Oh. Okay." Mildred didn't remember paying anything, but she must have. She started to leave but stopped. "Will they stop?"

The lady turned around and smiled. Her eyes were a perfectly normal chestnut color, not red at all. "They won't be hurting you no more."

"Thank you," Mildred said, and she lifted her helmet onto her head.

She rushed out of that unearthly house as fast as she could manage, which was rather slow by normal standards. Outside, the air felt different. Better. The ambiance inside had clouded her mind to the point that she hadn't even been able to realize how distorted things felt. How everything had seemed to be stretched on a rubber band, and only negativity could seep through the confusion. She took a deep breath and mentally let the clean air circulate through her.

Blam!

The door on the ramshackle cottage snapped shut behind her, sending her body into flight. The danger signs that had shown dimly when she arrived now blinked in neon red in her mind. *Bad place. Bad place. Bad place.* She had been so desperate for help she had ignored her instincts, but now they were alert. Goose bumps broke out on her arms. She shook as she put the key into her moped. Something serious had happened in there and there was no bullshitting about it. She didn't understand exactly why or how, but she knew the witch was right when she'd told Mildred the bullies would be stopped.

9

Mildred had every intention of going straight home, parking in her garage, and hiding in her house with a huge bowl of ice cream while crying until her fear of the strange magic shop dissipated. However, as she left that place behind her, a different plan came to her from somewhere dark inside. An idea that never would have occurred to her on any normal day. Instinct urged her to go somewhere else. Instead of turning right onto Sycamore Avenue, she found herself turning left onto Pine Street.

Dusk was plowing into full-blown darkness. She could already feel the cooler air that fall evenings brought, chasing away any warmth the sunlight had left behind.

An invisible string of fate tugged her along, and she found herself in front of Roanoke High.

The tall school building and neatly trimmed lawn sat still and silent, completely void of the life that inhabited it during the day. On evenings when she didn't have band practice, Mildred was sure to leave school grounds as soon as the doors clicked open to free students and faculty. This late in the evening, the school looked abnormal, like some empty, haunting scene from an apocalyptic movie in which almost everyone was dead. Mildred didn't like the feeling that thought gave her. She wanted to turn the moped around and go home, but when she accelerated again, she took a turn around the building, instead of going away. Soon, she found herself outside the high school football field, looking at the small concrete concession building. She came to a rest and shut off the motor.

What am I doing wasting time here? I hate this place. . . . Which was especially true about the football field, more so than the actual school. The only time she ever had reason to be here was with the marching band—another attempt for them to trip her up with her heavy tuba.

A few tall, square lights illuminated the field. They had been installed a few years before, after some kids from a rival team vandalized the field. Mildred felt weird being there. If there was any place in the world where she was more out of place, she couldn't think of it. She started to walk away, then she heard a sound.

Twump! In a few moments, it came again. *Twump!*

What could that be?

Curious, Mildred idly removed her helmet and peeked around the corner of the building.

Twump!

Even from this distance, the tall, sinewy boy throwing footballs across the big field was unmistakable. His hair and bare back were both slick with sweat. His shirt—probably Abercrombie & Fitch— was tucked loosely into a belt loop on his shorts. He bent and picked a final ball out of a wire basket at his feet, pulled his right arm back, and gave it a rough throw.

Twump!

"Ahh!" he said. He grabbed the shoulder of his throwing arm, that arm that had helped win so many games. "Frig!" he shouted and kicked the basket.

The mesh-metal basket slammed into the concrete building right at the corner from which Mildred was peeking. She whimpered. Aaron Renfro squinted into the shadows beyond the building. The basket had ricocheted and come to rest near Mildred, bent in half. The violence of the act made her limbs feel like jelly. She'd never seen him angry. Usually, he was the upbeat joker. Mean jokes, sometimes bad jokes, but jokes he found hilarious all the same.

"Who's there?" he demanded.

What if he thinks I'm a vandal from another team? Poor Mildred was petrified. She wanted to shout, "It's me!" but nothing louder than a squeak came out. *Speak to Aaron now? Alone? I can't!* Her words were caught in her throat.

"I said, who's there?" he called again, this time coming toward her hiding spot with a surly stride. He was intimidating and suddenly so close . . .

"Stop!" she shouted in panic.

Aaron stopped dead in his tracks and a cruel smile grew on his suntanned face. "Piggy, is that you?"

How many times had he taunted her, embarrassed her, and made her cry for him to stop? *Just please stop.* Mildred had no doubt he knew it was her the moment she'd let her voice squeak past her lips. He laughed as if he'd been silly for thinking it could have been anyone else, confirming her suspicions. She knew coming here had been a mistake. She could see the look on Aaron's face and knew what was in store. Practice was going badly, but now was the time for some fun. When feeling inadequate in skill, what better way to vent than to play with his favorite toy?

"What are you doing here?" he asked, as if he already knew but didn't want to deny himself the pure joy of taunting her.

Mildred was already trembling. It was dark, she was alone. No teachers would wander by and scare him into going quiet upon sight. No other student was around to see what he might do. There were no limits. Her heart pitter-pattered in her ears, a flapping moth in her chest. She gripped the strap of her helmet tightly as the weight of it rested against her right thigh. Aaron's hand smacked the side of the concession building above her head and she jumped like a timid mouse. Cornered.

"You followed me here, didn't you?" He cackled out loud. "You like to watch, huh? Like a freak."

Mildred shook her head. "N-n-n—"

"Get it out," he said.

He nudged her shoulder with his hand, but not hard enough to knock her backward.

"No." Her voice was almost a whisper, tearing up through her throat.

"You did. You probably watch me all the time. I've had that feeling of being watched out here. Now I know who it was."

"I don't—" Mildred said. Her face was flaming hot.

"Yeah, right. You probably cry yourself to sleep at night pining over me. Well, looks like you're out of luck." He made an unconvincing mock frown. "I'm just not into fat, pimply girls."

He guffawed as though he'd said the most hilarious thing. Mildred was speechless as she listened to the echo of the words in her mind, joined by other words he'd called her before. Like ghosts flying through her, blow after blow.

"You'll probably die a virgin," he said as he looked her over. "Because nobody is going to have sex with a disgusting pig."

The sting of his words scorched Mildred. It was as though fire had hit her square in the chest and flared outward, charging her limbs. Without thinking, she swung the helmet fast and hard. *Thunk!*

How could she have done that? She stared, wide eyed. Nobody could have been ready for her to react in such a violent way, not even Aaron Renfro. He stopped laughing immediately, and his eyes widened. He spit out bright blood and a tooth. Red spit swung from his lips as he came at her. She reacted instantly, letting all the hate she felt crackle through her like electricity and propel her arm.

"What the-*ack*!" *Thunk!*

Mildred was wound up and felt twice as strong as she ever had. The rage she'd tasted in the witch's house was as alive and destructive as wildfire. She pummeled Aaron again. *Smack!* Tiny wet splatters dotted her face. He swung at her but his injured shoulder made his punch weak. His fist flailed in the air uselessly. He tried to grab her with his left hand but she backed up just out of his grasp. Again, she swung and connected. *Crack!* This time, Aaron collapsed at her feet. He didn't move. He just lay there and bled some more and made an odd gurgling sound. She hit him a few more times for good measure. *Crack! Crunch!* He twitched but didn't fight, or speak . . . or breathe.

Something in Mildred, whatever it was that had led her here, celebrated. Her body tingled with pleasure that was not her own. Aaron was dead, she realized. From somewhere foggy, Mildred thought, *This is wrong. It's all wrong!* But at the same time . . . it was right.

She laughed as loudly as he'd laughed only moments ago. She'd never have to hear his cruel voice call her *Piggy* ever again. Her mirth faded into the night. Her joy was fast being replaced with something darker. Something sinister. A hunger. A craving.

A brief thought flitted through her mind—*What's happening?*—before she knelt next to his limp body. There, in the shadows, hidden from moonlight and stadium lights, she put her mouth to his cracked and distorted one. If a passerby happened along, they might think two lovebirds were making out. If someone with a sharper eye managed to see a slight glimmer of reflected light on the blood that was spilling out of the shadows, they might assume she was attempting CPR. They'd never guess what was really happening. What she was doing was inconceivable. Abominable.

She lowered her mouth to his; his blood tasted metallic. His lifeless lips didn't jerk away or twist in disgust at the sensation of Mildred's lips meeting them. She took his tongue into her mouth—the one that always had a taunt for her, spoke up in public, had jokes; the very same one that had a way of winning over the ladies—and she bit as hard as she could. She realized with a sinking feeling of horror that her incisors were sharper than usual, longer, and she couldn't stop herself from clamping down as hard as she could, but her new teeth still weren't sharp enough. She had to shake her head like the lions she'd watched feed on an elephant on the Discovery Channel. When his tongue finally severed from his mouth, Mildred stood up.

Blood ran down her chin. It coated her cheeks and some of her nose. She chewed while she strapped her filthy, dented helmet back on her head. She left him there and sped away on her moped, consuming his witty words and charisma.

10

In an odd euphoric haze, Mildred pulled into her empty driveway. She switched off the motor and slid off the seat. Her street, which had seemed indistinct to her before, came into focus. Like an anchor, the familiarity of her home helped put everything else in perspective. She had just murdered someone. Not only that, but she had *eaten* a part of him. As the overwhelming sense of rage seeped out of her fingers and toes, her body convulsed with fear and disgust at the terrible thing she'd done. Her hands shook violently as she desperately fumbled to enter the garage door code.

It wasn't anything she would ever even dream of doing. Where had this evil act come from?

She knew.

She had messed up by going to Crossroads Magicks and by asking for what she did. She was desperate. The woman was an evil witch. She took advantage of Mildred's weakness, like so many others in Mildred's life. As soon as she'd entered that shack, she'd known it hadn't felt right, but she had pressed on. By then, she had already fallen prey to the dark influence of that place, was already losing her grip on reality. There must have been some magic that had driven her blind. It had been so powerful.

The garage door went up too loudly. Mildred looked around, worried someone would see her, but the street was clear and the surrounding houses were unlit. She pushed her moped into the darkened garage.

Was the woman something more than a witch? Was she some evil being? Mildred struggled with her limited knowledge of such things. She recalled a movie she watched long ago with Patsy called *Wishmaster*, about a magical being that granted wishes in horrific ways. Patsy had said he was a djinn. Could the woman have been a djinn? She had granted Mildred's wish, saved her from the bully, but the circumstances were unbelievably twisted. Furthermore . . . why? Why had Mildred done what she did to Aaron's body?

It was all Mildred could do to hold it together long enough to shut the garage door behind her, closing out the night, before collapsing onto the cold concrete floor.

"Oh God!" she cried. "What did I do?"

She felt the dried blood on her face and the stream of tears that ran through it, making the blood sticky. The way he tasted, the mixture of saliva and blood, flashed through her memory. The way his eye had left its socket and dangled against his left cheek—from where she'd bludgeoned him in cold blood—taunted her. She gagged. Crouched on her hands and knees, Mildred thought, *No matter what happened at that place, I'm a murderer. I'm the one who committed the act.* She retched but nothing came up. Aaron's chewed-up tongue was still in her stomach.

She gripped her shirt, feeling her belly beneath, thinking of the thing she had done after she had killed Aaron. For a moment, she wondered if she could get any diseases from consuming his tongue. She had heard Caroline Miller had a case of mono. Aaron dated Caroline sometimes. Could Mildred catch it? She wished she could tear her belly open and pull every shred of him out of her. She got up and ran through her house. When she got to her bathroom, she snatched her toothbrush and knelt at the toilet. It did no good. No matter how many times she gagged herself, the tongue was there to stay.

A worse thought came to her while she sat by the toilet in defeat. *Prison*. She'd just left his bloody and mangled body out in the open. Her moped tracks were probably there, leading away from the parking lot. Maybe there was even some other type of forensic evidence that she didn't know could be left at a crime scene. Could she explain possible evidence away? Say it was perfectly logical for traces of her to be there because it was a public place that she frequented? Probably, she told herself. They could hardly say that her hair or fingerprints shouldn't be at the school. She took a deep calming breath at the thought.

Right away, Mildred decided not to go back to try to move the body. That would be stupid, she rationalized. If she moved him and someone found him, there would probably be traces of her being at that second site. *That* would be too damning. She wouldn't be able to explain that away with "I go to school there." Nope. Best to leave him where he died.

Her body shook, her nerves still on the brink. Even if they never found out it was her, she would know. She killed him and then she *ate* part of him. She would carry that guilt with her for the rest of her life. What exactly had caused her to act that way?

A curse? *It wasn't supposed to be real,* she thought. It was just supposed to be a desperate attempt to pacify herself, an act that should have just given her courage to face her classmates for a while longer. A twisted but harmless attempt to entertain the thought that they'd get what was coming to them one day. But not by her hand. Certainly not by murder, and not by cannibalism. What had she done?

Perhaps it had all been a dream, she hoped. The strange magic shop, the witch or whatever she was. Aaron.

However, it was not a dream. The blood and the dent in her helmet made sure there was proof against that theory, but Mildred couldn't come to terms with what had happened, so she ultimately decided to ignore it. She would pretend it hadn't happened at all. As far as she was concerned, Aaron Renfro was at home, making out with some popular girl or doing some other typical Aaron thing.

The blood on her clothes, helmet, and the garage floor were another matter. No way could she ignore it. She couldn't risk Naomi, her family's housekeeper, seeing this when she came into work. Naomi only came on Wednesdays and Sundays. Tomorrow was a Wednesday, and Naomi would surely be there at the crack of dawn. Mildred would have to clean the dark-red mess up before the young woman came to do her job.

Mildred searched frantically through the cleaning products for an item to clean her helmet and found Clorox wipes. She figured that should do the job and it did. There wasn't much she could do about the dent, however. She laid the helmet on the counter, then peeled her stained clothes and shoes off right there in the kitchen, and spent a moment feeling awkward being naked in a room that wasn't her bathroom. Could people see her? She felt like everyone was staring at her like this: naked, fat, and toting around bloody clothes she'd worn while committing murder. She barged into the clean laundry room, accidentally getting blood on the white door frame.

"Crud!" she said.

When she wiped it with a Clorox wipe, it smeared. It took some elbow grease to get it to fade away completely, but then she saw the brown wood peeking through the white paint—she'd scraped the paint right off. She hoped nobody would notice. Mildred wouldn't have noticed herself, because she never went into the laundry room. The area was frequented by Naomi, mainly. Her mom entered it only to restock supplies for Naomi, and only used the cleaning items on the occasion that something had been spilled and the housekeeper wasn't around. Her dad never bothered with the room at all. Mildred figured she had a good chance of getting by—considering everything else she had to clean, Naomi wouldn't care about a spot of faded paint.

Satisfied with the doorway, Mildred went to the washing machine. It was big and pristine white, with all kinds of buttons she didn't understand at all. Load size stumped her. Should she call it small, because it was only a few things? Would it wash them better if she chose large? Her clothes were a big size and they were filthy, so she decided that she should call it large. She pressed the button for Large and a little dot lit up in green, as if she'd chosen the right setting.

She looked on the shelves for detergent and found a jar of square liquid-filled packs. There were no directions on the jar. Her mother had designed the room for an expert cleaner to frequent—someone who didn't need instructions. Mildred desperately needed them now. She took a gamble and tossed three in, because it felt like a good number.

The other buttons were the most confusing of all: the cycle choices. Mildred stared at the choices, then closed her eyes and mashed one. The machine whirred to life and flooded with water. The noise was so loud in the quiet, empty house that it startled her into pressing Stop. She pressed it several times, sure that she'd done something wrong. What if the machine filled up and spilled over? Her house would flood and she would have to call 911 for help. And they'd find the clothes.

She panicked at the thought. She retrieved the soiled clothes, now somewhat damp, and ran back through the kitchen and out to the garage, where she opened the large trash bin and tossed them inside, out of sight.

In the shower, she let the warm water wash the blood away from her hair and skin. When it ran clear, she got out and readied herself for bed, but she didn't sleep for a long time. She kept feeling the blood on her even though it was long gone. She kept tasting the tongue even though she'd brushed her teeth multiple times. She kept remembering the thing she was trying to forget.

//

At six o'clock in the morning, Tyler was awake. Tuffy, his gray British Longhair, had woken him, demanding to be fed by smacking him on the face with her soft paw—claws retracted of course—and meowing relentlessly. It was her language for "Get up and serve me, human." He did, and while she was content and crunching, Tyler stood in the kitchen and gazed through his window, studying the Wacos' house. The hedges hid a lot from his sight in the kitchen, but from his room upstairs, he was able to see a lot more of their house. He could see their whole yard.

He'd seen the strangest thing over there last night. Mildred had appeared on her scooter with something smeared all over her. Chocolate? Mud? It was hard to tell. He guessed it was mud, because there was a lot of it, and it looked like she'd been splashed with it.

Tyler had laughed and snapped a photo while Mildred waited for her garage to open, which was easy since his phone was already in his hand. He zoomed in so that the dark splatters were more visible and captured the image. Then he texted his friend Aaron, who'd always called Mildred Piggy. And rightfully so, especially covered in mud like that.

You're right, she is a pig [Image sent]

Crunch, Crunch, said Tuffy in the background as Tyler day-dreamed about the night before.

Aaron hadn't responded, but now Tyler noticed the message was marked as Read. No big deal—bros get busy. Aaron was popular with the ladies, and Tyler had heard a certain swim star was recently into Aaron. He didn't blame Aaron for blowing him off for her. She was a ten for sure. Hell, maybe even an eleven.

But something about last night kept irking Tyler. Mildred had looked so alarmed. Crazed. She had pulled into the driveway like a bat out of hell, looking around like a maniac, as if terrified of being seen.

I saw you, Mildred, you freak, he thought.

Tuffy stopped chomping and came to twirl around Tyler's legs like a little fur tornado. He picked her up and rubbed her fluffy head absently while she purred. He thought of the noises he'd heard after the garage door shut behind Mildred. He'd been curious enough to tread downstairs, step outside, and what he heard from his front lawn had sounded like howling sobs next door. There was retching involved. It was all very gross and confusing. Had Fat Ass eaten so much chocolate that she'd gotten sick? Had she fallen in mud and hurt herself? Or was something else going on?

"What do you think happened, Tuffy?" he asked.

If Tuffy also found Mildred's night-capades curious, she didn't say so. She allowed Tyler to carry her back to his bedroom and leave her on his bed, where she cozied into his rumpled blanket for a snooze.

Tyler opened his nightstand. Inside, he kept a notebook filled with his business plan, schedule, and a savings tracker. So far, he had saved $8,372. *Not bad for a fella who decided to work on lawns instead of going to college,* he thought. He'd been saving for a few years already, but it was all part of the plan. One day, he would be able to afford proper equipment and be able to hire workers to get more lawns done in a day—it was a work in progress.

But what he was really interested in was his schedule, which was farther back in the notebook. He was working on two lawns today: Mildew's—as he'd written her name down—and Chelle's. If he worked Mildred's yard first, maybe he could get a close-up of her moped. Whatever was all over her was bound to be on it as well. He never saw her washing the thing—despite all the times he and others had bombarded it with trash.

Plus, if he went to Chelle's later rather than earlier, he'd have a better chance of spending time with her when she got out of school. And maybe she would also be interested in whatever weird thing Mildred was up to. Cherished were the moments he could manage with Chelle that didn't involve being some sort of servant to her. Her lawn guy, her personal assistant, her bodyguard—he'd filled all those positions for her. The position he really coveted was boyfriend. There weren't many guys in Roanoke who didn't want the same, Tyler figured, with the only exception being her stepbrother, Dashiel.

Dash had graduated Roanoke High last year with Tyler. They had not been friends. Tyler tried to hang out with him, but they had nothing in common. Tyler loved to work or lift; Dash loved to relax. Tyler liked movies; Dash preferred reading books. Tyler liked football; Dash said it was a joke and he ranted for hours about the amount of money professional athletes made, using the word *absurd*. That was all Tyler could take of the dude. He wasn't friendly with Dash after that, even if it meant he might see less of Chelle—but it had the opposite effect. He found Chelle wanting to spend more time with him. He was her first go-to guy when she needed help with anything, likely because it annoyed Dash after their falling-out. And so, he fell into another position with her: revenge pawn.

The bad thing was that he didn't even mind. Not at all. She was that hot.

What he did mind was the sneaky, tubby girl next door. Of all the people he could live beside in the world, it had to be her. Everything about her turned him off. Her hair, her weight, her laziness, her clothes, her face, and above all, her cowardice. Now she was creeping around, doing weird stuff at night.

He tried to forget it. A weight bench sat at one side of his room, and on the wall beside it hung a chart. *Lifting Goals*, boasted the chart. His highest weight benched was 270, but the main goal, written in black marker at the bottom, larger than the rest, was 300. He added 5 pounds to each side, making the weights a full 280. If focusing on that didn't take his mind off that weirdo next door, he didn't know what would.

By the time he finished lifting, he hadn't forgotten anything. He felt more like something wasn't right. Deep within his mind, he wondered if it wasn't something more disgusting that he saw her drenched in last night. He didn't want to think it, but he wondered if maybe it could have been blood.

But how would that freak have gotten blood on her? And why? Did she hurt someone? Or something? Tyler looked at Tuffy's furry body, resting content and safe on his bed. Was she one of those creeps you read about in news articles?

"He/she was really strange, they had no friends, and stuck to themselves."

That's what they always said about serial killers. Mildred sounded like that kind of person . . .

Tyler scoffed and shook his head. Mildred Waco wasn't capable of killing anyone. She was terrified of everyone who came near her. The thought was . . . what word was that Dash had used? Absurd.

But Tyler heard somewhere that when serial killers started on the path to serial killing, they started out killing animals. *She could be capable of that,* he thought. If the stuff on her last night was blood, which he'd now convinced himself it was, she had to have gotten it on her from somewhere, and if not a human, then what? A friendly dog? A cat, like Tuffy? This thought sent Tyler into a fury. If there was one thing he couldn't stand, it was animal cruelty.

He changed into a dry shirt, picturing horrors all the while. Animals crying out in pain as Mildred bathed in their blood, laughing, fully aware that they weren't a danger to her like the people she cowered away from for so long. Knowing that she could torture them in secret . . . Tyler's stomach knotted at the torrid of macabre thoughts. If only he hadn't seen her—but no. It was better that he *did* see her, because he was going to go over there to check stuff out. If he found any proof, any at all, he was turning her in.

If she was doing this, would it really be different from the way they'd treated Mildred for years? *Yes,* he told himself furiously. She was weird and gross. She was all-round unpleasant, and she could have stood up for herself at any time, but she always chose not to.

He looked at the photo again. Mildred's eyes were wide enough to see the whites shining in the light outside the garage. Her irises looked solid black. Dark splatters spread across her cheeks and nose, poured down her mouth, chin, and neck, as if she'd vomited whatever it was. And it certainly did look like blood. Could it be her own? Tyler hoped it was. Better her than some poor animal she'd taken her frustrations out on. *Any girl who looks like that has to have a lot of frustrations,* he thought. Either way, he would find out.

His parents were still asleep as he slipped quietly by their bedroom. The morning air was slightly chilly, but comfortable, not that he paid much mind to it. His thoughts locked onto the Wacos' garage. He had the code because he used some of their lawn equipment stored in there. If anyone caught him going inside, he'd just grab the hedge clippers. Just another normal day, doing the job they paid him for . . . not investigating anything suspicious at all.

12

Vaguely, as if in a dream, Mildred heard the clink of the metal curtain hoops sliding on the metal rod above her bedroom window. A burst of sunbeams exploded into her dark room. She felt like jumping up and screaming, the way a vampire might, but she was much too comfy in her soft bed. Instead, she groaned her displeasure and squinted her eyes.

"Wake up," Naomi's high-pitched voice said. "Millie, wake up. You have school today."

"No, sleep," Mildred grumbled. She pulled the covers over her head. A vision of Aaron beaten and bloody flashed in her mind and she threw the covers away. "Okay, I'm up!"

"Did you have an accident?" Naomi asked. Her eyes were fixed on Mildred with concern.

"Huh?" Mildred asked. Her mother would have cringed to hear her say it. *It isn't a word,* she always insisted, *It's an ignorant sound unintelligent people make.* Mildred had gotten used to never saying it. It sounded strange to her own ears but Naomi didn't seem to find it odd.

"Accident. Did you have an accident?" Naomi repeated. She held up Mildred's helmet. It was clean but dented on the side.

If Mildred told Naomi that she'd had an accident, she would undoubtedly tell Mildred's parents and her parents might make a big deal. It was a slim shot, but still a big enough chance for Mildred to not want to say.

"I dropped it," she said. She was shocked at herself. Normally, she would have stumbled over her words and sounded very suspicious.

Naomi's brows raised into the straight line of her thick bangs as she studied the dent again. "Where did you drop it from, a five-story building?" she pressed.

"Don't worry about it," Mildred said. "It's no big deal." Okay, her voice was definitely strange today. Instead of the hateful, shrill sound that she typically used to indicate her annoyance, it was calm and had a carefree undertone. In her ears, the sound was sort of like Aaron's style of speaking. That nonchalant way he charmed people, almost without even trying.

Naomi was no exception. "Okay, Millie, but come on, let's get up," she said.

Mildred was bewildered by the housekeeper's reaction, but she went with it. "How about you make me some breakfast, toots?" The words rolled right off her tongue, and this time she didn't marvel at them. They were quickly growing on her.

"Toots?" Naomi giggled. "I'll make you some eggs and bacon. You get dressed, okay?"

She sat the dented helmet gently on the dresser beside Mildred's perfume bottles—never used—which Barbara insisted on buying her from every city and country she visited. As if those little glass bottles could make up for her absence. Naomi walked out of the room with a polite smile, and for the first time in a long time, Mildred smiled back.

Mildred threw on clothes without really caring how they looked. All her clothes were so basic and plain, so uncool, that it wouldn't have mattered anyway. She ended up in a faded green tee and a pair of tan corduroy pants. She looked in her full-length bathroom mirror.

I look like a walking palm tree, she thought. *No, a palm tree is skinny. More like an oak tree. A fat oak tree.*

What's more, her hair was flat and oily again—even though she'd showered the previous night—and she had a huge pimple on her nose. It was more than huge. It was mammoth. Colossal. And bright red.

"Have a great day, Rudolph Waco," she said to her mirror self sarcastically. She'd never had a habit of constructing or voicing such horrible opinions of herself before. Most things she thought of herself were negative things other people had already said about her. This was something totally new, but she didn't spend much time pondering the development.

In the kitchen, the bacon was sizzling. She found a seat, and as soon as the food hit a plate and landed in front of her, she felt like vomiting.

"Enjoy. I'll go clean Mr. and Mrs. Waco's office," Naomi said. "I'll clean up here when you leave."

"Okay," Mildred said.

She didn't think she'd enjoy any of the food. It smelled rancid. None of it was appealing to her. Not even Naomi's freshly squeezed orange juice. She threw it all down the garbage disposal, so it wouldn't hurt Naomi's feelings that she hadn't eaten it. Her stomach felt empty, but something was off about that food. She searched through the fridge to find something else but came up empty. Despite a fully stocked variety of foods, nothing appealed to her.

Downtrodden, Mildred retrieved her helmet and walked into the garage—where she immediately bumped into Tyler, her neighbor. *Oh right,* she remembered, *he's working at our house today.* His boulder-sized body barely budged when Mildred plowed into him, but he looked angry anyway. It must have been the idea that someone as unimportant as Mildred didn't see someone like him. Regardless of his sports career not getting him an easy ride through college, Tyler had always given the impression that he was tough stuff. To himself, he was a huge deal. He had always viewed her as beneath him, and took every opportunity to show her, even though her parents signed one of his paychecks.

"Watch where you're going, Mildew," he said, working up a nasty tone he reserved just for her.

"Sorry," Mildred spouted. "Maybe you shouldn't have been standing in the way."

She clapped her mouth shut. Those words had come from nowhere. She barely even registered that they were coming from her at all. They were smooth and automatic. Aaron! He'd already gotten her in trouble.

Tyler scrutinized her. His neck was as thick as a tree trunk. Huge muscles bulged at his shoulders and down his arms. Hedge trimmers hung limply from one of his beefy hands.

"You shittin' me?" He set down the trimming sheers. "Tubby has attitude now, does she?"

"I didn't—I didn't really mean that . . ." Mildred said.

He was big and tough and could crush her with hardly any effort. He was obviously aware of that, yet he chose to press matters. Chose to flex his size and intimidate her. *If he actually hurts me, nobody will know,* Mildred thought. Naomi was cleaning the office, a room that had a special soundproof feature so her parents wouldn't be bothered with noises—Mildred—when they worked from home.

"It seemed like you meant it."

He was closer, standing over her, proving that he was big and bad. She hated him. Hatred rumbled in her stomach. It rose into her chest. She tried to fight it down, steadying herself, breathing deep.

"I didn't. I meant *I* shouldn't have been in *your* way." She laughed nervously. "I was talking to myself."

He glared at her then said, "Yeah, you are that type." He turned away from Mildred and her heart pounded in her chest as he crouched in front of her moped. "Weirdo."

All her life, Mildred had been called much worse than *weirdo*, but this time it gave her feelings she'd never felt. Anger and an urgency for retribution. A red-hot hatred inside her snapped open, like a roadside flare.

"You finally cleaned this heap of junk?" he was saying, but it was far away in her mind.

In a daze, she went for the hedge trimmers, took them in both hands, and spread the blades apart. Tyler must have felt her coming upon him, because he started to turn, but she'd already buried the blades in his back. He struggled on his knees, trying to reach the trimmers. His muscles were too big to allow him to reach far, so the shears stayed there as Mildred ran and slammed the button to close the garage door. She came back and pulled the blades out. A red line sprayed from the wound and from his mouth. The bright color should have taken hold of her, snapped her out of it, but it did not. She kept the trimmers open and shoved the blades right through Tyler's eyes. Her hands, as they plunged the blades in and pulled them out again, surprised her. They weren't her usual hands. Her nails were longer, sharper, like claws. She could dig right into his skin with them. He stopped struggling, going limp on the garage floor like a giant sack of flour. She let the gory trimmers, with one of his eyes still clinging to a blade, fall next to her feet.

He's so strong, she thought. *But he fell so easily. A waste of all that muscle.*

She was still burning with hate, and just as hungry as she'd been when she'd woken up that morning. He was wearing a muscle shirt, of course. Blood spattered the tight skin at his shoulders and biceps. Mildred licked her lips and felt her teeth had sharpened, like they had when she'd attacked Aaron. She went down next to Tyler and lapped up the splatters on his arm, then sunk her teeth in. She ate until nothing was left of his arms but bone, from shoulders to hands. Everything happened quickly and she never seemed to feel full, but once it was over, her anger washed away, like dirt in a shower. The grotesque claws faded into her normal fingers, with her usual short, chipped nails. The sharpness of her teeth dulled to normal. Unfortunately, the body and the taste of Tyler's blood remained. As well as her instant regret.

"No!" she cried. "Not this. Not again!"

But it had happened again. Tyler's face had gone as pale as a ghost, with two gory holes where his eyes should be. The missing flesh from his arms sent a shiver of disgust through Mildred. She wept for what she'd done to him, even though she had hated him.

She would have rather hated him as he was alive and well than be the cause of his death.

She was a murderer twice over now. She wondered if that made her a serial killer, and that thought begat another one, a more frightening one: how many times would this happen before she would be free? Would she kill everyone who had hurt her in the past? Would she continue to kill those who hurt her in the future?

The questions were too much for her. She felt as if they were pounding her on the head from every angle. Her mind shut them down to protect itself.

Just focus on the tasks at hand, she told herself.

She had only twenty minutes to get to school, where she would have to act like everything was normal before they found Aaron. Now she had another body to deal with, and this one was far more damning, being in her garage. It was just luck that Naomi hadn't stepped in to check on the commotion. Mildred knew she had to hide this quickly or she would go to prison for something she was unable to stop. It wasn't as if she could tell the jury she had simply been cursed by a witch and get out of two murder convictions. She shoved Tyler's body with all her might until she managed to get him into the corner with the lawn mower. She threw a tarp over both him and the machine. It would have to do until she had time to plan something better.

She threw away her clothes and, checking for Naomi the whole time, ran to her bathroom to rinse herself and retrieve another outfit from her bedroom.

Naomi was in the kitchen when she came back through. "Oh, good idea, that outfit looks much better!" She smiled cheerfully at Mildred. "You have a good day, Millie!"

"Thanks, Naomi, you too," Mildred said.

She was careful to keep the ghastly murder scene hidden from Naomi's view while opening the garage door. There was a drain in the floor of the garage, so Mildred hosed the concrete floor before she left.

She had to be at school in ten minutes, which she could do today because for once she didn't feel like stopping at her favorite bakery. She would have just enough time to get to school and find her seat in her first class.

Mildred kept reliving her violent acts, and by the time she made it halfway to school, they were weighing on her heavily. In the moment, they felt like sweet revenge for everything that had been done to her. They had felt justified. But now they made her feel wicked. Also, what was up with her hands changing during the attack? Sharp nailed, tougher purplish skin. They weren't her hands at all. And her teeth—she felt like she was turning into an animal. What was happening to her? Overwhelmed, she pulled over to the shoulder of the road and, careful to hide her face from passersby, bawled.

She had just pulled into the school—six minutes late—when she saw something that made her stomach and heart sink. Cop cars. At least five of them, with the bold words *Roanoke Police* stretched along their sides. Blue strobe lights on their roofs were still flashing. Two officers held back a growing crowd.

13

Patsy sat quietly in Seth's passenger seat, pondering deeply. The night before she had pulled out her special wooden box from behind the picture frame. Inside was something she'd promised she'd hide forever. This special, secret thing had been locked away since she'd locked away her friendship with Mildred. A longing nagged at her to have both back in her life, but she was afraid. The thing in the box was the first valuable item her mother had ever given her, and it was also the worst. Box in hand, the scene had been all the more vivid in her memory.

ø

"Pretty girls deserve pretty things," Kathy said, a sly grin on her narrow face.

Patsy's fingers explored the pearls and diamonds with wonder. So smooth. So shiny.

"I saw you looking at them," Kathy said.

"But they're not mine, Mommy," Patsy said.

"They are now," Kathy said. "You deserve them more than that rich girl because you'll love them. She doesn't care about them. She left them lying on the floor, forgotten."

Ø

She felt sick as she recalled the words of her mother.

Ø

"Just one rule," Kathy demanded. "Never, ever tell anyone how Mommy gets things, or she might go away for a while, like Daddy. We don't want that, do we?"

Imagining her mom being taken away made Patsy's heart feel heavy and her eyes sting. "No, I don't want you to go!" She plowed into her mother's arms and wrapped herself around her waist.

"Then don't tell," Kathy said. "Promise?"

"I won't, I promise!"

"Cross your heart?" Kathy gently pushed Patsy away from her and made an X over her own chest with her slender finger.

"Cross my heart." Patsy mimicked her mother's gesture.

She really, really meant it. Daddy had been gone for months and if Mommy was gone, too, Patsy would be all alone.

Ø

Alone.

Mildred. She was all alone at Roanoke High and it weighed on

Patsy. Sitting on her bed last night with the box, she knew why Mildred had slammed the door in her face hours earlier.

I should just give it back and apologize, then she can stop being mad at me, thought Patsy.

But what if Mrs. Waco decided to press charges? They might have suspected all these years that Kathy had taken the pearl and diamond necklace, but they didn't know for certain. Bringing it back would be like signing a confession. Patsy could barely keep her life together *with* Kathy's help. What would Patsy do without her?

Patsy glanced over at Seth, his eyes on the road, lip-syncing to a popular song on the radio. He hadn't noticed her gloomy mood and Patsy wondered how much he cared. What would he think if she turned her mother in? What if she was homeless because she couldn't pay rent without her mother? What would they all think?

On impulse, she turned down the radio.

"Hey!" he said. "I'm the driver, I choose the volume."

"Do you love me?" Patsy's face was serious.

"'Course I do, babe."

He said the words but was he really feeling them?

"Would you love me if I wasn't a cheerleader?"

He chuckled. "Why would you ask that?"

"Just would you?"

Shrug. "Yeah, of course."

"What about if I was sick?"

"What?" Finally, some concern. "Patsy, are you sick?"

"No, it's just hypothetical."

"Yes, I would love you."

"What if I was poor?"

He laughed. "Sure, babe. You're being really weird, by the way."

The way he laughed her off in such a flippant manner, it

seemed like a joke to him. Patsy didn't feel his words at all and she didn't think he was feeling them either. He pulled into the school parking lot and immediately the blue flashing lights of the police cars drowned out all Patsy's thoughts. Panic and confusion settled in their place.

"What the hell?" Seth mumbled.

They got out of his truck and followed a sparse trail of confused and curious students; as they got closer, they saw the traumatized faces. Some were crying, some were comforting others with hugs, some were being comforted. Patsy saw faculty members on edge, in a state of sadness and struggling to keep control, calming students. Police officers were huddled around something beside the football field.

A cry broke out in the crowd and Patsy saw Joan Renfro. There were a few noticeable people among the faces around her—Chelle, Yvette, Donna, Herman—but someone was missing.

"Aaron Renfro." The name came from nearby, a student telling another latecomer. "Dead."

Patsy's thoughts were jumbled as she ran over to Joan's crowd. She was one of them, after all, and this was her place. All thoughts from a few moments ago about walking away from all of them disappeared in the face of such tragedy. *Dead? Dead how? Why?* Questions that everyone was probably asking, no doubt, but nobody louder than Joan.

"Why?" she cried in a raw voice that ripped through Patsy.

She had to look away, and when she did, she saw Mildred. Horror was etched on her former friend's face as she stood yards away. Alone.

14

Mildred's troubled, sunken heart pounded rapidly somewhere into her lower abdomen, or so it felt.

"Back it up," an officer said as he waved people back.

A crying blond girl fought against the officer's outstretched arms before breaking away toward the concession stand, her moist face zeroed in on the ground where something unbelievable lay. Like an anchor, a tall officer held her by the waist while her legs swung in turbulent desperation.

Mildred recognized her right away as Joan Renfro, Aaron's younger sister. She was a freshman, two years behind Mildred, but Mildred knew who she was. Everyone did, thanks to her brother and her position on the cheer squad. At that moment, she was making full use of those infamously powerful lungs all cheerleaders seemed to possess.

"No! Nooo! Aaron!" she cried.

The other cheerleaders and some of the football team were near her. Some of them—like her best friend, Donna—were crying with her. Some of them—Chelle—looked afraid. Mildred saw Patsy rush up to the crowd with Seth at her heels. Last time she'd seen Patsy, she'd shoved the door closed in her face, knowing the others couldn't be far. Seeing Patsy there with the popular group, instead of next to Mildred, solidified what she suspected. If Patsy cared, she would have seen the terror and worry on Mildred's face and come to her. Instead, she was caught up with *them*. A tinge of anger sparked in Mildred, but then tears spilled over Patsy's eyelashes and Mildred gasped. Patsy may not be her best friend now, but she had been, and seeing her cry was a slap back to reality for Mildred.

The blood drained from Mildred's face. She felt a sharp stab in her chest. All the turmoil happening before her was her fault. She had taken someone's life, and in doing so, she'd hurt and terrified all these people, and she was sure she would go to jail because of it.

You knew it, Millie, you knew they'd find him, she thought miserably.

Her terror-stricken eyes focused on the curiously shaped sheet spread out on the ground, the dark-red grass around it making the white sheet seem even brighter. She saw the place where his nose would be tenting the sheet if she hadn't broken it flat. And even though she knew the terrible state of his body, she thought, *Wouldn't it be great if he would just stand up right now?*

He would likely be the darnedest gruesome sight any of them had ever beheld. Their screams would reach outer space. That would scare them bad enough for picking on her—she wouldn't have to punish any more of them. He would be alive and if he could be alive, Tyler would be alive as well.

Wait. She hadn't meant to think *punish*, and she knew that

neither of those boys was alive. She felt them in her in a way that let her know they couldn't possibly exist anywhere else, and she couldn't even begin to understand what that meant.

The dark-red splatters on the concrete building beside Aaron's body were being scraped into a vial by a casually dressed guy wearing gloves. She hadn't worn gloves.

They're going to know.

She wanted to vomit but knew it was out of the question. Just like she couldn't vomit Aaron's tongue the night before, she wouldn't be able to vomit Tyler's arms. Thanks to dark magic, this was what her life had become.

A gust of wind blew the sheet up, partially revealing what she had done. Aaron's face was a scarlet mess. The tall officer left Joan and rushed to cover the body, but it was too late. Chaos had already filled the air, confirming that everyone had seen. Shocked, Joan's knees hit the ground and Donna rushed over to wrap her long arms around Joan's shoulders.

"Who—who would d-do such a th-thing?" Joan sobbed.

"That's precisely what we want to know, miss," an officer spoke softly to her. He was copper skinned and buff, with a notable set of vibrant green eyes. If Mildred had to guess, she'd assume he was in his midtwenties. "I'm Detective Hyde. You're the victim's sister?"

Joan nodded and sniffled. Herman Bernstein, nerdy-looking as always in a white polo, rushed forward to help Detective Hyde lift Joan to a standing position. He stayed among the group of popular students at her side, sharing their pain, and they accepted him, because he had known Aaron well.

"Is there anyone your brother argued with? Any problems he may have had with anyone?" he asked, keeping his calming tone steady.

Joan didn't seem to be in the mood to discuss her brother's life at the moment.

"No," she said, as if insulted that he'd accuse her brother of being disliked in the least. "Everyone loves him. Loved . . . loves . . . everyone—" She howled an agonizing cry.

That's what she thinks, Mildred thought. *Her brother was an ass.* But it also stung her eyes and made her chest feel heavy to hear the girl in so much pain. It was tough to bear. Mildred wondered if she could slip away without being noticed but decided it might make her look guilty.

"It's okay. You don't have to talk right now." Detective Hyde patted Joan's shoulder in a friendly, comforting sort of way. "Your counselor will escort you to a more private area for now. Your friend can go, too, if you'd like." He indicated Donna as the specific friend he was referring to.

"Thank you," Joan said.

As Joan and Donna were led away by Mr. Turner, a tired, aged officer and Miss Spade made their way to the center of the group. They spoke in low voices with Detective Hyde. The crowd's noise grew. Cries, sobs, students calling their parents to tell them what had happened. When the officials finished their private conversation, the older officer had to raise his voice to make his next words heard.

"Everyone, I'm Detective Carter. My partner—Detective Hyde—and I,"—he indicated the younger officer at his side—"will be the lead investigators on the case. Who found the body?" he shouted.

Herman raised his very skinny arm. *Figures,* Mildred thought, feeling bitter. He had cost her the extra time she had hoped for, and though she hated to admit it, she had always been just a smidge jealous of him. *Dorks are supposed to be bullied,* she thought. *But they don't bully Herman.* They let him in their circle. Instead, they saved the bullying for Mildred.

She was aware, however, that his life wasn't exactly ideal. The cool kids didn't bully him; they used him. Herman was the football team's lackey. He practically worshipped the ground they walked on. Always helpful and eager to please, he did anything they asked. In return, they let him hang around them. From washing their uniforms to chauffeuring them on long drives during dates so they could make out in the back of his sensible hybrid car, Herman did it all. He was the kind of pal they would call in a jam but wouldn't invite to their cool parties.

Mildred did not like Herman, and, like his idols, he didn't like her either. He often talked down to her for her lack of intelligence and motivation.

He said things like "You are always late because you don't care about your education. You just come to disrupt class and waste the time of people who *do* care about their education."

Mildred could picture how it had gone: *Herman comes to school early to make sure all the football players get their homework to turn in so they can pass classes and stay on the team, but he can't find the smoothest mouth in Roanoke, Aaron Renfro. Lo and behold, he discovers the grisly scene next to the football field where Aaron had had some of the best times of his life. Gasp and shudder.*

She soaked in Herman's surly expression. The way he locked eyes with the officer, seeming somewhat proud that he'd been the first to discover this nefarious deed. *He's probably thinking that he can help solve the case. Annoying, nosy Herman.* Mildred wished he had gotten mono from Caroline Miller and missed school today.

"I need to see you privately," Detective Carter told Herman. He then raised his voice to speak to the crowd. "If any of you has any information, please leave your name and number with Detective Hyde. If you feel that it is too important to wait, please go to the station. You're welcome to bring your parents to join our interview or you may conduct it on your own. For now, we need everyone to vacate the area. This is a crime scene."

Nobody left. Some people started to complain. They wanted to know what was going on. What was going to happen? Who had done such a thing?

"That'll do, that'll do, students." Miss Spade took over. "You heard the officer. We must leave the crime scene to the investigators. Considering this tragedy, school is canceled today." Her eyes were red and troubled.

This display of emotion was puzzling to Mildred. Was she reading the expression wrong? Could the bad principal actually care about the students? Or was it only students who weren't Mildred? "Anyone who seeks counseling may see Mr. Turner. His office will be open today, otherwise, please return to your homes and if you must be out, stay in groups. We don't know what kind of lunatic is out there."

Mildred couldn't stop her eyes from narrowing at Miss Spade. *Lunatic, indeed.* Couldn't anyone simply make a mistake? It's not like she was a bloodthirsty maniac. She was just . . . temporarily possessed? Cursed?

"Excuse me," a soft voice from the crowd said.

Students separated to let someone through, and Tiffany Cosby strutted out of the bunch. Her white socks were pulled up to the bottom of her knees and her blue skirt was pulled down to just above them. She wore the same pompous look she always wore, like she'd just smelled something stinky.

"Sorry, Miss Spade, but we have rehearsals today. Regionals is only a week away and rehearsal is mandatory at this point," she said.

Tiffany was the band's most talented member. She played the keyboard and her fingers were magical. Mildred was also in band, but she was wretched. She hated it. When Barbara made Mildred join an after-school activity, Mildred had chosen music. She hoped that the racket produced while practicing at home would annoy her mother so much she'd let Mildred quit. She had chosen the tuba to further annoy her, but also because she felt a bit smaller next to its girth. She was horrible at making music with it.

A moment ago, she'd thought band practice would be one less nuisance to have to deal with. She thought she'd get home and get rid of the body and filthy clothes in her garage. She'd hide away from everyone until she could figure out what was going on and stop it from happening again.

"Very well, Tiffany," Miss Spade said. "Stay inside except for band rehearsal students."

Mildred's eyebrows raised in disbelief. Her expression didn't go unnoticed.

"I said *mandatory*, Mildred," Tiffany said. "So don't even think about skipping out."

Mildred's plans would have to be put on hold. She glared at Tiffany as she tossed her curly hair back and bounced away. Mildred scowled, knowing Tiffany would be back for practice before any of the others, waiting to condemn Mildred for not making it there first, as usual.

As the other students dispersed, Mildred realized what she was doing. She wiped the look of distaste off her face. When she glanced over at Hyde, his green eyes were locked solidly onto her, soaking in the entire exchange.

Ø

Mildred was moments away from backing out of her parking spot when someone tapped her shoulder. She was surprised to see the handsome face of Detective Hyde when she looked up. His 60-watt smile was almost painful up close and Mildred was reminded of her own crooked, yellow teeth. They pressed against her lips uncomfortably. One sharp corner of a tooth grazed her tongue and she felt ashamed that she couldn't match his easy grin.

I bet he was popular in school, she thought. *He has no idea what it's like for someone like me.*

She let the motor on her moped die down and lifted her helmet so that it leaned back and rested atop her head. "Yes?"

"Cool ride," he said, friendly.

Mildred knew what Hyde was doing by pretending to be nice to her. Open with a compliment, gain her trust—tricks he'd likely picked up in some type of detective class. She thought of saying, "Sorry, I'd prefer to have my parents present before answering any questions." But to say such a thing would probably look suspicious. Aside from that, it didn't seem as if he was asking her questions about the crime . . . yet.

"Thanks," she said, unmoved. "It gets me from A to B."

"And with good mileage, I'm sure. I like the helmet, it matches," he added.

Cut the crap, Mildred thought with a fake smile on her face, careful to give no indication of the annoyance under the surface. Instead of running away, like her body wanted to do, her new gift of the gab—thanks to the lifeless body lying a few yards away—took over completely, and she found herself giving in to Detective Hyde's attempt at friendly chatter. She could alter the situation, take it to a place that made Hyde uncomfortable.

"Thanks," she said with a lilt in her tone. "Pink is my favorite color. There are lots of interesting pink things." She smirked in a flirty way that she'd never dared to before. Honestly, she was shocked at herself, however pleasantly. If there was anything that would make him run for the hills, unwanted flirtation should be it.

Hyde cleared his throat uncomfortably. "Would you like to talk about Aaron?" he asked nonchalantly.

Damn, Mildred thought. He was good at his job. Now was the time when the point for a present parent should come into play. But that might hint that she had something to hide.

"Not particularly," Mildred said. "Such a tragedy. It's too sad." It was a lie that slithered right through her teeth, but a skilled lie, borrowed from a skilled liar's tongue.

"It is. It's very sad," he replied, matching her. "Looks like you narrowly missed a tragedy as well," he added, pointing to his own head with a grin.

Mildred, not being very smart, twisted her face in confusion. "Huh?" she said. There was that word her mother hated again.

"The helmet," he said, pointing to her head this time. "That's a nasty dent. Must've been a close call."

"Oh." She giggled nervously. "Yeah, it was."

He nodded, but then his brows drew together in deep thought. "But there isn't a mark on your bike," he noted.

His expressions were the easiest Mildred had ever had to read. She coupled the look with the words and had an internal panic. *Crap! He* knows *something . . . or* thinks *he knows something . . .*

"Oh, there was. It's been repaired. I just couldn't bear to change the helmet. Figured the battle wound only adds character." Mildred finished with a mimic of Hyde's grin that would have worked for Aaron but probably looked nothing short of bizarre on her.

"I see," he said, without batting an eyelash.

Reading body language must have been one of Hyde's strong suits. Could he have been analyzing every little twitch Mildred made from the time she showed up? In return, he seemed to effortlessly make his expressions easier to read than others around her. Coupled with her new advanced tongue, she was holding her own, but Hyde was a tough opponent. She tried not to look bothered as he continued to speak.

"Well, I'll just take down your name and number. If I have any questions, or bump into an especially cool, undented pink helmet on sale, maybe I'll give you a call."

Mildred kept the awkward grin. The muscles around her mouth were being pressed to their limit today. "That would be great. Mildred Waco, that's *W-A-C-O*. My phone number is 660-570-1999."

As she spoke, Hyde scribbled in a little notebook, just like an old detective in the movies. She wondered why he didn't upgrade to a tablet or something, like he was living in this century. More importantly, she wished he'd lose the little notebook *and* her number. She knew he was suspicious of her already. The big red flag was waving. He was just too observant.

Once free of Hyde's scrutiny, Mildred sped away. The moped was small enough to slip right by the little traffic jam of distraught, dumbstruck students leaving Roanoke High. For that, she was thankful. She didn't want to stay anywhere near the school for even another minute. She'd heard of killers who stayed close to their victims and sometimes even disposed of the bodies near places where they could always keep an eye on the site. She wasn't like those twisted people. The farther she could be from Aaron, the better. If it wouldn't have looked odd for her to miss school, she wouldn't have shown up at all today. Good thing they called it off—even if she did have to show up for after-school band practice in the evening.

The world whizzed by Mildred in a haze as she made her way home. Trees melted into houses and houses blended into cars. All that mattered was getting home and getting rid of the body and evidence. She tried not to be afraid. Nobody could prove she had anything to do with Aaron's death, so she had plenty of time to get rid of Tyler. There was no reason for the police to show up on her doorstep or to ask to search her garage. No reason for them to even look her way. Except Detective Hyde had. He nagged at the back of Mildred's mind. He could be a problem, and she pondered ways to knock him off her trail. Continue to be friendly with him? Fabricate suspicious characters to divert his attention?

She started to reach for the button on her keys to open the garage door, but noticed it was open about a foot already.

No, no, no, no. What's going on? She came to a stop, knocked the kickstand out, and crept up to the garage. As she reached for the garage door, she thought that maybe she *should* be caught. It would be easier than having this feeling for the rest of her life. Maybe she should turn herself in. The whim hit her, and she immediately dismissed it as ridiculous. None of this was her fault. She was somehow being forced into these crimes by the witch. It was the witch who deserved to go to jail, but Mildred couldn't turn her in without admitting what she'd done—

Smack!

The sound within the garage stopped Mildred dead. She heard hissing whispers, something rattling, thumping. She had joked to herself about Aaron waking up back at the school and scaring all the people who had been mean to her, but she hadn't really thought it possible. Now, away from other people, her mind went wild. Had Tyler gotten up? Was he fumbling around in there, blind and mutilated? Had he come back to exact revenge on her?

She wanted to scream. She wanted to run. But she didn't move at all.

"Eat later, take now, no time to waste," a voice said. It was screechy, like air whizzing from an untied balloon.

It didn't sound like Tyler. They'd spoken of taking something. *Burglars.*

This was a different situation. Normally she wouldn't face a burglar, but on a normal day, there wouldn't be a body in her garage that a potential burglar could find. To call the police would mean risking them finding Tyler. To leave the burglars would risk *them* finding Tyler. Maybe they would blackmail her for ransom. Maybe they would get to a safe place and turn her in. Burglars weren't exactly murderers, after all, and maybe they would feel obligated to report her. Thieves with a conscience. It could happen. Bravery came from desperation. Mildred flung open the garage door, sure that being revealed in the open would be enough to scare her burglars away. *Sorry, not this house, and definitely not today.*

But what she found inside was not a human stealing her family's precious silver.

She didn't know what to call the things she was looking at. One of them stood about the height of a child. The other creature was double the size of the short one, though it hunched over as if trying to appear smaller. If it was to stand it could easily reach over six feet. They didn't appear to be the same type of creature; one—the short one—had skin like a lizard, whereas the other was covered in a bear-like fur. Their faces weren't human in the least and it frightened Mildred most of all to see their unusual, glowing eyes.

As she looked on in shock, the short one's thin reptilian lips spread into a grimace, giving her a wide view of its rip-blade teeth. It let out a dangerous shriek that resonated like a pipe organ at a Sunday mass, and Mildred joined in, providing a special kind of harmony. Ode to Terror.

She tripped over her feet trying to get away. Her legs were fluid. They were rippling waves and wouldn't work like legs; she was scared, and they were failing her. The hairy one came toward her, cackling madly. When the light of the sun touched it, its fur began to smoke, although it hardly noticed. With the concrete driveway below her, and nothing surrounding her, Mildred knew she was done for. *This is what I deserve,* she thought. *This is what my victims felt before I ended their lives.* This was her payback—she could accept that, but she didn't want it.

"No, no, please," Mildred cried.

The reptile-like one remained in the shadows, whistled for the other's attention, and said, "No time to play. Come."

"Bye-bye," the hairy monster said.

It went back to the other monster. Together, they lifted Tyler's body out of the corner and vanished.

It took some time for Mildred to gather herself. That instant had been so traumatic, she had trouble processing it. Her body trembled at her near-death experience, but she was overjoyed that she was somehow still functioning. Finally, it occurred to her that she had seen claws like the reptilian one's before. They had been her own, as she murdered Tyler.

And they had taken Tyler. Why?

"Eat later," one of them had said. Eat. The thing she had done to Aaron and Tyler. Whatever those things were, was she becoming one of them? *No. Impossible,* she thought. Those things didn't look as if they'd ever been human.

The witch must have known the thoughts Mildred had about going to the police and sent the creatures to frighten her into not telling anyone. Fine. Point made. She wouldn't tell, but she was going to go to the magic shop and get rid of whatever whammy that crazy old lady had put on her. Murder and cannibalism were not what she signed up for.

Mildred thought of band practice and sighed. She couldn't miss it.

15

The only thing worse than seeing Aaron dead, as far as Yvette was concerned, was enduring the long wait for questioning. They wanted all people closest to Aaron to give information. This meant all of his closest friends, Yvette assumed, but as she waited in the cafeteria for her turn, she'd seen several people who barely knew Aaron: the girl whose locker was below his, the boy he sat next to in Spanish class. It was really making the whole process take ages.

Yvette blew through her questions and felt that she'd connected somewhat with the younger officer, Hyde. She remembered his name because it was like that book she'd had to read in her world literature class the year before. Other than that, his exceptional appearance and ability to sympathize with her had made her want to remember.

Ø

"*How well did you know Aaron Renfro?*" he asked.

"*We were dating.*"

"*Was it serious?*"

"*I wasn't dating anyone else.*"

"*I'm sorry,*" he said. "*This must be really hard for you.*"

Nobody else had taken the time to care how Yvette had felt through all of this. They were all worried about Joan, but they didn't notice that Yvette mattered too. Aaron was sort of her boyfriend and he was dead, and nobody had thought to ask, "How are you feeling about this, Yvette?"

Nobody except Hyde.

"*Thank you,*" she said.

Ø

Yvette blinked and thoughts of Hyde faded as she realized Chelle's car had stopped moving. They were in front of a house on Winchester Street. The English Tudor-style house was on the smaller side, but what it lacked in size it made up for in yard, which would have been lively with children playing had they also been let out of school early. Fortunately, no students had died at the other schools and classes remained unaffected. Jump ropes and soccer balls lay discarded on the grass, while a trampoline and swing set remained dormant in the absence of Yvette's brothers and sisters.

Yvette stared at her home. Through the kitchen window, which was framed with bright-white curtains, she could see her mother laughing as she wiped a dab of cake frosting on Yvette's little sister's nose. Four-year-old Maria—a small clone of Yvette— tried to lick it off her nose with her tongue and fell short, which made her mother laugh harder.

Yvette sucked in a breath, as if she'd been holding it since they'd climbed in the candy apple–red Audi and left the high school.

"They look so happy," Yvette said, with gloom in her voice. "Mom doesn't know."

She pictured going inside with her joyless face and having to tell her mother what had happened at school. Having to tell her mother what she'd seen. That moment when the wind had blown back the sheet—Yvette couldn't bear to watch the two of them anymore. Their bright cheer amplified the sadness and confusion around her. At the same time, she couldn't stand the thought of telling them and wiping the joy from their faces.

What she had seen back at the school would wipe the joy from her own face for a long time. When the wind had lifted the sheet over Aaron slightly she was just at the right angle to see underneath. The image was seared into her visual cortex. She shook her head at the memory, but unfortunately her mind didn't work like an Etch A Sketch. She saw the vibrant, deep wounds and the pasty, dead skin, and she thought, *It could be me lying there, with my skin cold and its beige tone drained of vibrancy. Waxy. Gone.*

How could she explain that feeling to anyone? That dread?

"I don't think I can do it, Chelle," Yvette confessed. "I can't go in there and let Maria see me like this. She will be terrified."

"I know; it's really messed up," Chelle said. "I can't believe this is happening."

"Yeah . . . I just feel numb. And kind of scared," Yvette admitted. "Can we go to your house?"

Ø

Chelle was scared too. Aaron was a medium-sized guy, bigger

and stronger than her. If this thing that attacked him could do that to him, it could do worse to her. She was probably more afraid than Yvette, she figured, because at least Yvette was tough and fast. When it came down to a cheerleader versus a swimmer/track star/softball player, Chelle knew what side she was on: the losing side. But on the other hand, Yvette was a good choice to have by her side right now, and she was glad to keep her close.

"Yeah, we'll go to mine," Chelle said. "Dad's out, but Clarissa's there."

Clarissa was Mrs. Martin number two, and had been with Mr. Martin since Chelle was six.

Chelle's mother, Denise, had been a New Yorker and a rising model. Her father, a designer of homes, moved to New York from the South in his early twenties, hoping to try his hand in the fashion world with his brother. Fashion wasn't in her father's future, but Denise was. They met, were married, Chelle was born, and shortly after, Denise met an untimely end. It was a mugger who stole the life of Denise Gellar, something that Chelle's father felt there would be much less of in his hometown.

Apparently, Chelle thought, *there are worse things . . .*

"That's fine. Clarissa won't freak like my mom will."

"True. She probably won't care at all."

"My mom will probably want to pull me out of school when she hears, until whatever did that gets caught."

"That's the difference, I guess. Clarissa isn't my mom."

Chelle was already driving down the road, leaving the Darling place behind. To be honest, maybe she would have liked a mother who would be so worried about potential danger that she'd rather have Chelle home with her instead of in school.

There was no trampoline or swing set on Chelle's lawn. The Martin yard was strictly for looking at, not playing on. Sometimes Tyler would be at work on the hedges or cutting the grass, but otherwise it was a no-man's-land type of situation. Mr. Martin was huge on aesthetics—their house always featured the most modern renovations—and the yard was as important to him as the home, which was why it was so odd for the grass to be getting as high as it was, Chelle noticed.

As they walked up to the front porch, Chelle pulled her phone out of her Louis Vuitton backpack purse and clicked on Tyler's name. She sent a quick text:

Lawn looks like shit.

Then she put her phone away; she was tired of seeing all the messages about Aaron.

"Hi, girls!" Clarissa chirped when the girls walked through the front door.

She was standing with one foot behind her, one forward, and her arms stretched out to either side. The mahogany coffee table had been pushed back to make room for Clarissa's yoga mat, which she'd spread out in front of the seventy-five-inch television screen in the living room. Her tracksuit was bright yellow—the sort of color that screamed for attention. Chelle would have liked it on herself, but it looked awful on Clarissa. The top was much too small for her chest and the bottoms were low enough to show an ugly appendectomy scar above her hip.

"Hi," Chelle replied offhandedly.

A man on the screen was instructing the pose that Clarissa was attempting. He wore thin, white pants and a plain white tee. His hair was pulled back into a bun.

"Butch Pacheco," Clarissa said, as if Chelle had asked for an introduction. "The ladies say he's the best out there."

By "the ladies" she meant the other trophy wives from the country club, whom she met up with every Sunday at brunch. He was instructing another pose and Clarissa went for it.

Chelle nodded.

"Cool," Yvette said, even though she didn't sound like she really meant it.

A normal parent might have stopped what they were doing and wondered why their child was home so early from school. Would have hugged her after finding out the terrible news and would have been so happy that Chelle wasn't hurt.

"Want to join?" Clarissa asked.

"Nope," Chelle said. "Have at it."

She led Yvette down the hall to the kitchen, where the countertops were white marble and the cabinets were even whiter because, as Clarissa had insisted to Mr. Martin, it was "really *in* this year."

"Skipping school?"

The deep, snide voice made Chelle groan. Dashiel; stepbrother from hell. A blond, chiseled devil. He strolled into the space as if it belonged to him alone, jerked open the refrigerator door that Chelle had been inches from, and pulled out a Diet Coke.

"Coke?" he asked Yvette.

She nodded shyly. He gave the Coke to her, got himself one, and shut the door without offering Chelle anything.

"Dad's gonna be mad when he finds out you skipped school," he said and popped open the soda.

Before he could lift it to his lips, Chelle took it from his hands and raised it to her own. Gulp. The bubbles stung her tongue but she didn't care; she was making a point.

"*Dad* will be glad I'm away from school and safe when he hears what happened," she said, making sure to put a lot of emphasis on the word *dad*. She was trying to drop a huge reminder that he was biologically her father, *not* Dash's.

"Rude." Dash took the soda back and Chelle let him have it now that she'd had her fill and had proved her point. "What do you mean? What happened?"

The girls shared an awkward look. It wasn't easy to bear the news of someone's murder. "Don't you watch the news, dork?" Chelle said when she couldn't think of how to say it.

"Nope," Dash said. "Too depressing."

Ø

"Our friend . . ." Yvette said. Should she have said boyfriend? She was supposed to go on her second date with him tonight. No, they weren't official yet. They hadn't even kissed. "Our friend was killed at the school."

"Oh shit," Dash said, looking more serious. "Anyone I know?"

"Aaron Renfro." As the words left her lips, Yvette felt her chest tighten and her vision blur.

"Bummer," Dash said to Yvette, then he turned his attention to Chelle. "Guess it'll take a lot of *Dad's* money to heal from this one, huh?"

Ø

Chelle's face contorted into a sneer. "You're an insensitive prick." She took the Coke from him again and stormed down the hall, Yvette on her expensive heels.

The stark white and pale-gray surroundings stopped abruptly at Chelle's bold, gold bedroom door. Turquoise walls inside made the atmosphere more relaxing than the hospital vibes the rest of the house had going on. The only different wall was the one at the head of her gold bed frame, which had been painted in aqua, turquoise, and gold stripes.

"I really hate him," Chelle said.

She threw the soda into a wastebasket by her closet. She hadn't really wanted it; she just didn't want him to have it.

"Death makes some people act strange," Yvette said, as if she was an expert.

To the best of Chelle's knowledge, Yvette didn't know anyone who had died, except maybe a grandparent. Even then she'd been much younger. It was just her silly crush on Dash that was driving her to make up excuses for him, which Chelle had witnessed before, but it still puzzled her how anyone could have a crush on Dash.

"He's evil," Chelle reminded Yvette. "Puppies don't even like him."

"He's allergic."

"My point exactly."

Chelle let her bag slide from her shoulders and land on her bed. She couldn't fight the urge to look at her phone anymore.

"I hate him," she repeated in a grumble. Tyler hadn't replied to her message. "Hmm . . ."

"What?"

"I haven't heard from Tyler," Chelle said. "I texted him almost ten minutes ago."

"But he always texts you right back."

"I know."

"You don't think—"

"No, he's probably just mowing or something. Right?"

Yvette shrugged as if it was a possibility but her face looked worried to Chelle. Her brows weren't usually that close together, and her lip was caught between her teeth, as if she was holding back words she didn't want to say out loud.

"Never mind," Chelle said, deciding she didn't want to hear anything else about it. This whole death thing was a real downer and she'd had enough. "Come on."

She put her purse back on, phone still in hand, and headed out.

"Where are we going?"

"The mall," Chelle said.

She hated that Dash had been right, but it wasn't difficult to discern that Chelle shopped when she got upset. Something about handing money over always lightened the pressure closing in on her. From the way she felt now, she had a lot of shopping to do. Before she got into the car, she sent another text to Tyler.

Meet me at the mall in an hour?

Because she needed him to carry her bags, but she didn't say it.

Ø

Yvette hoped to be around Dash some more. His nearness, even in different rooms of Chelle's big house, made her pain from the loss of Aaron a little lighter. She and Aaron had only just started dating, but she'd liked Dash for a long time. It was just too bad that he and Chelle always had the sibling rivalry thing going on. On the other hand, it had played in her favor once, a few months ago. Dash had caught her in the hallway coming out of Chelle's room and slipped his arm around her waist.

Wonder if Chelle would get mad if I stole her best friend, he'd said.

Yvette blushed as she recalled the moment, but suddenly the memory of his face was replaced with the gruesome sight of Aaron's she'd glimpsed earlier. She felt like crying, but she held it in, because she hated that sort of thing.

"I'm kind of hungry," Yvette said, hoping to stall.

"We'll get something on the way," Chelle said.

"Do you really think we should be out? They did suggest we stay indoors," she said.

"We will be indoors at the restaurant, then at the mall. Do you know any wild, vicious creatures who hang out in restaurants or at the mall?"

Yvette couldn't argue with that. There were tons of people at restaurants and security guards at the mall. And if she knew Chelle, she would have some big guy meet them at the mall so he could carry her bags. Yvette knew what it was like when Chelle went on one of her spending sprees, how the mountain of bags could pile up. The first guy on Chelle's call list for those sorts of tasks was always Tyler.

Tyler didn't reply earlier. Yvette felt a chill up her spine. *Stop it,* she told herself. *He's a huge strong guy, so not the victim type. You're just being paranoid, Yvette.*

"You know what I need?" Chelle asked. "A new bikini. And some new tops. What about you?"

"I could use a bikini too." Yvette tried to keep her voice level, and as they spoke about stops they'd make and things they were going to buy, the stress melted away. All the places had the same thing in common—other people. Whatever happened to Aaron, he had been alone and outside. Totally different from their situation.

Safe, Yvette thought.

16

Music spilled into the street from the two-story brown house on the corner as Tiffany played her grand piano. Pompano Street wasn't in the best part of town, nor was the brown house in the best of conditions. Paint was peeling, a shutter was loose, and the door was just a little off so that they had to lift it slightly as they opened or shut it. However, the piano was in perfect working order and Tiffany's fingers danced across it as if they'd been born to do so.

Eyes closed, Tiffany let the music flow from her, through the instrument, and into the world. In her mind, a couple performed a ballet with elegant stretches and turns that fit her flow. The pixie-like female in her mind's eye wore formfitting pale pink. A chiseled male was in white, his pants tight and his shirt billowy. The female twisted away from the male as the tempo picked up, but when she stopped turning, something went wrong. Her face became a mask of horror. One side of the male's face looked at the female with confusion in his eye. The other side of his face was grotesque. Muscle was visible, small shards of bone mixed within, as if he'd been broken open. His eye socket had been broken away until the eye protruded, falling away, dripping. Cheek crushed.

Aaron.

A sour note slipped in.

Smack!

The back of her hand stung like alcohol in an open wound, but she didn't cry out. She used to, when she was a child. As a teenager, she merely stopped playing. A red rectangular welt rose on her hand, reminding her what it had been like when she was eight years old, perched on the piano bench beside her mother and her thick wooden ruler. Back then Tiffany had made a lot of mistakes, but now there were very few. Practically nonexistent. The ruler hadn't touched her hands for months.

It's the stupid murder. It's got me distracted! I can't concentrate on the story, she thought.

The story was everything when it came to music. What she played wasn't just random notes that matched; it was a journey of love or heartbreak. Bravery. Loss. Loneliness. Tiffany had told so many stories with her music while the scenes in her mind flooded onward, while the dancers played their parts and she played the keys.

She fumed but kept her voice at a reasonable level as she spoke to the stern woman next to her.

"You know I have a huge competition coming up," she said.

Tiffany's mother sat stark straight. Her hair was slicked back into a low bun, her eyes an abyss of deep blue. She was unmoved by her daughter's disruptive complaint.

"It'll be fine. You won't break," she said simply. "Continue."

"I think I'm done for now," Tiffany said. "I have prac—"

Smack!

Tiffany uttered a startled cry this time. This one was more intense than the last swat had been, and hurt so much more for being on the same spot. Her hand throbbed.

Bitch, Tiffany thought.

"You're done when I say you're done," her mother said. "One more song."

She may not break, but the pale skin stretched across her metacarpals was already tinged a light purple from the latest assault, and what she really wanted to do was slam the keys and say, "To hell with it!" She felt the notes so easily. It was effortless and, in another life, she might have loved music. If she could have played for fun, it would be different. But day after day, hour after hour, practice, practice, practice. She glanced down at her mother's left hand, where her ring finger and her pinky were missing.

Her mother had once had the gift of music as well, until suddenly she didn't. It was an accident on a sailboat that had taken Stella Cosby's fingers. Before then, her life was promising. She was seventeen and a star. Her boyfriend had talked her into sailing with him. He'd talked her into trying a lot of new things. She thought he was good for her.

Then there was the accident. Stella blamed him for the loss of her fingers and her career, and broke up with him from her hospital bed. Shortly after the accident, she learned she was pregnant with Tiffany, and Tiffany's future was written for her in that moment.

Now, what Tiffany wanted to say was, "I'm done playing! You can't live vicariously through me!" but she gathered herself, straightened her back, stretched her fingers, and played until the last note faded.

Her hatred, however, didn't fade at all.

"Check on Nonna before you leave for band practice," her mother said.

Nonna stayed upstairs in her bedroom. She was old and couldn't maneuver about the house the way she used to when Tiffany was a little girl. Each year she'd grown weaker until now she practically stayed in bed all day.

"I heard you playing, *piccola*," the frail woman said. "Beautiful. Almost as good as Stella was."

"Thank you, Nonna."

"It's like hearing myself play again. But these hands." She held her twisted, arthritic hands in front of her. "They aren't as nimble as they used to be. The gift is yours alone now."

An ache lurched deep in Tiffany. It was a sad and jealous one. She didn't want to be the one to hone "the gift," as her mother and Nonna often called it. It felt more like a curse. Nonna didn't know, but Tiffany would gladly have traded her talent if it meant she'd never have to touch a piano key ever again. If she didn't have to be the one everyone's eyes were on. Constantly. Play longer. Play better. Play, play, play.

"But, Nonna," Tiffany said. "You've still got your memories. You've performed in the most majestic places . . ."

"Oh," Nonna said. "Did I tell you about the tour? The theater in Budapest? Every seat was full . . ."

Nonna went off into a long-winded story about her performance and Tiffany wasn't truly listening. She'd heard the story a thousand times over, so her mind wandered to things more suited to her actual feelings. These were desires she'd never spoken about.

Boys. Namely, Herman Bernstein.

Since the age of twelve, boys had been labeled off-limits as per her mother's harsh orders.

They'll only distract you, she had insisted. *You'll be a famous musician as long as you keep your eyes on the path and not on some idiot boy. They'll never be worth giving up your gift.*

Tiffany felt like that wasn't true at all. Herman wasn't an idiot. He was one of the smartest students in school. He was handsome, in a dorky way, and he always smelled so good. No matter how much her mother insisted boys only wanted one filthy thing, he had never said or done anything like that. He was a true gentleman and Tiffany didn't see anything wrong with liking him at all. He asked her out a lot, although his offers seemed very casual.

You should come watch that new Reese Witherspoon movie with me tonight, he'd said. *I mean, friends should hang out.*

He mentioned friends, but the Reese Witherspoon movie was a romance, so did he have more in mind? Mixed signals like that plagued Tiffany. Sometimes she thought of just asking him flat-out if he was interested in her romantically, but then she reasoned that there was no point. Even if he liked her, she couldn't have a boyfriend, so she'd only get to see him at school. Any other time, she was under the thumb of her mother. Every moment of her day was planned, every activity was timed. If she slipped away after school to watch some movie, her mother would lose it.

But she still thought Herman was one of the best guys she knew, and if she was able to date, she'd date him.

Herman was heavy on her mind that day. Not only because she adored him, but because he had found Aaron. The thought made her skin prickle. Herman must have felt terrible after finding something like that. It would be nice if she could check on him. Maybe she could sneak away just this once instead of going to—no. If she missed practice, Mr. Philpot would be terribly concerned. He'd call her mother, and Tiffany didn't even want to think about what would happen after that.

But maybe she could sneak through the woods afterward, instead of going to the parking lot where her mother would be. She could go to Herman's house, spend some time with him, then come back later and make up some excuse for why she was late. She'd never cut through the woods before, so her mother would never catch her.

". . . but oh, listen to me rambling on and on," Nonna was saying. "You have to go, don't you?"

"Yeah, I do," she said, a little perkier than she had felt before. "Sorry, Nonna. I love you."

"I love you, too, sweetie."

Nonna's skin was as smooth and thin as silk as Tiffany brushed her lips against the old woman's cheek, then she rushed away, feeling like the day had just gotten a little brighter.

17

Mildred loathed the thought of band practice in the middle of this nightmare she'd suddenly plunged into, but she knew that if she didn't go, there would be hell to pay from Tiffany Cosby. Compared to Mildred, Tiffany was pint sized, but she wielded a powerful influence over the artistic and intellectual groups of students at Roanoke High. Mildred was already on rocky terrain with both groups and didn't want to risk backlash from them. There was also the matter of behaving as normally as possible.

The Waco house was empty and squeaky clean, with Naomi nowhere in sight. Mildred went to her bedroom and reached for her tuba case with the same effort she often applied to pick it up, but tumbled backward from the excessive force. The instrument was lighter. She flung the strap of the clunky case over her head so that it rested across her torso from right shoulder to left hip. It felt as heavy on her back as it ever did. Tyler's girthy arms flashed in her mind.

She pressed onward, past the thought of her terrible crime, and got on her moped.

Only a few cars littered the parking lot when she pulled in, but it looked like all band members had arrived. Unlike Mildred, they'd made it on time. In her haste, Mildred stumbled a few times under the swinging weight of her tuba before she took it off her back and held it more steadily in her arms as she shuffled to the school's door. Music notes floated out of the music room, then stopped flat.

"You're late, *Mildred*," Tiffany spat, her tone very condescending. "You should try to be early. You need more practice than any of us."

One look at Mr. Philpot, the music teacher, told Mildred that he was certainly not going to reprimand his prize student at Mildred's expense. His lips were tight and his arms crossed as he glared at Mildred with contempt. Normally, she would cower and apologize, but this day was different. She faced Tiffany. Mildred didn't look away as Aaron's attitude spilled out of her.

"I'm sorry, it just took longer to wade through the air of bitchiness you left behind on your way in here," Mildred said brazenly.

Tiffany gasped as though she'd been physically hit. "Did you just call me a bitch?"

"There are a lot of *other* things I could call you," Mildred said. "Would you prefer cu—"

"Miss Waco! That is enough!" Mr. Philpot finally spoke, his words loud and sharp.

Tiffany didn't retort but her eyes narrowed menacingly at Mildred, then she flipped her hair and settled in front of her keyboard, her delicate fingers spreading across the keys.

"See me after practice, Mildred," Mr. Philpot said.

Of course, I'm *the bad one,* Mildred thought. She got in position with her clunky tuba, bumping into a few students in the process. Mr. Philpot tapped the metal music stand in front of him with his conductor's wand. Everyone readied their instruments.

Practice went on forever. Mildred messed up just as much as usual, but everyone else's playing was improving, making hers worse by comparison. When everyone left, Mildred stayed behind as told, though she dreaded it.

"If I hear you speak to Miss Cosby like that again, you're out of band," Mr. Philpot said simply.

Mildred's jaw dropped. "What? But she said mean things to me as well. She says nasty things to me *all the time!*"

"You heard me, Miss Waco. I will not have my best student belittled by my worst. Heed my warning and have a pleasant evening," he said as he gathered some papers and hurried to the door.

Mildred was floored. After all that Tiffany had said and done to her in his class, he had the nerve to single Mildred out and threaten her. Treat her as if she didn't try at all. She did. She put in innumerable practice hours. She worked with private tutors in her spare time until the muscles in her face ached. Sure, they were hired and insisted upon by her mother, but that shouldn't matter. Whether she did it of her own will or because her mother made her, Mildred still had to put forth the effort. No matter how hard she tried, she just wasn't as good as Tiffany. Did the girl eat, sleep, and breathe music? Perhaps, Mildred pondered, it was something deeper. Some sort of musical gift. A natural talent. If only Mildred had that too.

She was still fuming by the time she got on her moped and headed home, but instead of going the normal route on the road, she had the urge to take the trail through the woods. Dirt and rocks bounced the moped around, jarring the soft parts of Mildred, but she didn't care. Even if she wanted to turn around, she couldn't. For some reason, this felt like the way to go, like she was being drawn in this direction against her will. She could feel her frustration over the injustice of the situation boiling up and ready to burst, but, although she didn't know how, she knew this way would lead to some type of relief.

Tall grass and trees drifted by. Mildred turned a sharp curve and about twenty feet up she saw Tiffany. Mildred recognized her pink and purple Nike backpack and her light-brown ponytail bobbing along as she walked with her usual bouncy stride. Hate washed over Mildred, drowning out any other logical thought. Tiffany must have heard the moped's motor speed up because she glanced back right before Mildred zoomed by, throwing out her arm to hit Tiffany across her throat. Clothesline.

Tiffany went down, and Mildred stopped. She flung the tuba off her shoulder and let it fall beside the moped. Tiffany was trying to get up, but she was hurt. Scrapes marred the left side of her face and Mildred could already see a bruise forming on her neck. Tiffany opened and closed her lips, but gasps came out instead of words and she reached toward Mildred with a trembling arm, her eyes pooling with tears.

Mildred might have cared a few days ago. She might have taken Tiffany's hand and held it while calling for help. But Mildred wasn't the same person she was a few days ago. She lacked any empathy. On the contrary, the way that Tiffany lay there and did her fish-out-of-water routine was a little comical to Mildred. *Let her be the one to struggle for once,* Mildred thought. When she laughed, it was manic, and she hated Tiffany so much that it felt good.

Driven by that same insane emotion, Mildred stooped forward. Tiffany turned over and tried to crawl away, but Mildred took hold of Tiffany's necklace and the neckline of her shirt. She pulled them tight around Tiffany's neck. The chain was so tight it sank into Tiffany's skin until it popped and fell into the dirt. The charm spelling *Band Girl* slipped off the broken chain and landed in clear view of Mildred before Tiffany, struggling, knocked it away. Mildred was strong now, and she held Tiffany up off the ground by the neck of her shirt. Mildred kept pulling as the other girl struggled weakly. Tiffany reached backward and clawed at Mildred's powerful arms. The same words—*Band Girl*—were emblazoned on a ring of white gold that matched the broken necklace. A moment passed while Mildred held the girl there. Another. And then there was no more movement.

Mildred let go. Tiffany's head thumped on a rock below her but she didn't flinch or cry out in pain. Her bloodshot eyes stared at the leafy trees with a complete lack of recognition. Her tongue protruded from her blue lips. Her musical career had ended abruptly, but her talent didn't have to go to waste.

A disturbing animalistic hunger took over Mildred. She felt the sharp points of her teeth growing, stretching against the inside of her cheeks and lips. She dropped to her knees and tore into Tiffany's talented hands, tasting the burst of flavor as Tiffany's blood and flesh filled her mouth. Mildred discovered that she didn't have to force the flesh apart. Her strong fangs—*Is that what they are now?*—sliced through like a strong blade. Even bone was no match. She swallowed chunks of flesh and bone whole until there was nothing left at the end of each of Tiffany's wrists.

Sated, Mildred gradually came back to herself and realized what she'd done. She stumbled back, tears streaming down her face and blood on her chin.

"Why?" she cried, but she knew why.

She knew exactly why, and she was going to get that magic lady to take it back.

Thanks to a mud puddle nearby, she was able to rinse the blood from her hands and face. She left Tiffany lying there and went back to her moped. There was nothing anybody could do for Tiffany now. Mildred flung the tuba case–strap back across her chest. There was still some of Tiffany's blood across her shirt front, but she didn't care; after all, it was a maroon shirt and the blood kind of blended in. All she cared about was that she couldn't keep going around killing and eating people. As Mildred started the moped and twisted the handle for the gas, the white gold words *Band Girl* slowly appeared on the skin of her ring finger. Before her eyes, the words became more defined, then rose and separated from her, until they formed a ring exactly like Tiffany's. Mildred gasped and pulled at the ring. *Only one person has a ring like that,* she fretted, but it wouldn't budge. Then Mildred had an idea; she'd flip it around so that a plain band showed instead of the words. Nobody else would know, she told herself.

18

Mildred had the strange thought that perhaps she would go back to Crossroads Magicks and all traces of it would be gone. There would be no scary witch. There wouldn't even be an address called 6 Hollow Grove. She imagined she'd drive up until solid forest blocked her way, the way she remembered that closed-off little road being in the first place. The whole thing would have been naught but a figment of her imagination, because they'd finally driven her crazy. Chalk it up to extreme stress due to years of inflicted mental abuse. Or maybe someone had slipped a strong hallucinogen into her food. Either way, she was sure everything since yesterday was completely made up.

Normal people didn't do the things she'd been doing.

It made no sense. The reckless feeling she'd felt, as though something was hijacking her mind and emotions. Bending her ability to make logical decisions. She'd never even struck someone, let alone *bludgeoned* them or run them over . . . it just wasn't in her. She didn't have that kind of ability. If she had, she would have fought her bullies a long time ago, would have shown them she wasn't one to be messed with. But that was never the case. She let them beat her up day after day, mentally and physically, and she never beat back.

Once, Mildred's father had set out mousetraps. Ben and Barbara had left for a business trip the next day—as usual—and Mildred set out to find all those cruel mousetraps so she could toss them out before they could do any damage to anything. To her horror, one had been tripped. Even worse, the mouse wasn't inside it. It turned out, the mouse was much bigger than the trap. The mouse wasn't a mouse at all. It was a rat, and it stood stock still, bleeding from its face when Mildred found it. It looked at her accusingly when she opened the bottom cupboard in the kitchen. Mildred was mortified. She left the house in tears. She was so disturbed by it, she refused to enter the house again until her dad phoned a friend in town who could come take care of the rat. The friend, a vet, nursed the rat back to health and Mildred kept him as a pet for years afterward.

She had compassion.

How could she have done those things to Aaron, Tyler, and Tiffany with her own hands?

Her heart pounded as she turned off the main road onto the dirt path. This was it. She would see that everything was fake, and that everything had all just been a horrible nightmare.

But the little mailbox with the skinny, sprawled scrawl was still there. Crossroads Magicks looked the same as it had the day before. Mildred's heart ached. Being crazy would have been much easier to deal with. There were options: Medication. Hospitals. If it wasn't insanity but *evil* that she had to battle, her chances were much worse.

She slipped off her moped and hooked her helmet to the handlebars. Courage had begun to bury itself, withdrawing into her. The more she looked at the decrepit shop, the less brave she felt. Tombs were less creepy than this place. It smelled of rotting wood, moist earth, and something else that Mildred couldn't pinpoint. It made her skin prickle, but she stomped into the place anyway. The witch was rummaging around on her shelves, standing on a tall ladder that was every bit as rickety as the floor it stood on. She paid Mildred only the slightest note of recognition. It was as though she'd known Mildred was coming.

"What did you do to me?" Mildred demanded. The accusatory words poured out of her mouth.

"Gave you what you wanted," the lady said simply.

"What I wanted? What I wanted! This is *not* what I wanted!"

The lady found those words funny, but only slightly. Only enough to make her cackle one loud *Hah!* "What do you mean? I asked if you wished death for them, you said yes."

Mildred didn't remember that. Not at all.

"I said you will gain what they have, you said sure."

Did she really? Mildred wasn't sure about it.

"You said you would do anything for the help you needed."

Yes, she did say that. She was sure of that one.

"But I didn't know . . . I didn't mean it. I didn't mean—I was just sad and hurt. I didn't mean for this to happen."

"Be careful what you wish for, they say . . ." the witch said, unmoved.

She obviously didn't get it. Mildred gaped at her.

"Do you know what I did last night and today? I hurt people. I hurt them badly, and then . . . then I ate parts of them," Mildred said, lowering her voice for fear that someone else may be lurking about, trying to catch her confession on a voice recorder—or in an outdated tiny notebook. "Take it back. Please. You have to."

The witch regarded her with doubt. "You get what you asked for, and you want to give it back? It's too late, the deal is done. Osveta is doing a good job for you."

"Well, listen, Os-whatever-your-name-is—"

"Ruza is not Osveta. Ruza is Ruza," she said loudly, jabbing a finger in her own chest.

"I don't care; just take it back," Mildred said, grinding her teeth.

Ruza's voice grew deeper and it made Mildred shudder. "I warned you it was black. Told you it would darken the soul. You agreed. It's too late now. Everything is final." Ruza pointed at a sign near the counter that said all sales were final. It hadn't been there moments ago; Mildred was sure of it.

Ruza continued shuffling jars around on her shelf and started singing a song in a language Mildred didn't know. She wanted to cry and beg, but when she opened her mouth, a hissing sound startled her into shutting it again. Movement from the edge of her eyesight caught her attention. A large, furry creature was hunched over, its long arms resting against the floor, like a sitting cat, but looking more like a cross between an ape and a bull. The same tall beast Mildred had seen in her garage.

"I knew it!" Mildred said.

Ruza was unmoved. She said something to the creature in another language and it left the room swiftly.

"I knew you had something to do with them," Mildred said. "Why did they take Tyler's body? What are they? What kind of evil crap are you up to? Did they use to be people like me? People who came to you for help? They ate him, didn't they?"

Mildred was desperate for answers to tons of questions, and she was angry. Taking advantage of people who were at their lowest point was despicable. Ruza may even be worse than the bullies that hounded Mildred for years.

"Your evidence is cleaned up and you complain." Ruza scoffed, and then continued, "Don't mind Pohlepa, she does not concern you. You just worry about your desires. Who is next? What will you take from them, greedy girl?"

Her accusing words stung Mildred. The thought that she was greedy had never crossed her mind. She'd never cared about having things before, but now that she was killing people and taking parts of them, she couldn't dispute it. It was a very greedy thing to do. It was a vile thing to do. They were all dying horrible deaths simply to fulfill some twisted desire within Mildred. It was true—she did want to be like them—but she'd never wanted to murder them. She didn't want to hurt anyone.

"It's all your fault," Mildred said. She was crying and the words hurt to get out.

"You blame me, but I am not the one spilling blood." Ruza's words were harsh and final, spoken in a loud, demanding way that left no room for a counterargument. No room for pleas.

Mildred wanted to shout back at her, demand whatever whammy the witch hit her with to be taken away. What came out instead was, "Fine."

Instead of walking forward to shake Ruza until she rattled, Mildred fled out the shop door.

At that moment, she felt a cruel happiness deep within her rise. It was wrong, but she couldn't stifle it. It soared with glee, and when she climbed on her bike, it carried her away.

19

Ruza watched the nasty little American girl with Osveta inside her climb on her scooter.

She wondered how Osveta was adapting. Ruza had seen only a glimmer of her within the girl. She was lying low for the time being, Ruza thought. Once the demon gathered more strength from more souls, she would have more power over the girl and eventually control the body all the time. Ruza laughed out loud. Once Osveta had used the girl up and claimed her flesh, she would serve Ruza. It was Ruza, after all, who'd found her and planted her in a willing vessel.

Soon, Osveta would belong to her, just as Pohlepa and Ubiti were hers. Ruza stepped into her hidden room where her demon minions dwelt. She threw some chicken innards and reptile parts she'd taken out of some jars onto the floor. A thin beam of sunlight shined on them, making the slick blood glisten. The demons scurried from the shadows. Pohlepa reached her long arm out to snatch a handful. The sunlight made her arm smoke but she pulled back quickly enough to not catch fire. Ubiti wasn't as eager. He sat on his haunches and watched Ruza for a moment. He was probably thinking about stabbing her with one of his horns, as he'd tried before. Let him try. She would just heal or resurrect and lock him in a small cage of jasper—which drained his demon powers—for months or years afterward.

"Have it your way," she said to him in her native tongue. "Eat or don't eat; you will still belong to me either way."

His yellow eyes burned at her with scorn, but his clawed hand moved toward the snack. Pohlepa hissed at him and grabbed another handful. He roared at her and rammed into her, knocking her against the wall. Then he ate the treats she dropped while she lay on the floor, grunting in pain.

Ruza laughed fondly, excited to know that another would be joining the family soon. As suddenly as it came, her laughter died. She felt the presence of strangers near the shop.

Ubiti's scowl faded, replaced with hopeful alertness. Ruza was quick to catch this change of demeanor. She knew Ubiti was capable of much more than she. The thoughts of humans came to him the way birdsong carried on the wind, a demonic attribute that had been most useful.

"How many?" Ruza asked.

$\varnothing$

Ubiti snarled, irritated that he had to share his knowledge. Bound to serve Ruza, his knowledge was her knowledge. There was no choice in the matter. She had released him within the body that made Ubiti flesh and bone rather than mere demonic spirit—a flimsy existence. He had known that passing into this life would lock him in this troublesome predicament, but the lure was irrefutable. His host had been the most delectable—

"Ubiti! How many?"

"Two. A boy and girl. The girl is worried. The boy is angry." He felt the roiling emotions and shivered with anticipation. The girl was so complex. Hope, sorrow, worry, and he even picked up on her underlying contempt for the boy. "He wants the girl to obey him. She does not care what he wants."

That's how fights happen, and fights are how murders happen, Ubiti thought. He could feel it in the boy, the potential. If Ubiti had his spirit form, the boy would be the type of person he would cling to. For a while he would buzz around, lending influence on reprehensible deeds. An easy influence.

But not the girl. The girl was a whirlwind and, to Ubiti's dismay, nothing in her was useful to him. She was not his flavor.

"She's nosy. She's going to enter," Ubiti said. "He will wait outside."

"Take on your human host's form," Ruza said. "Talk to her but tell her nothing. I'll handle the boy."

Ubiti's image wavered and pulsed as his demonic side faded into a young human male. On the outside, he was now seventeen. Tall, blond, with piercing hazel eyes. On the inside, he remained a three-thousand-year-old demon that had been of flesh for only a few years. He hated his human form. He would rather be flesh as his demon self, however, the human form was useful for a lot of things. The only drawback was having his will be controlled by his captor.

"As you wish," he said, sure to fill every word full of malice.

20

Patsy and Seth almost crashed into Mildred at an intersection a few miles back. She didn't even notice them as she flew through the stop sign, but the sight of her frightened Patsy. She was 90 percent sure there was blood on Mildred's shirt.

"Follow her," Patsy said.

"What?" Seth asked. His face twisted in confusion.

Before he had time to protest, Patsy said, "I'm serious—follow her."

Seth obliged, grumbling something about how they were supposed to have date night and date nights didn't include Mildred Waco. "No date night has *ever*, in the history of man, included Mildred Waco," he said.

"Why are you so mean?" she asked. "Couldn't you see something was wrong with her?"

"I've been saying that for years! There's *so* much wrong."

"Just go faster, please."

Mildred was really leaning on the gas, weaving through traffic in ways that Seth's truck couldn't maneuver. Somehow, they kept up and saw her turn off into thick woods, which alarmed Patsy. To Patsy's relief, Mildred hadn't purposefully driven into a tree. A narrow dirt road, hidden from view, was cut between two maples. Patsy had lived in Roanoke her whole life and had never seen that path before. Seth followed Mildred's dust trail.

The dirt trail took them to a ramshackle house. Careful to stay out of sight, Seth drove a little past the house and parked behind some trees. Mildred stomped up the aged porch and went inside. Patsy was mystified. Why would Mildred ever go into a place like that? She came from a nice neighborhood, had lots of money, and Patsy knew this sort of place was way out of the comfort zone of the Mildred. The shack didn't even look fit for a hobo, yet Mildred had walked right inside. But why? Patsy didn't like it. Something could happen to Mildred in there.

"Gross," Seth said.

"I'm going in," Patsy said.

"No. Are you crazy? Anything could be waiting in there."

"Yeah, *Mildred*. And I'm going to go get her out."

"She's not your problem—"

Thump!

Something smacked onto the hood of the truck and stared at Patsy. She startled but then let out a heavy breath.

"It's just a chicken," Seth said.

Patsy supposed it was, but it was more haggard than any chicken she'd seen before. It had rumpled feathers and strange red eyes. It glared at her through the windshield of Seth's truck, as if Patsy posed a threat to it. Patsy's attention drifted beyond it to the yard, and she realized that the chicken wasn't alone. Others had stopped pecking the ground to stare at the truck. Other animals in the yard had turned on them. Pigs, goats, even a duck, had frozen and locked onto them with a steely red glare.

"What the—" Patsy said, and then something jarred the truck.

The cab shook at the impact. When it stopped rocking, Patsy saw a goat edging backward. It propelled itself back into the truck, hitting Patsy's door at full speed. The truck trembled, and Patsy yelped and jerked her hand back from the door handle.

"Hey! Knock it off!" Seth said. "Crazy goat."

The goat didn't butt into the truck again. Patsy didn't think it had much to do with what Seth had shouted. Deep in her bones, she had a feeling its goal was to keep her in the truck. She went for the handle; the goat bowed its head at the ready. She let go; it lifted its head. Confirmed. She left her hand off the door. This was getting weirder by the minute.

"This place is nuts," Seth said.

"Yeah, which is why Mildred definitely shouldn't be here," Patsy said.

"Why do you care?"

That question was a perfect opening for Patsy to say how she really felt. *I like Mildred a lot more than I like you. I've never liked how you all make fun of her. How you all torture her. She's a cooler person than you or your vapid friends.* But if she said those things, she would be labeled a loser at school faster than she could blink. If she'd had to endure even half of what Mildred did Patsy didn't think she could handle it. So she lied.

"I just think it's weird, okay? Something is definitely up with her."

The door opened and Mildred trundled out. Through the trees and across the distance, Patsy could still tell that Mildred was upset. Her face was downcast, and her stride was urgent as she rushed to her moped. She threw her head back and let out a wild chuckle that confused Patsy. She had never heard Mildred laugh like that. It was almost as if it wasn't Mildred at all.

"Good, she's out. Let's go," Seth said.

He twisted the key in the ignition but the engine didn't scream to life. He tried again.

"Crap, I just changed this starter."

Patsy's attention drifted toward the house. The peeling paint made her think of dirty bones, dug out of the ground. There was a sign on the door that was too far away to read, and she wanted to know what it said. The chicken left the truck hood and joined the others, idly pecking the ground. The goat had likewise abandoned its post. They weren't even glancing at the truck, when a minute ago, they were staring at it as if they'd been enthralled.

Patsy put her hand on the door handle again and nothing came to stop her. She clicked it open. The goat was busy munching on grass and didn't seem to care about anything else. She pushed the door wide.

"What are you doing? She's already gone," Seth told Patsy.

"Come on," she said. "We have to find out why she went in there."

"No way."

"Please? It might be safer if there's two of us."

"Nope. Suit yourself, but I'm not going in there." He folded his hands behind his head and leaned back in his seat, unbothered.

She knew he thought that without him she would be too afraid and would change her mind. It annoyed her. He could have made it easier on her if he'd supported her, but he acted aloof and tried to use her fear to force her into submission. She wasn't going to give in. She wouldn't let fear hold her back, especially not when he was acting as though he could control her. She had a point to prove now. She hopped down onto dead grass. That far out in the woods, the sound of the door shutting echoed loudly. She had meant it to be quiet but her edgy nerves threw off her perception. It was hard to focus on anything other than the morbid house in the middle of the woods. She made it onto the rickety porch and saw the words on the door: Crossroads Magicks. A dreadful chill passed through her.

What was Mildred doing here? she wondered.

She raised her hand to knock but the door screeched open. The scent of herbs and smoke filled the air.

"Hello?" Patsy's voice trembled. She called out louder. "Hello? I'm a friend of Mildred's."

"Hello, a friend of Mildred's," a boy said.

She could see him standing in the next room, but she didn't move toward him, preferring to stay near the open doorway. Something about the boy was familiar. She felt she had seen him somewhere recently. Then again, he had the kind of face that could be on any number of commercials, so perhaps she'd seen someone who looked like him on television.

"Patsy, actually," she said. "Is this, like, a witchcraft store?"

"Kind of like. I'm Owen."

Ø

Seth leaned back in his seat, thinking about how psycho it had been to follow Mildred Waco into the woods. He looked at the ugly shack his girlfriend had just gone into, all because of that social reject. There was probably nobody inside. Most likely, Moldy Mildred had seen them following her and had decided to prank them into wasting time, snooping around a broken-down old house for nothing.

"Hello," a woman's voice said softly.

Seth's breath caught as he took in her beauty. She looked so much like Patsy . . . then she looked like Donna. Or a mixture of the two? But how could that be? The girls were so different. Somehow, she favored both of them in different ways. Her hair was textured like Patsy's but was dark like Donna's. Her lips were pouty like Donna's, but her eyes were green like Patsy's.

Seth rubbed his eyes. "Erm . . . who are you?" he asked.

"I'm Ruza," she said. Her teeth looked like Patsy's when she smiled. "You're Seth Montgomery."

How could this strange lady out in the middle of nowhere know his name? If he hadn't been freaked out already, that was enough to do it. His heart started racing and he thought, *Screw Patsy, I'm out.* He gripped the keys and started to twist the ignition.

"Don't be afraid," she said.

At her words, a stupid grin spread over his lips as his hand drifted away from the steering wheel and he dropped the keys on the floorboard.

"I'm not afraid," he said, but he was. Somewhere inside he was cringing and screaming, but he looked at her Patsy/Donna smile and it was mesmerizing. "You're pretty."

"Am I?" she said, as if she didn't know she was a dime. "As pretty as Patsy?" As she asked it, she looked more like Patsy. "Or Donna?" And she was Donna.

"Wha—"

"Who's your favorite?" she asked, and she was both again.

"Patsy," he said, and meant it.

"Then why bother with Donna?"

"She's just a side piece. That's all." Why was he telling her that?

She clicked her tongue in a disapproving way. "That's a fast way to lose dear Patsy."

"No way." He was suddenly feeling very defensive, and he didn't care why he was admitting it. "Everything is going smooth. Patsy doesn't know about Donna, and Donna has a crush on Aaron, so she won't blab about us."

"That's nice. Except . . ."—she held the thought in the air for a second and then kept going—"Aaron's gone now. Right?"

Paranoia hit him like a dozen Red Bulls, making him jitter inside. "Do you think she knows?" That feeling was the worst.

"Maybe," she said. "Maybe you should mark your territory. Prove who your favorite really is."

"How?"

As soon as the word left his mouth, she was already giving him a knowing look. She stepped toward him with her Donna-not-Donna-but-Patsy legs and craned her neck through the open window of his truck. She pursed her lips as if she was about to kiss him and blew. Her breath was rancid. Raw steak and burning plastic.

Ø

Owen came closer but didn't remove the distance between them completely. He only came halfway, allowing her the choice of whether or not to close the rest of the gap, then held his hand out to her. She remained in the door, not wanting to leave Seth's line of sight. Owen dropped his hand.

"You're afraid," he said. "I don't blame you. This place is pretty creepy if it's your first time."

You think?

"Sort of. So what do you sell here?" she asked.

"Herbs. Candles. Love spells." He waved a hand at the walls of the room he stood in. "You're welcome to come see. Maybe you'll find something you like. A nice perfume that's supposed to help you feel more relaxed during exams?"

She had to admit that sounded tempting. Could there be something that would help her get money? That way she could move her and her mother out of the slums and live in a house like one of the many her mother cleaned. Or something that—

What was she thinking? This wasn't the reason she was here.

"Maybe I'll just have what Mildred bought."

"That's no longer for sale," he said.

"What was it?"

"You should try our bottled wealth. A potion that will help you turn ordinary paper into cash."

Patsy's heart skipped. The exact thing she wanted was being offered up. How did Owen know?

There could be something about her that clued him in. She tried to always look tidy and chic, but maybe she'd missed a mark. She was poor—he knew that somehow, and that frightened her. If a stranger could tell, who else could? Had people known all along? Maybe they talked about her behind her back.

Did you see that outfit she wore today? I wore that last season!

It's so sad how she wears drugstore makeup and tries to pass it off as high end.

A desperate need burned within her. Money would change her life. She wouldn't have to steal clothes to fit in at school anymore. She wouldn't have to depend on Seth for rides, have him pick her up at her mother's employer's house, where she pretended to live. Debts would be paid and investments would be made. Dollar signs filled her mind. Could it be true or was it all just smoke and mirrors? It couldn't hurt to try it . . .

Seth was still waiting in the truck when Patsy left the shop. She hadn't learned a thing about Mildred's purchase, but Patsy now had her own. She was a little unclear about the payment, however. He'd said it would take effect once she used the potion, but he had been vague about the whole thing. Maybe it was just a sales technique. Give them a little something to get the customer hooked, then they'll come back and spend the big bucks.

She noticed Seth looking at her with a burning stare, as though he knew what she'd taken. Heat rose to her cheeks.

"Why are you staring at me like that?" Patsy asked.

"I just never noticed how beautiful your hair is."

He brushed a strand of hair away from her face with his hand and tucked it behind her ear, exposing her neck. Out of nowhere, he began working his lips on her neck and earlobe. Patsy pushed him away.

"What are you doing?" she asked.

"What? We're in the woods." He went in again and she held him back.

"We're still not alone."

"As good as." He scooted closer to her, until a sheet of paper couldn't have passed between them.

"I'm not in the mood," she said. How could she be after the way he'd acted when she needed his help?

"I'll get you in the mood."

An impish grin flashed on his face and Patsy felt his hand in places she'd rather it wasn't.

"Stop!" She shoved him hard and retreated until her back

touched the door. "What is wrong with you? I said no. You're acting like you're possessed or something."

"Come on, Patsy, you always shut me down. I have needs!"

Patsy couldn't believe what she was hearing.

"What you *need* to do is take me home."

"Fine!"

His face was red. He didn't look at her the whole drive back to
her fake house. It occurred to her that he might break up with her.
She'd be a loser again if he did. The spot on the cheer squad would
probably be history. No more popular friends. Panic started to
settle in.

"I'm sorry, I'm just not ready," she said. "And you should
respect that."

"Will you ever be ready?" he asked.

"Sure, I will. Just . . . give me time."

"Time. I've given you so much time. Maybe I need someone
who doesn't need time."

All her worries flew out the window at that. Let him break up
with her, let them kick her off the squad. It wasn't worth being
threatened and pressured into something she didn't want to do.
The truck door slammed loudly behind her as she stormed out
of the passenger side. She made sure it did. Tires squealed as
he pulled away, and she started the ten-block walk to her actual
home.

Ø

Seth sped away the moment he heard the passenger door shut. He
didn't know why he was taking this so hard. She'd turned down
his sexual advances before. He only knew that today he wanted to

be with Patsy terribly, only it hadn't worked out and now he was very angry.

Why? He'd never been so angry at her before. Now he was heading to Donna's after being out with Patsy, knowing it was Patsy he really wanted to be with. But Patsy's purity just didn't seem to have an end in sight.

He pulled into Donna's driveway and had a thought: *Maybe I should just leave Patsy. She's a nosy prude and I could do without toting her around, following Mildred Waco.*

He didn't really feel like that, but he was thinking it, and underneath it all swirled so much confusion. He stepped up to Donna's door and knocked. She came to the door in the cute little nightie he liked, but she also had runny mascara on her face and he could see Joan over Donna's shoulder, crying on the living room couch.

Great. Looks like it's my lucky night, he thought sarcastically.

Ø

In Patsy's pocket, the vial of liquid felt bulky against her thigh. She let herself into her dingy apartment. Her mother was already home, sitting on the couch, chain-smoking and watching some game show on television.

"Calico! Calico!" she shouted at the game show contestant.

"Tabby?" said the contestant.

"Aw! You moron!" she said, and then she glanced at Patsy. "Hi, honey, did you have a good day?"

"No," Patsy said as she passed through.

She sat the vial on her chipped gray desk. Clear, jellied contents filled it to the halfway point. The potion. As embarrassing as it was, she was certain she'd been duped. Owen had played her like a fiddle, and the bad vibe in that place helped make her vulnerable. She felt ignorant now, and believed that the goo in the vial wouldn't create anything other than a mess. She knocked it into the wastebasket below her desk.

21

Mildred felt the tug. It was leading her down Lincoln Drive. Shopping areas were down that way, and she really would rather not go there. She drove right on by Lincoln Drive, but as she did, panic consumed her. She felt as if not listening to her instinct would result in something very bad. *What?* She had no idea, but the possibility scared her enough that she turned around.

She stopped outside the mall and took up a whole parking space with her moped. An inner voice told her that she needed to go inside. Something she needed was in there.

I'll just browse the shops, Mildred thought, since she had nothing else to do. Maybe she'd check the bookstore to see if the new issue of her favorite zombie graphic novel had come out yet. She had been waiting for that one. Or maybe she could find something new in the manga section.

She didn't make it to the bookstore. As soon as she passed Secret Threads, she heard familiar voices that drew her in.

". . . what is the football team going to do now?" Chelle asked, her voice coated in excitement rather than remorse. Her motives bent toward the gossipy aspect of events rather than the actual loss of a fellow student.

Mildred slipped inside and hid discreetly behind a rack of yoga pants. She pretended to shuffle through them so as not to attract the attention of the sales associates as they wandered the area straightening up random things.

"Our date was tonight. I just had my legs waxed yesterday, and this morning, he shows up dead?" Yvette sobbed. "I can't go on a date with a dead person!"

Mildred frowned as she peeked around the yoga pants and saw Chelle's forced look of concern as she patted Yvette's slim, tan shoulders. Yvette was wearing a bright floral-print bikini. She was so broken up over her date's death that she'd decided to shop for swimming attire. Mildred stared Yvette up and down, hating her and admiring her. Her slender legs were so shiny and smooth, they looked like sculpted sand.

Yvette held a different bikini top up to her chest. "Wait, I can't decide which matches these bottoms better," she said.

Matching bikinis probably shouldn't overrule dead dates, Mildred thought. A burning sensation flared within her.

Yvette was perfect for the swim team; it was no wonder she was captain. Her tall frame and toned physique looked mightily impressive in the two-piece. Mildred had never worn a two-piece. If she had it her way, she'd never swim. Of course, when your mother was a marine biologist, it was hard to avoid water altogether. Barbara had insisted on swimming lessons when Mildred was ten. She had worn a one-piece, but always kept a shirt over it—even in the pool. Even at that young age other kids had let her know that her body shape wasn't okay.

Chelle and Yvette had changed back into their normal clothes and were paying for their purchases when Mildred's mind returned from her past swimming memories. She watched as they opened their designer wallets and slid their credit cards across the counter, as if all thoughts of their slain classmate had evaporated. When all was done, they had two handfuls of bags and a much airier disposition—if that was even possible. Yvette strutted out of Secret Threads like a proud Clydesdale, with Chelle at her side.

Their movements were as graceful as ballet dancers. When they laughed together, their voices were a duet of nightingales. If they met a stranger's eye, the stranger smiled and said hello, instead of averting their gaze. Everything about them was entirely unlike Mildred. She hated how they seemed perfect on the out-side yet were so ugly inside. It made Mildred furious. An almost blinding rage settled in.

As the girls went into another clothing store, Mildred joined, staying far enough behind that they wouldn't notice her. They were in their own world, zeroing in on fabrics and price tags, while Mildred zeroed in on them. When they moved, she moved.

"I need this in a size two," Chelle said to a nearby salesperson, an older woman wearing a bright-red dress.

The saleswoman pawed at the racks but came up short.

"Looks like we're all out here, but I can check in the back," she said.

Mildred was looking at Yvette's silky legs as bright red over-took her line of sight. She barely had time to step away as the saleswoman pushed past her on her way to the back room. The woman didn't say she was sorry. She didn't acknowledge Mildred in the least. It was almost as if Mildred was completely invisible. Considering how helpful the salesperson had been toward Chelle and Yvette, Mildred found it odd that the woman would completely disregard her. Then again, she didn't look like the type of customer who would really spend money in this type of store, where the fabrics weren't blended and the fur wasn't faux.

"Did you see that god-awful dress she was wearing?" Chelle asked.

"Yes," Yvette said. "Gag."

"I don't know if I want to buy anything here or not. They're clearly lacking style."

"Yeah, let's ditch."

They slipped away while the saleswoman was dutifully hunting down a size two specially for Chelle.

Selfish, Mildred noted.

She trailed behind, as though an invisible string tied her to the girls. She saw them turn to each other, their lips moving as they walked and talked, but she couldn't hear their words. Her mind was ranting deep hateful words of its own. Soon, the hate turned into longing and even some very tempting suggestions.

Look at those legs, it said. *They are goddess legs. Why does Yvette have them? They would look much better on you. So would her long arms and fit body. And Chelle's chest and her pretty face! Why, you should have those too. They'd go great with your beautiful new legs and slim waist.*

The girls, completely oblivious to Mildred, disappeared behind a door with a LADIES sign on it. It was as if the door had flipped a switch within Mildred. Standing outside, staring at the sign, she knew they were in there, but she didn't have to go in. She'd followed them for a while. Was this stalking? It hadn't seemed like it, but now things weren't so clear. What she was doing could, by an outsider, be called stalking and she could get in serious trouble.

Don't let them get away! Get them, she—or something in her—thought. *You* need *them. Remember the last time you were in the restroom? How they taunted you? How they hurt you? Now it's your turn.*

Haunting voices replayed in her memory: *Go home and cry, you're just making us hate you more by sticking around . . . Why should we care about Moldred's fat ass, she obviously doesn't care about it . . . go home and cry . . . fat ass . . . why should we care . . . hate you . . . loser . . .*

All the pain that had been inflicted by them for years rushed back to her. It filled her and made her want to cry out, but then the anger came, coating the pain. Saving her and overwhelming the parts of her that were afraid.

Yes, you remember. Don't let them get away with it! Go!

Nobody during this whole time had paid any attention to Mildred. They probably wouldn't even be able to pick her out of a lineup to say, "That's the one, the girl who was stalking those two beautiful goddesses."

She walked in.

Yvette, in all her tall and bronze loveliness, was primping in front of the mirror. Her brown-green eyes never even left the image of herself as the door swung open and Mildred entered. Just another mall patron, needing a pit stop. None of her concern. Yvette cast her eyes down, focusing on a dark spot on her shirt that she was now trying to get out. Mildred came up behind her and filled her fingers with Yvette's long chestnut hair. She slammed Yvette's head downward, knowing as soon as she did that her new strong arms were being put to good use. Yvette crashed into the counter, but she had thrown her arms up to protect her face from the impact. She kicked backward at her assailant.

"What the hell?" Yvette said.

She was never known for fighting, so Mildred hadn't expected it, but Yvette did have a competitive spirit and a fighter's mentality. The kick knocked Mildred off balance and into the tiled wall with a grunt. Yvette flung her fist out to punch; Mildred ducked and sidestepped. As she did so, Yvette got a good look at her, immediately registered what she was seeing, and froze. Mildred saw herself in the mirror, the same terrifying sight that Yvette saw. Wild red eyes that weren't her own. Tough leathery skin and a mouth full of jagged fangs. It was only a glimpse, but it was the first time she'd seen what this side of herself looked like, and it was horrifying. Mildred smashed the mirror with her fist. A large part of the glass shattered, breaking the monstrous image into dozens of pieces.

"What's going on out there?" Chelle cried shrilly from one of the stalls.

Mildred grabbed a big piece of pointed glass and slashed it through the air. Yvette snapped out of her stupor, attempted to punch Mildred again, missed, and ran for the door. The handle to freedom was within Yvette's grasp. The sharp glass in Mildred's hand gouged Yvette's neck. Yvette's eyes widened in shock but not a word passed her lips. Mildred pulled out the glass with a wet sound, and Yvette crumpled to the bathroom floor. Blood squirted out of the deep wound. Yvette gripped it and applied pressure as she tried to call to her friend, but could manage nothing more than hoarse gasps that would never find a voice. She tried to crawl away on the floor. Mildred grabbed Yvette's ankle and pulled her back. She slid easily over the slick, reddened tiles.

While she was still struggling, Mildred went to work. Her teeth sank into Yvette's skin and bones as easy as biting into pecan pie. *Crunch. Slurp. Crunch.*

Ø

"Hey . . ." Chelle's voice shook. "Yvette?"

Blood pooled and spread, seeping under Chelle's stall door. The bright red liquid oozed, inching toward Chelle's size-seven Jimmy Choos. Alarm gripped her chest and squeezed. Sloppy sounds greeted her ears. It sounded like someone eating. Lips smacking and opening, slurping, and a strange throaty noise as though someone was trying to swallow something large. The loud pops and cracks were most alarming.

Something was out there and it had hurt Yvette. It could even have been the thing that killed Aaron.

Trying to be quiet, Chelle stood up, pulled up her lacy panties, and let her skirt fall back into place. She slipped off her shoes and held them heel out in her hands like weapons. Her breaths were shallow. She lipped the mantra "Please let it go away, please let it go away."

Silence. Utter fear. Silence.

SLAM! The stall door jarred, rattling on its hinges. Chelle cried and begged as the door broke away from the stall and revealed the monster. Its anthropoid face was bathed in Yvette's blood. Chelle swiped feebly with her heels and took off for the exit door, shrieking hysterically. She got the door open for a split second, but the monster rose from the floor in a swift motion and closed in on her. The door crashed shut, catching Chelle's fingers in it. When she yanked her hand back, it was already bruising and her yellow manicured nails were a broken mess. She screamed in pain, frustration, and fear, and a smile spread over the creature's bloody lips. It was Chelle's last sound before her body was slammed against the wall hard enough to knock the breath out of her. She coughed blood and gasped, tears spilling over her very black MAC mascara.

As she lay belly down, she saw her friend's face beside her. Her legs were gone. Her torso was bare, and most of the skin was gone. Chelle wanted to scream, wanted to run out of there.

But she never would.

Ø

Mildred stood on Chelle's back, pressing her into the hard floor. The weight that Chelle had always teased her about had become a weapon, squeezing the life out of Chelle underneath her. Gasp. Black tears. Gasp.

Mildred felt the life leaving Chelle and it felt great, like getting a tough stain scrubbed off a surface after struggling with it for years.

As Chelle lay staring blankly, Mildred went back to finish her meal of Yvette's waist. Once she slurped down the last muscle, she flipped Chelle onto her back and started in. That same metallic flavor danced on her tongue as she chewed Chelle's face, but the unnatural taste of all the makeup turned her off slightly. It made the flavor bitter, but she still swallowed it. The flesh of Chelle's chest was bursting with flavor and as soon as the last chunk was consumed, the rage in Mildred settled, satiated.

The overwhelming hatred for her victims dissipated and she felt as if she'd woken up there, in the mall bathroom, surrounded by complete and utter carnage.

Mildred stared around her in terror. Chelle's warm blood had mingled with Yvette's. Mildred looked down at herself to see that their blood covered her hands, coated her knees. She barely knew what had happened, but she was seeing it all. Broken bodies. Missing parts. She remembered sinking the glass into Yvette, the way it opened her up. The look on Chelle's face as she saw what Mildred had become. That thing she saw in the mirror.

She was a monster.

"No . . ." she whispered.

22

Mildred could hear the uneven lop of the cleaning trolley rolling down the hollow hallway outside the restroom door. Her startled heart skipped a beat. What would she do? Explain to the cleaning person that she was cursed? Tell them she was really a good person and she'd never have killed anyone if she hadn't had a dark curse on her? Then ask them to please not tell anyone?

Nobody would have believed an excuse like that. Not a chance.

Oh no! She panicked silently. *I'm caught. There's no way out. The cleaning person is going to come in, see this, and—*

Mildred's eyes were shut tight, her back against the wall with blood pooling around her Converse sneakers. Squeaking at the hinges, the door swung open and she heard the trolley roll inside. Her heart thudded a mile a minute. The door swung backward, shutting noisily. She couldn't breathe. It would all be over the moment the cleaning person saw the blood, thick on the floor, and the mangled, half-eaten bodies.

But nothing happened.

Mildred opened her eyes and saw . . . no one. Next door, a toilet flushed in the men's restroom.

Safe for now, Mildred breathed again. But it was no time to relax. In a matter of minutes, it would be the ladies' room door swinging open. She had to get out of there on the double. As she stood, she slipped a little on the slick, messy floor, but she was able to keep upright. She stopped at the door and glanced back. The bags that held Yvette and Chelle's expensive merchandise were sitting on the floor by the sinks. On a whim, Mildred snatched the bags—seven in total. Then she ran out, streaking blood all the way down the hallway to the back exit.

Ø

At home, wrapped in her pale-pink bathrobe, Mildred sat on the edge of her bed. Her wet hair dripped on her comforter. She stared at the bags on her floor, stained with remnants of the girls who had bought them. Pretty hot-pink and white stripes splattered with bright-red droplets. Spattered with proof of her crimes.

Mildred lurched up and turned every bag on its end, letting the contents fall on her carpet. She scurried to her bathroom and got her bloody clothes and shoes. For good measure, she also grabbed the toilet cleaner with bleach and a cloth. Then she carried the bags, clothes, shoes, cleaner, and cloth to her garage.

Usually, Naomi took the trash to the dump when she left on Wednesdays, and put a fresh bag into the trash can. Mildred wasn't even sure when the garbage truck came around. She thought it might be Thursday, but it could also be Tuesday. It was definitely one of those days that starts with a *T*. She balled up her clothes and tossed them, along with her shoes and the bags, into the big trash barrel at the back of the garage. It was empty. The shoes thunked on the bottom of the aluminum can.

This had been the most gruesome situation she'd been in thus far, and she was certain there had to be blood on the footrest of the moped. Sure enough, when she sprayed the cleaner and wiped it, her white cloth was turned various shades of red. She kept wiping, kept spraying. The seat, the handles, everywhere. Once satisfied her bike was completely clean, she threw the cloth away as well. She tied the trash bag and dragged the barrel to the end of her driveway. The neighbors' trash cans sitting next to the road on either side let her know she was in luck. Thursday was the day to get rid of things you didn't want to clutter up your house . . . or your police record.

All the moving around had caused her pants to slide off her waist. They felt droopy at her back end. She pulled them up but they felt looser than they had an hour before. They slid down again. She ignored it and went back inside, where she pulled out her laptop.

She went to the search engine and typed *how to get rid of a curse*.

Several hits came, but they all focused on what exactly a curse was, rather than how to remove one.

She changed the phrase and tried again. *How to break a curse.*

Her heart sank as she read the results. *It's impossible, you're cursed for life.*

It can be broken only by the one that put it on you.

Another result instructed her to buy crystals and special candles infused with herbs and coated in oils. Black fluorite, tawny agate, basil, frankincense, Dead Sea salt, sage, a purple pillar candle, three white votive candles, and three black votive candles.

All the ingredients could probably be found on the shelves at Crossroads Magicks, but Mildred was determined not to set foot back in that place. She bookmarked the page so she could find it again when she got all the ingredients and needed the spell.

Her next search was for an online occult store. It was easy to find a nice Wiccan store, where she ordered all the stones, oils, herbs, and candles she needed with her emergency credit card. She ordered a one- to two-day rush on the package. Two days sounded like a long time. Waiting wasn't preferable, but she had no choice. The other options she'd bumped into seemed to just insist that she was doomed. This was the only hope she'd found, and she clung to it.

She took off her robe, put on pajamas, and crawled into her bed, exhausted. Her head sank into her cozy faux-feather pillow, but her mind was troubled. Two possible days. So many people could die within that time frame. So many had already died because of her.

It's the last time, she told herself as she struggled to drift off to sleep. *I'm not ever going to kill anyone again. I didn't mean to at all. I'm not a bad person. Please, just don't let anyone find out.*

Her nightmares flared to life in a vivid bundle of gore. Flashes of broken bodies. Blood on her hands. Monstrous hands. She saw herself, a devilish beast. When she screamed, her mouth opened with jagged daggers, and when she cried it was the evil red eyes that shed the tears. Her small voice echoed in this giant evil body, and she was trapped inside.

23

Garrett Hyde snapped his office door shut to drown out the buzz of the police station. As far as offices went, his was rather minimal. A desk, a lamp, a laptop, and paperwork. Lots of paperwork. Inside his desk drawer, where some detectives might keep gin or whiskey, Hyde instead kept worn copies of *One Flew Over the Cuckoo's Nest* and *The Silence of the Lambs*.

He tossed the latest file that had been assigned to him on his desk and opened it to the first page.

This is a tough one, he thought as he glared down at the report, roughly scribbled in his scratchy style. Black letters on stark white should be plain to see, but none of it made much sense to him. This case was different from others he'd handled. Still, the sergeant had been breathing down his neck, eager for Hyde to do what he did best and fast. *Easier said than done, Sarge. It's been only twelve hours.*

Truth be told, Hyde wanted nothing more than to work whatever magic he'd been blessed with and solve this case lickety-split.

Most times, a case fell in his lap and the answers came to him the way musical notes had come to Mozart so long ago, but this time all the chords were crossed, and his brain-piano was playing off-key.

Something wasn't factoring in, and that something was the missing puzzle piece that would complete the whole. His job was to find that piece. Find the piece and he could find the killer. Everything left a trail. Everything, everyone. Even seemingly normal neighbors moonlit as murderers—*that* he knew from experience. Said murderous neighbor had almost killed Hyde's mother and his memory of that night was never far from his mind. It was the reason he'd joined law enforcement as an adult. He wanted to be one of the good ones, helping to outweigh the bad.

He went over the photos in front of him again.

A dead boy.

The kid had been a star athlete, charismatic, well liked. He was easy on the eyes, going by the small school photo attached to the file. Could have been a jealous classmate. Maybe an ex-boyfriend of one of the dead boy's dates—of which there had been a pretty long list. He was popular with the girls, just as Hyde himself had been in his high school days. He knew how the most trivial things could seem calamitous for teenagers. Another kid could have been so jealous of his crush going out with Aaron, he could have lashed out. Eliminated the competition.

But that explanation didn't feel right to Hyde.

The scene was gruesome, the worst he'd set eyes upon in all the time since he'd become a detective. The kid's eye had popped out, hanging by the nerves like a macabre paddleball dangling from a string, for Christ's sake. It was lying in the bloody dirt, the pale blue iris covered in flecks of deep red and earthy brown. His head was caved in. The scene bore all the signs of a rage-fueled jealousy murder. That could be the answer . . . if it wasn't for just one thing: the kid's missing tongue.

Hyde studied the photo, trying to put the killer's thoughts in his mind. *I'm a romantic adversary. I'm fed up and out for blood. If that a-hole jock was out of the way, I'd have my girl.*

He leaned back in his uncomfortable chair.

What do I bring with me to confront the jock? A bat? Crowbar? No, it would have to be something wider. What things around a school are wide? Think!

In his mind's eye, he saw the boy's wounds again. A smashed-open skull.

When he was six, Hyde's older brother had reluctantly taken him out during Halloween, at the behest of their mother. This was before the deranged neighbor had broken into their house and attacked her, and long before Hyde became a cop.

Hyde still remembered the strong plastic scent that filled the night, courtesy of the old cheap costumes from those days. That Halloween, big bro Ern had met up with his pals and done more tricks than Hyde had done treats. Ding-dong ditching, a few flaming bags of dog turds on porches, toilet-papered yards. A small and disturbed Hyde had watched in terror as Ern and his goons gleefully trashed Pumpkin Alley—a street in his home-town where people would decorate hundreds of pumpkins and leave them alight on Halloween night. Jack-o'-lanterns, lit up with different expressions, were a favorite thing of Hyde's. The thing he liked most was that with all the choices of expression available to people, they chose to carve smiles instead of frowns or snarls.

Hyde was crushed inside when Ern lifted a widely grinning

pumpkin and slammed it down. Pumpkin pieces flew every-where. Half the fruit lay crushed and broken—like the kid in Hyde's crime scene photo.

Hyde sighed and tried to remove the splattered pumpkin from the brain matter in his fantasy reconstruction. He was tired and probably shouldn't have been thinking of it until after a bit of rest, but he couldn't stop.

The kid on the side of the field at Roanoke High . . . it made Hyde's guts bubble. It made him feel six again, disturbed and afraid. But he would never let anyone know. He would stomach it, because he was a twenty-six-year-old detective now, not the little boy back in Pumpkin Alley, or even the eleven-year-old kid who came home and found his bloody and unrecognizable mother on the living-room floor.

It was hot in his office. Hyde hooked his finger on his tie and loosened it. He stared at the less gory photo next to the crime scene photo on his desk. A pretty girl with a ponytail smiled at the camera from a photocopy of her latest school photo. Below it, it said MISSING. Her name was Tiffany, and she was a band star, a straight-A student, and a weekend volunteer at the local veter-inarian clinic. She hadn't been seen since band practice several hours ago.

If the jealousy card was off the table for Aaron's murder, then maybe the two were connected.

Kids like her didn't just up and run away, Hyde knew. Funny that she would go missing when all of this started. Could she be involved? Could she be a victim? Hyde gave it a moment of thought and decided that there was a connection. There had to be, but where?

He was almost sure of the connection, because Tiffany had

also known the restroom girls. These were the girls in the next photo Hyde pulled from the bottom stack and sat atop. He had watched the surveillance cameras from the hall outside the restrooms, had seen the girls walk in alone and then something strange happened to the video. It was as if it blinked. That was the best way he could explain it. The time skipped, showing nothing. Somehow, it missed everything. All the cameras in the mall, from the southern entrance door to the restroom exit, had malfunctioned last night, making his job harder.

The scene had been another bad one. So bad that a few of the other officers had vomited and one had refused to go inside. Blood splashed the walls, mirrors, stalls. Broken glass, slickened red, was scattered across the floor. The girls were mangled, as if attacked by a wild predator. Something with sharp teeth and strong jaws. If Hyde was making a wild guess, he'd say they'd been killed by a shark, but that was ridiculous. Sharks didn't attack out of water. He'd thought of a bear but bears didn't attack inside malls. The assailant had to be a person, but that thought felt most insane of all, because how could a human being do something like this? Hyde had seen his share of horrific crimes, but this one raised the bar. This one set his nerves tingling, as if the ground had opened in the room and shown him a flash of hell. The impressions he got at the scene were foul and chaotic.

For all the physical clues they found at the scene, the crime could have been committed by anything. There were no fingerprints, no evidence, no witnesses. They had less than nothing. An unexplainable nothing. Nothing tangible at the boy's scene, nothing tangible at the mall, and no trace of Tiffany.

What Hyde did have was instinct and experience. He could tell these crimes weren't planned. At the ball field, he'd seen the footballs strewn about where the kid had been practicing his throw. This told Hyde that someone had either waited while the kid practiced or happened upon him while he was practicing. The intensity of the kill didn't strike Hyde as being from the type who would waste much time waiting. It felt very sudden and violent. With the girls, it seemed that their deaths came quickly after they'd entered the restroom with only a short amount of time skipped on the hallway camera between when the girls entered and when blood began pooling in the hallway from beneath the door. Both scenes felt very much like convenience kills.

At the same time, it couldn't possibly have been a coincidence that all the victims and the missing girl had been popular students at Roanoke High.

Hyde wiped his tired eyes with his hands. He wished he could wipe away the photographs as simply, but he needed to study them. He needed to know the positions, needed to remember every wound—but he could take a short break from the scene and focus on another angle: the crime scene crowd. He pushed the photographs away and opened his little notebook. The first name he saw was Mildred's. Her description read: brown eyes, dark hair, pudgy, poor hygiene. Suddenly, before his eyes, the words faded and new ones appeared just as though he'd written them himself. Hyde blinked. He shook his head as though a fly had landed on his nose. He forgot what he was looking at, then he remembered his notes. The note before him read: brown eyes, dark hair, athletic, pretty. Right. He remembered her now.

24

Joan didn't know it was possible to feel such pain—the kind that tore through your core and stripped away part of your soul. After her mother left, she thought she had endured the worst pain she would ever experience. But with her mother, they had seen it coming. She had warned time and time again that if their father didn't stop the drinking, she would leave. When she finally left, there had been time. Joan had held her hand as Mary kissed her cheek. Mary had been able to tell Joan she loved her and would miss her, that she would come back someday. But years had passed. The idea of never seeing her mother again came slowly.

With Aaron, death had come like a stealthy bandit and snatched him away from her. No warning. Like a lightbulb that had been there and had suddenly blown out, never to light up again. Thrown away. Only that comparison was stupid, because lights didn't matter as much. They were replaceable, not like Aaron. So full of life. So charismatic and lovable.

The Renfro house was quieter than it had ever been under its cloak of sadness, so when the door to Joan's bedroom creaked, her head snapped up. She saw the silhouette of her father in the doorway, framed by the warm light from her muted television. Jason Renfro's short hair was sticking up on the right.

"You're awake," he said.

He didn't sound drunk, which caught Joan by surprise.

"I've been awake," she said. "Can't sleep."

He shuffled inside soundlessly and sat on the side of her bed. He didn't smell drunk. But all the years she'd spent building walls hadn't been forgotten in light of his being sober—she instinctively drew her legs up closer to her and made room for him, not wanting to be within vomit or spittle range.

"I just . . ." He stared at the wall and avoided eye contact. For a breath or two, words seemed to escape him. Then he picked back up. "I'm sorry. I'm so sorry, Jo. It's my fault and I—if I hadn't . . ."

"It's not your fault, Dad," she said, because watching him struggle was difficult, even if somewhere deep inside, she felt like he deserved this guilt. "You didn't know there was something dangerous out there. You had no way of knowing."

"I was . . . such a shit. I'm a terrible drunk. I didn't mean for any . . ." He faltered, then howled and put his head in his hands in despair. He blubbered, "I'd take it back if I could. All of it. Losing Aaron . . . losing Mary . . ."

Joan stiffened, but it wasn't because of the mention of her mother. The television screen had grown brighter, casting more light upon them and grabbing her attention. Two familiar faces beamed at her from their school photos. Chelle Martin and Yvette Darling.

"Dad, look." She took the controller from her nightstand, pressed a button, and voices came to life.

"*. . . both students at Roanoke High. We're speaking, of course, of the same Roanoke High that Aaron Renfro*"—Aaron's photo replaced the girls on the screen—"*attended and the site where he was found. All deaths appear to have been of an animalistic nature. We've asked if the murders were connected, but—*"

Joan's mouth dropped open in shock. No . . . this couldn't be happening! A drunk sort of swimmy-headedness hit her.

"Oh my God," Jason said.

"*. . . a missing persons case may also be connected. Tiffany Cosby—*" The girl's school photo came onto the screen. Joan recognized the similar school photo background and her Roanoke High Band shirt.

"*Could her disappearance be connected to the murders of her fellow students? We'll have more information as the story unfolds.*" The image went back to Chelle and Yvette. "*Once again, the two bodies found inside Roanoke Mall's east restroom area have been identified as Michelle Martin and Yvette Darling. Officials say that they're working on recovering footage to see what exactly broke into the restroom. If you have any information, please call—*"

Joan muted the television again. All her breath had been vacuumed out by the news of more deaths. These were all people she was close to, except for Tiffany, though she definitely knew who she was. But Aaron? Chelle? Yvette? What was happening? What kind of animal was doing this?

Animal. As she thought it, it didn't seem right. If it was an animal, how had it perfectly targeted only Roanoke High students? Wouldn't there have been reports of a wild animal seen wandering around by now? It seemed more like someone was purposely staying out of sight. One thing was certain: something terrible was going to keep happening to people unless someone found out what was causing it and why.

"Why?" Joan cried, and it was not the first time. Her father had been no help that morning and she left with the question still on her mind. Now she was sitting in the back seat of Seth's truck, Donna in the passenger seat.

"I'd like to know myself, but are you sure you want to do this whole school thing?" Donna asked.

"I have to go," Joan said. "Someone has to know something. And Dad is a wreck. I hate seeing him go through this while I'm trying to work through it myself." She waited a beat, pondering. "I have to know why this happened. What or who did this?"

"So you're saying you think it could have been a person?" Donna asked.

"You heard the news this morning. It was inside the mall. I don't think a wild animal would be in the mall. And without anyone knowing?" Joan speculated aloud. "No way. This had to be some*one*."

"But who?"

"You know who I saw sneaking around yesterday?" Seth asked. "That girl Millie."

"The really pretty one nobody likes? Well, pretty except for her hair and gross teeth, I mean, I don't know what's going on with that," Donna said.

"Yeah, her."

"Weird," Joan said. "I've had a feeling about her since I saw her at—at the field, you know where Aaron was . . ." She couldn't finish but felt confident that they knew what she meant. "Did you see her? She was scared senseless."

"Everyone was scared senseless," Seth said.

"Not like her," Joan insisted. "I can't explain it . . ."

"Do you think she did it?" Donna said.

Seth cackled loudly. "You serious? That girl weighs a buck ten and probably can't lift for crap. Uh-uh. That kind of damage took serious strength."

"I didn't say she was a suspect," Joan said. "But I do think she knows something."

"She probably doesn't know *anything*," Donna said. "It's not like anybody would tell her anything. She has no friends."

"That's true," Seth said.

The three of them grew silent. Joan gazed out the window, watching trees and houses float by. Pine, spruce, maple, maple, pine, and they were all living, those trees—but Aaron wasn't, even though he should be. Donna and Seth didn't understand how much this meant to her. The last thing she'd said to Aaron never left her mind. It burned in her like the Olympic torch. *I hope neither one of you comes home tonight!* Aaron would never come home again.

That girl Millie . . . she knew all the victims, didn't she? Joan sighed. *Lots* of people knew all the victims. She knew all the victims, Seth knew all the victims, Donna knew all the victims—everyone in the truck could be a suspect.

"Hop in the back, Donna," Seth said.

Donna gave him a mean look but he didn't seem to notice or care. Joan's lip curled as she watched her best friend unbuckle and then squeeze between the two front seats into the back part of the king cab. They rolled their eyes at each other, knowing he was picking up Patsy. It wasn't that Joan hated Patsy; it was just that she hated seeing Patsy continually being chosen over Donna. She wondered why Donna even wasted her time on Seth. There was a slap as Seth's hand made contact with Donna's bottom while she climbed in the back. Donna squealed and laughed.

"Stop it," she said playfully.

Joan wanted to hurl. Their horseplay was kind of gross, seeing as he was clearly using Donna. He was never going to leave Patsy.

"Can you guys be serious, please," Joan said. "We could all be in danger here."

"The reports say animal attack," Seth said. "It sucks, but we have no proof it was anything else."

Heat rose in Joan's cheeks. "How would an animal get into the mall restroom?"

"I don't know, Joan," Seth said. "Maybe it found an open door."

Joan knew that when Patsy sat down, the passenger seat would be warm, and that wasn't the only thing Donna was keeping warm for her. Joan saw Donna's face grow stony as they pulled up next to the sidewalk. Patsy wasn't standing there, waiting for her boyfriend. Her house looked dark and quiet.

"So where is she?" Donna asked smugly.

Seth shrugged.

"Maybe she's had a change of heart," Donna said.

"Or maybe she's just running late," Seth said.

Holding in all the secrets and questions made Joan's head hurt. She just wanted to scream at Donna, "He doesn't care about either of you!" But she settled on saying, "Then go knock."

Clearly Patsy was mad. She was always here, but now she wasn't, and Seth had said they'd had an argument. *Maybe now he can finally start focusing on Donna more? Or maybe,* Joan thought,

Donna will wise up, too, and leave this lousy cheater.

Seth stared at them and they stared back. Surely he didn't think one of them would go up to the door and knock.

"It's all on you, dude," Joan said. "I've got enough to deal with."

Seth nodded, looked at the solemn house, put his hand on his key . . . then dropped it and pulled away. "Screw her," he said.

Joan and Donna shared a knowing smile, although Joan's was forced. At least now they could get back to the real issue, which was who'd killed her brother.

25

Sharp beeps cut through Mildred's troubled sleep. She was so on edge from all the nightmares that she almost tumbled out of bed. Reflexes she hadn't possessed before helped keep her steady enough to stand on her feet instead of hitting the floor hard on her bottom. As she stood, her pants and underwear—already loose around her—fell right off her bony hips, slid down her trim thighs, and pooled on the floor. She gasped and tightened her pajama top against her to cover herself, even though she was alone. The top hung limply on her, as though she'd shrunk several sizes during the night. Her stomach felt tight and slim underneath the fabric. She unbuttoned the shirt and let it fall.

In the bathroom mirror, a stranger looked back at her. Her eyes, hair, and teeth were the same, but her face and body were both like and unlike the late Chelle and Yvette. There was a hint of herself but it was buried deep beneath the others. She studied her new self, pleased and amazed. Her arms and legs were toned.

Her breasts and butt were perky and round. Her unblemished skin was as smooth as a baby's—

What was that?

A small tattoo below the right side of her right breast. An anchor? Mildred must have gotten this tattoo from someone. It had likely been on Chelle. Mildred hadn't noticed it, but then again, she hadn't been in her right mind the night before.

She remembered another time, when she overheard Chelle bragging about how much her tattoo had hurt. It was her way of letting everyone know that she had one.

Ouch, my tattoo is so sore, she'd said.

But Mildred had never seen it. She wasn't cool and couldn't possibly be permitted to be shown the thing. She'd just overheard and had shoved it to the back of her mind.

Now she inspected it on her own body through the mirror. It was cute and small. Hardly anything that would be sore for a week. Mildred kind of liked it.

What are you thinking? she thought, ashamed. *You killed for this body, for this face, these hands, and arms. You killed three innocent girls and two innocent guys . . .*

Something else in her piped up. *Innocent? No, no. They were cruel and narcissistic. The girls would do the same thing to you to be beautiful, if they were in your shoes.*

But I'm not like them.

Why shouldn't you be? Don't you deserve it, after all they put you through? After all the times they ridiculed you? Hurt you?

Mildred bit her plump lip as she mulled over the truth of the thoughts. They were so different from the lips she was used to. Softer. Thicker. She pursed her lips in the mirror and turned from side to side. So different, and yet when she smiled, her lips fell instantly into a frown. It was her own smile. Her uneven teeth showed through lips that parted the same way her old ones had, instead of more like Chelle's.

Wait. What was she thinking? She had this new amazing body and she was upset that she didn't look *exactly* like Chelle? What was wrong with her?

Weight settled in her chest; she was unsure if she could handle the type of person she was becoming. Even though the curse was making her commit evil deeds, it felt more and more as if it had been what she'd wanted all along.

As she stood there, she noticed more differences. Her arms were a couple of subtle shades darker than her chest. Her legs and torso were about five times more tanned than the rest of her. Not as brown as Yvette had been, but more so than Mildred's usual tone, sort of a color in between them.

She wasn't them. And she wasn't herself. Who had she become, some version of Frankenstein's creature?

I can't keep dwelling on this!

She threw up her hands and stepped away from the mirror.

Only a second later, she realized a new implication of what she'd done when she opened the closet door and saw all her old, frumpy clothes hanging there. Those gawky fabrics wouldn't cover this body. They would hang off her and fall away. She looked greedily at the clothes she'd emptied out of the Secret Threads bags. Old Mildred wouldn't have been able to fit any of those bottoms over her knees. But now, anything in that pile would fit her.

It did. She chose a lacy black bra with matching panties. The lace felt itchy on her skin, but it was sexy. That alone made her feel comfortable in them. Comfortable for the first time ever in any underwear of any fabric. She marveled at herself.

Next, she searched through the pile until she found a long pink top and a pair of pink and black leggings to wear. The top slipped off one shoulder and showed her lacy bra strap. She wasn't entirely sure it was supposed to do that, but she'd seen other girls wear them that way, so she let it stay there. As a bigger girl, she'd never worn leggings. She thought her legs would look like frog legs in them and the bullies would have new ammo to tease her with. But now, she wore them with pride. They hugged her muscular thighs and felt extremely comfortable. Sitting at a desk all day at school might not be so bad.

The second alarm on her clock beeped.

What the hell?

She never set a second alarm. Somehow, in an instant, she knew what it was. She must have set it some time last night. Hearing it triggered something in her. The thought of Yvette running on a treadmill came to mind. That alarm was her cue that it was time to stop running and start getting ready for school. Mildred didn't have a treadmill, but she was aching to stretch her legs. Going for a run would be great. It made perfect sense. Even though she'd never run from anything except maybe a spider or a basketball during gym class, now running felt perfectly natural to her.

She slipped on her normal black sneakers and headed for the garage. She'd ride to school early and use the treadmill there. But after entering the garage and seeing the moped, it just didn't seem necessary. It wasn't far. She'd just run to school.

She pressed the garage-door button and as it lifted, a figure came into view. He was looking curiously at the trash barrel at the end of the driveway. Tall. Muscular. Dressed in a suit. Mildred recognized him right away. Detective Hyde.

What the crap was he doing nosing through her garbage? Her very *incriminating* garbage. It had to stop, now.

She took off down the driveway, ready to chase him away with taunts. Tell him he was acting like a cheap private detective instead of an official police detective, out snooping in people's personal discards without a search warrant. Many nasty insults came to mind. The types of things some other people might say, people like Aaron or Chelle or Yvette, but Mildred had never dreamed of being so harsh. Halfway there, her steps slowed.

Poor dense Mildred. She suddenly realized how her new appearance might affect others. She started to go back and hide, but he had already noticed her. Jogging up and facing him was the only choice now. Her heart pounded.

"Hello, Mildred," he said, looking up with a grin. His grin wavered as his eyes met her face, so different from the one he'd met yesterday. She waited for it. For the confusion and then perhaps fear, suspicion . . . but his grin came right back. "Bad hair day?"

Not "Why are you different?" No "What happened to you?" He had recognized her easily as she'd come from the house. She could have been a cousin of Mildred's, or even a sister for all he knew. A slim figure coming down the driveway who was definitely not Mildred Waco. Couldn't have been. That's how she looked. Yet he'd called her by name, as if she looked as normal as the rising sun had that morning.

Mildred worked hard to keep the puzzlement free from her face, but her words came as naturally as ever. "Can't do a thing with it. What brings you around this side of town?"

"You mean the side of town where recycling is so popular there's nothing but empty bins out on garbage day?"

This time, Mildred's perfectly plucked brows—now a soft, brown hue rather than her normal borderline-black color—pulled together, all efforts of hiding emotion abandoned. "Huh?" she said, dumbfounded.

She stomped over and peered into the barren can and racked her brain. The garbage truck hadn't been around this early before. She glanced over at the Lankford's trash can, which had a hint of white bag poking out of the top last night. Still there, so they hadn't been by yet. Why was her can empty?

Ah! Of course. The witch's monsters.

She plastered on a smile. "My parents are both hard-core environmentalists. Always working toward a better tomorrow." The sentence sounded generic, like a commercial voice-over, but she didn't care. It made her look like a silly kid, and that's exactly what she needed Hyde to see her as.

"That's good. Admirable." He nodded and smiled politely, eyes still studying her. "So why bring an empty can down to the street?"

Mildred hesitated. "Raccoons. I think there was a bag with some food in there, but you know how those critters can be."

"Oh, of course."

A moment of silence passed while he waited, and Mildred finally spoke up. "Can I help you with anything?"

"Now that you mention it, I do have a few questions for you," he said thoughtfully.

"Can they wait? I'm going to be late for school—"

"It won't take long," he said quickly, pulling out his old little notepad and flipping it open. "Were you in or near the school on the night of the twelfth?"

"At night?" Mildred said, scrunching up her face, pretending to be thoughtful. "Nope. Can't say I was." *Literally,* she thought, proud of herself for not lying entirely. She honestly couldn't *say* she was there.

"So there would be no reason for your moped to be there either?"

Stay calm. She wanted to grab him and shake him. Scream, "Okay, what are you getting at?" but she stared wide eyed and said, "Of course not."

"Ever park at the visitor's lot near the football field?"

That was exactly where she'd parked that night. Mildred took a deep breath, looking more annoyed than nervous.

"I don't know. Maybe. If the student parking lot is full I might park over in the visitor's lot."

"You stated that you'd had an accident, correct?"

"That's right. What does it have to do with the investigation?"

"Just curious. How did it happen?"

"I . . ." Her eyes roamed for a moment. She'd gotten a smooth tongue, but she still had the same old slow mind as Mildred and no idea what to say. "I . . ." Just then, a squirrel darted across the Lankfords' yard and up an old sycamore tree. "A squirrel. I dodged a squirrel and hit a mailbox. I wasn't going very fast, though. Not much harm done."

"I see. Any chance you've seen Tiffany Cosby around anywhere?"

Mildred shook her head. "Not since band practice."

"Uh-huh. And did you, by chance, visit the mall yesterday?"

A-ha! He was trying to catch her off guard, ask her random questions before he asked the big one, hoping she'd just spat the truth. *Well, not this time,* she thought. "Nope."

Hyde jotted all her info in his little notepad. She wondered what else was in there. Was he drilling everyone for any little thing, or did he know something she didn't know he knew? Was the crime scene evidence list in there? Did they find Yvette and Chelle? And evidence of her moped at the mall? No. No way. He was just nosy. The kind of nosy that likes to rummage in people's trash cans. He just locked onto her because her awkwardness made him a little suspicious. That's all, she was sure of it. All she had to do was keep her cool.

Or find someone with a better brain to take, so you can out-smart him, something said.

She startled but didn't think back at the inner voice that didn't seem to belong to her. Instead, she spoke quickly and loudly to Hyde, as though she was trying to drown that other voice out. "Has something happened to Tiffany?" Mildred asked, knowing full well where Tiffany was.

"She's missing. Given these attacks, she may be something worse . . ."

"Oh. Well, I hope you find her," she said, as sincerely as she could muster. "So if that's all you need for now, I really have to get to school."

"I hope we find her as well." It sounded like a threat. The pleasant kind, said with a smile. "You have a nice day, Miss Waco." His gleaming, newscaster-worthy smile flashed and Mildred saw a little dimple in his left cheek. She wondered if she had dimples now. She'd like to have some, because she'd always heard other people say how much they liked that sort of thing.

"Thanks, Detective Hyde. You have a nice day as well."

It was eerie how perfectly chipper she sounded giving the line, when inside she was a storm of worry and terror. Hyde had no idea how close he was getting, and she couldn't have that. He turned to walk back to the curb where he'd parked. She didn't want to hurt him, but it would be so easy now that his back was turned.

"Mildred, yoo-hoo," a voice called to her from the next yard. "Millie!" Mrs. Vaughn was poking her head over the hedges.

Hyde stopped in his tracks and turned around.

Rats!

"Sorry, Millie, dear, I didn't mean to interrupt you and your friend. I was just wondering if you've seen Tyler lately?" she asked.

Her hair was already fixed neatly, even at seven in the morning, which Mildred couldn't fathom. No wonder Mrs. Waco liked her; they were soul mates.

"No, I haven't. Sorry."

"It's just that, he went out to finish your yard yesterday morning and I haven't seen him since. His bed doesn't even look slept in. Do you know where he went? I've tried calling his friends. Nobody has seen him."

"That's weird," Mildred said. "No, I don't. He didn't do our yard yesterday." She tried to ignore Hyde's pen scratching against his little notebook.

"Oh no! I hope it's not drugs."

"Hello, ma'am, I'm Detective Garrett Hyde," he said, walking closer to the hedges.

"Oh, hi, Detective," she said brightly. She fidgeted with her already nice hair, smoothing the surface.

"Are you the mother of the missing individual?"

"Yes, sir."

"And is this usual for him? Does he often disappear? Is he on drugs?"

Mildred felt her nerves jitter inside, tingling at her fingertips.

Her yard was the last place Tyler was supposed to have been and this was the last thing she needed. The air felt heavy. Their words faded.

"Um, excuse me," she managed to say. "I'm going to be late for class. Feel free to call if you have any questions for me, Detective Hyde."

He turned toward her. "Will do. Have a great day at school, Mildred."

She gave a closed-mouthed smile and turned away, heading down the driveway at a jog. He was so friendly, it annoyed her. Every kind thing he said felt like a sugarcoated threat. *Have a nice day at school, it's going to be one of your last, because I'm onto you and it's only a matter of time before I lock you up.*

She had to stop running and wait when she reached the light near the school. The sharp sound of a car horn made her jump. Her first thought was that a car was plowing toward her, and she flinched, but it was only a guy in a convertible smiling and waving at her.

Weird, she thought. *This must be what it's like to be pretty. People like looking at you and want you to know it.* It made her feel a little awkward. Maybe it was easier for people who had grown up being pretty. She still felt like the same old Mildred—nobody had ever honked at her for being pretty; they honked because she was in the way. This was something that would take some getting used to.

26

Chatter filled the halls of Roanoke High as students gossiped away with reckless abandon. Like Hyde and Mrs. Vaughn, no one reacted to Mildred's new body—it didn't seem as new to everyone else as it was to Mildred. A few people said hi to her, and one boy winked at her while she stood at her locker, which was a new development. The majority of the student body seemed to be focused on other issues.

One death was big enough news on its own, but now that three deaths and one missing student were reported, it was all anyone could talk about. Luckily for Mildred, they seemed to have no idea what actually happened at all.

"Yeah, torn in pieces," a girl with thick, black-rimmed glasses told her friend.

"I heard they found her head in the dumpsters outside," one of the guys on the football team told a cheerleader.

"I heard they didn't find her head at all," the girl replied.

". . . just like Aaron Renfro, chewed up by a wild animal," a girl with French braids said between smacks of gum.

A locker door slammed, sending a metallic rattle through the halls. Joan Renfro stood beside the locker, which had been assigned to Aaron. She had a black bag that probably carried personal things he'd left in his locker. Complete silence fell as she marched up to the girl with braids.

"My brother was *not* killed by a wild animal. He was killed by one of *you*!" Her puffy, red eyes roamed angrily over everyone in the hallway. Roved right over Mildred, and it felt like Joan glared at her in particular for an eternity. Then Joan stomped away.

The chatter started back up, as though a spell had been broken. Mildred reeled from the aftereffects of Joan's emotional outburst. She felt like she was being smothered. She ducked into the ladies' room to gather herself.

She said "one of you." She knows, she knows, she knows, Mildred thought.

Shut up. She doesn't know anything.

Mildred gasped. There it was again. That voice that sounded nothing like her. "Who's there?" she asked out loud.

"Who's asking?" a tough female voice replied from inside a stall, startling Mildred.

"Oh, sorry," she said, then rushed out of the restroom and back into the buzz of the hallway.

I'm losing my mind, she thought. At which an involuntary chuckle overcame her. She stifled it quickly just as a few of the girls from the swim team walked by. They shot dirty looks her way, personally insulted by her mirthful outburst—

Or did they know something? Could one of them have seen

her? Followed her home? What if the monsters hadn't taken her trash? Could someone else have stolen it? One of those girls?

It could be any one of these people, Mildred thought. She had to find out who, before they caused her to get locked up in jail or a hospital. *I probably belong in both.* Maybe they just wanted to blackmail her for something.

I don't have anything that anyone would want or need, but I would gladly give up this curse, she thought miserably as she slammed her locker and scurried off to biology class.

A note posted on the door of the classroom directed her to the next door. The lab. All sorts of things could go wrong in the lab, with chemicals and fire and glass and needles—*gasp*—needles. What if they took her blood for some reason? When they looked at it through the microscope, would it show everyone that she was a monster? Her chest and forehead felt damp. She forced a few calming breaths and passed through the open door to find no needles or microscopes. Dark green lumps sat atop metal trays on the tables. Frogs. The teacher had warned them there would be a dissection at some point this semester. It looked like today was that day, even though a lot of students were away dealing with their grief. Science class prevailed, apparently.

Half-wit cheers struck Mildred with distaste as the boys in class shouted "cool" and "awesome." Nothing about cutting a creature open was cool or awesome to her. More like "gross" and "sickening." If she had it her way, she'd walk right back out. Walking out wasn't an option, though—that had been one of the key points in Mrs. Kline's talk about it earlier in the year. She had informed them that the dissection would count for a large portion of their grade, and for that purpose, she'd be springing it on them at a random time so that nobody could skip that day to specifically avoid it. *She must've had it secretly scheduled since the beginning, knowing Mrs. Kline,* Mildred thought. Lucky for the mourners that they managed to slip by the rules on this one.

There Mrs. Kline was—already having seen Mildred—and there were all the frogs. Mildred could smell the chemical scent of formaldehyde and knew that the frogs had been dead a while and embalmed. They wouldn't be wiggling around or hopping up from the table.

Good thing for them, Mildred thought.

"Okay, class, looks like most of you are here," Mrs. Kline said. "By now, I'm sure you know what today is. Pair up."

Students scrambled to find their partner but Mildred stood in place. There was nobody in the entire room she wanted to pair up with. Jeff Gregory started toward her at one point, but was sideswiped by Ellie Pickler, thank goodness. Mildred didn't think she could power through class with him. He smelled worse than the frogs with the body spray he habitually wore. Besides that, he had called her an offensive name just last week and forced her to move her desk away from him to let Ellie sit closer. Why he wanted to choose her as a partner now was beyond her.

He let Ellie lead him off to a table, but he glanced backward at Mildred with a longing smile. She grimaced.

"I guess it's just me and you again," Laura Bell said.

Mildred figured as much. Laura wasn't the brightest crayon in the pack, and she had a habit of annoying people. It wasn't the first time they'd been left to partner up. She and Mildred trotted over to the only open table left. Two pairs of gloves and goggles, a scalpel, and a work sheet awaited them. The diagram on the paper showed a frog on its back, legs akimbo, and the skin pulled back, exposing its innards. Lines stretched out from each organ to blanks waiting to be filled in with the proper name.

Queasiness brewed in Mildred as she looked at the diagram. She hesitated to write their names on the top of the papers, so Laura picked up the pencil and scribbled *Laura* and *Milldread*. Mildred didn't bother to correct her. She was far too hot and uncomfortable, thinking of the actual frog spread out like the diagram.

"Now, gloves and goggles on," Mrs. Kline said to the class. "And make sure those goggles are on properly. The last thing you want is to be squirted in the eye by formaldehyde." She gave the class time to get adjusted before she said, "Begin."

Hands trembling, Mildred picked up the frog and flipped it over. It felt like a wax mold of a frog. She strapped it onto the little tray, but then had to catch her breath. Without meaning to, she'd been taking shallow breaths.

"Be careful not to cut too deep," Mrs. Kline reminded the class as she wandered among them, observing.

Mildred didn't reach for her scalpel. "Come on, you cut, I write," Laura said.

But Mildred didn't want to cut. She knew what was in there. The same things that had been inside Yvette when Monster Mildred had torn her open. Vivid flashes of that moment were etched in her memory. Glistening, warm organs. What if she picked up the scalpel and the monster decided to come back and attack the class with it? With her strength, she could hurt so many people. Would they even be able to stop her?

"Ugh, if you're going to spaz, I'll just do it." Laura shoved the paper at Mildred and took the scalpel.

With an unsteady hand she made a cut. Mildred tried to get a hold of herself. It was just a seventy-five-minute class, then it was over. She'd never have to dissect anything again. Or would she?

"So, where are the lungs?" Laura asked.

Mildred stared down at the dissected frog without seeing it. She was picturing Chelle's lungs, which had shown between her bare ribs. Little details kept popping up, even though she tried hard to block them out. The faint heartbeat she'd seen beneath Chelle's ribs. The mushy feel of Yvette's intestines.

"Do frogs even have lungs? I mean, aren't they anfibins or something?" Laura prattled on.

Mildred's face screwed up. "What?" She was still trying to forget the things she'd seen.

"You know, anfibins. They breathe water, silly." Laura rolled her eyes as though she was trying to win Most Dramatic at an eyeroll pageant.

"Amphibians, you mean, Laura," Mrs. Kline said from behind the girl.

Mildred startled as though Mrs. Kline knew she'd just been thinking of last night's dirty deeds. Mrs. Kline didn't notice.

"They live on land and water. Some amphibians breathe straight through their skin without the need for lungs." She patted Laura on the shoulder. "But frogs do have lungs."

The teacher. She's smart, the voice in Mildred's head said. *A vault of yummy knowledge. Her brain would be useful . . .*

"No," Mildred blurted out loud.

Mrs. Kline gave a surprised expression. "You can't?"

She must have been asking Mildred a question, but it was so hard to focus. Mildred panicked, struggling hard to contain it. It would be okay, she told herself, because there was no way that whatever kept happening would happen in a classroom full of people. Right? No way would she lose it and attack Mrs. Kline here.

"Oh, no. Sorry. I missed the question," Mildred said smoothly. "I was just noting that there's no uterus."

"You're right, Millie. This one appears to be male."

When did people start calling me Millie?

Mrs. Kline smiled sweetly. "I'd like to talk to you after class, by the way." She still had on the smile as she walked off.

After class? A portion of time in which she would be alone with Mrs. Kline . . . alone with all the scalpels.

Oh no. No, no, no. Mildred thought desperately.

The voice in her cheered, *Yes, yes, yes!*

27

Beneath the bed, hidden in the blackness of shadow, Pohlepa worked her strong jaws on her latest prize: a shoe she'd slipped out of the pile of junk Ubiti had brought back after his special outing. He could hear Pohlepa purring as she slurped greedily at the dried blood on the sneaker.

Ubiti looked over the stolen phone in his hands—from the first dead boy—and sneered at her. Her simplemindedness annoyed him. Greed demons like her were so plentiful, yet so dim-witted. Nothing like himself, cunning and resourceful. She'd be content enough to lie about surrounded by her hoard of stolen goods for the rest of her existence. She seemed troubled only when Ruza ordered her to separate from her stuff for any length of time. Ubiti, on the other hand, needed full freedom. This was something he knew—from the instant he was first in Ruza's clutches—wouldn't be easy to acquire. He had made the mistake of underestimating her once, when she had first lifted his soul from the underrealm. He had played the memory back numerous times during his captivity.

One moment, Ubiti had been having fun torturing a damned human soul, and the next he was on Earth without solid form. Others—some he knew, some he did not—were with him, tens upon hundreds of them. In the center, Ruza and her magic. She appeared to him as her true self—she could not hide her form from demons the way she could easily dazzle humans into seeing what they wanted to see. To him, she was skeletal and rotten, with slime dripping from her ancient bones. Ubiti recognized her right away as an old associate. It had been ages . . .

Ruza's booming voice called out. "From this moment forth, you are all Earthbound souls."

Ubiti didn't hear the words as a human hears the words, but he felt them vibrate through him and knew their meaning. Black flames danced amid a circle of dust—crushed bone of slaughtered innocents and dirt from the underrealm. Ubiti was aware of this because it was the only way the witch could have summoned so many demons against their will.

"You may roam the Earth as wisps. Find human dwellings to inhabit and haunt. Or you can be more."

She let the vibrations of her words linger within the air. Ubiti seized the moment to will confusion toward her, to make her drop the bowl of nefarious ingredients she held over the fire that locked the demons in place, forcing them to hear her lunatic cries. She didn't even flinch. This form had rendered him unable to perform magic.

"Should you choose to be more, know this: the cost of a demon crossing over into flesh is eternal servitude to the flesh bringer."

Ø

He left that day thinking he could get flesh on his own. He had been wrong. Now he sat in his flesh form—which was often the same small, gargoyle/reptile–like form he'd always had in the underrealm and sometimes like the form of Owen, the human boy who'd once hosted him—seething, with the stolen phone in one hand, the mate to Pohlepa's shoe in the other. It smelled very human, and he didn't care much for the taste. He had loathed every bite of the human boy they'd devoured the previous day; he was already tired of Osveta's leftovers. Human meat was fine for some of their kind, but he'd rather have something cold-blooded. However, he wouldn't be going hunting at his leisure any time soon. He glared at the flimsy wooden door of his prison. A frail human barrier, nothing more. But the chains that bound him to Ruza the witch kept him from freedom.

Gather these things, Ubiti, my wretched little beast, she had said. The voice of his captor still echoed loudly in his memory. And so, reluctantly, he had.

Not that he wouldn't enjoy this type of behavior of his own free will. Obstructing justice was just one thing murder demons liked to do regularly. Especially from kill scenes as bloody and as gruesome as the one he had beheld in that human waste room. Those two girls, torn to shreds. Devoured. What an admirable skill Osveta had. Tingles coursed through him as he pictured it again. The splattered walls, the exposed bones. He barely had to even hide anything there. Just the brownish-red shoe prints leading to the parking lot. He was delighted to see that Osveta had grown strong enough to use the power of stealth mode, barely ever showing in camera footage while following the other two through the mall. Her skill fooled the people around them, he noticed, as he watched the saleswoman almost bump right into the girl in the clothing store. That neighbor boy had managed to take a clear picture of the bloody girl in her driveway—Ubiti had seen it on the dead boy's phone—but Osveta had killed only once at that point. It was different now. Most of the time, cameras didn't register her at all. Even *he* had difficulty masking his presence from humans sometimes. But Osveta . . . she was a pro. There had been only one brief slip, right before she entered the restroom, when Ubiti saw a flash of the girl clearly on the camera. He hid it but memorized the image and savored it. In that flash, he was able to see a glimpse of Osveta peeking out of the girl's form—the skin changing shades on the girl's arms, fingers growing slimmer, longer. The whole thing was exhilarating.

But the bottom line was that he'd gone there on Ruza's orders, and that filled him with resentment and loathing.

Pohlepa slurped loudly from her hiding place. Redirecting his anger to his fellow demon, Ubiti threw the shoe across the room at the bed, hard. It hit the bed, bounced to the wall behind him, then flew back onto the floor near the bed. A moment of silence, and then Pohlepa's furry arm slithered out and quietly withdrew with the shoe in her paw. The gnawing sound resumed.

One way or another, Ubiti was sure he would be free of Ruza the witch and this annoying Pohlepa. Even if he had to call upon the darkest of resources.

28

The pencil fell out of Mildred's hand and hit the linoleum floor, the lead tip skipping off in another direction. "I can't!" she cried, startling everyone in the room.

Mrs. Kline nodded understandably and said, "There's a squeamish one in every class."

Mildred ignored her and ran from the room with the cruel laughter of Osveta ringing through her head, leaving them all to think that cutting a dead frog had creeped her out. It was not the dissection of the frogs that had scared Mildred away. The thing that frightened Mildred followed her as she ran all the way down the hall—blind with fear—into the nearest restroom. She stopped at the sink, grabbed both sides, and stared into the mirror, determined to face her tormenter.

"Please don't, please," she begged, her eyes wild.

There's nothing you can do to fight me. I'm strong now. If I want her, I will have her. You've made the deal . . .

"The deal? I didn't mean it. I take it back!"

Mildred's arms flew up and then crashed down on the sink. At her unnaturally strong blow, the porcelain cracked and a corner broke off. The action terrified Mildred, who hadn't willingly caused it, and she whimpered.

Can't take it back, stupid girl. Make them pay. Make them pay. The voice vibrated within her, and she didn't like it. It felt overpowering. Scary. But she tried her best to stand firm.

"No!"

Must make them pay.

"I can't—"

"What on earth is going on in here?" a nasally voice demanded.

Mildred tore her fearful, teary eyes away from the mirror and saw Herman Bernstein staring back at her angrily. A wooden stick was in his hand. It was one of the custom restroom passes made by workshop students.

He'll do for now, the voice cooed triumphantly.

"What are you doing in the boys' room, Millie? You know you can be suspended for this?" His long, pointed nose scrunched up as though appalled at her.

"I-I didn't—" Mildred started.

"You really are creepy, you know, sneaking around in the boys' restroom. You're a real pervert," Herman said.

The words scorched, and a switch inside Mildred flipped. *How dare he?* Mildred thought. *How dare he accuse me of being such a thing? How dare he give me that look? I have every right to look at him that way! He followed me in here. It's what he always does, follow.*

"Don't you have some football players to follow around? You know, keep them from doing anything stupid, like shoving forks into electrical sockets or something?" Mildred said.

Herman appeared angry and maybe even embarrassed for just a moment, then he grinned. "You're going to be in so much trouble." He spun to go back out the door.

In a flash, Mildred was buried beneath the unbelievable rage. Old scenes passed through her mind of Herman's pointy face laughing along with the jocks as they teased Mildred.

Ø

"Look at Mildred's lunch," Aaron said.

She was sitting alone, as usual, her lunch spread before her. He, the other jocks, and Herman had stopped to gaze at Mildred while she chewed, the way people gaze at animals at the zoo.

"A cellulite smorgasbord," Herman said.

"Fried chicken, fried chicken, and more fried chicken. Ever heard of fruits and vegetables, Mildred?" Tyler asked.

"And how many pudding cups can one person eat?" Seth asked.

"About as many as she can fit in that backpack she calls a lunch bag," Aaron said.

They all laughed. Mildred felt hot, and wanted to cry, because it was true. She shouldn't eat so many puddings, but she loved them and eating them made her feel happy. They were all staring at her as she chewed her fried chicken. She wanted to spit the chewed bits out at all of them, especially Herman, standing closest to her and laughing the hardest.

Ø

His wide smile was highlighted in her mind's eye. It pulsed in her memory, causing the anger to tear through her, like a flood had been released. It contorted her face and controlled her limbs. Herman's smirk was replaced with alarm as he watched her morph into something inhuman. Serpentine skin and sharp teeth bared like a deep-sea anglerfish. Animal-like, she crouched and pounced, clearing much more space than any normal human could.

Before he could react, she was upon him. His back was against the floor. When he tried to swing the wooden stick, she took it from his hands. He tried to shout, but the sound was cut off when Mildred slammed the stick down across his throat, cutting off his airway. Her jaw unhinged, showing him a wide view of his fate. She chomped through his skull, spit the scalp and bone out, and went straight for the brain. By the time his body stopped convulsing, his brain was gone.

Mildred, her sense of reality seeping back, jumped off him. Blood pooled around his body. The knees of her leggings were soaked and warm. Her hands and face were a horror. The worst part—the part that really set her heart pounding—was the school bell, letting everyone know the first class was over. Dozens of voices spilled into the hallway. Students rushing to open lockers, exchange books, and use the restroom between classes if need be.

Mildred panicked and started to drag the body, but it hit her: where would she hide it? And the blood, she couldn't clean up the blood within a few seconds. She was in the boys' restroom; how was she going to explain that if someone saw her walk out? The hall was crawling with students who would see her come out for sure. Then someone would find Herman and know that she knew but had said nothing. She'd look so guilty. There were no windows and the only exit was into the hallway. She was backed into a corner. End of the line.

Suddenly, a solution came to her. It was a huge risk, but she had no other choice.

Mildred took a deep breath and screamed. The door flew open.

29

Mildred's scream rang through the school. Patsy knew right away it was her. It shook her to her core, as if she had suddenly become stuck inside a Jell-O mold. The unsteady world around her, the fright, the inability to act. She didn't know what was wrong with Mildred, but the scream sounded desperate. Painful. Others braver than Patsy ran toward the source of the sound and she felt some sort of small relief for it.

Please let her be okay, please let her be okay, Patsy prayed.

More devastating screams broke out. One student came away with blood down his side.

"I fuh-fuh—I fell," he said.

Oh God, what happened? Please let her be okay.

Patsy didn't realize she was crying, hugging her books tight in an attempt to cling to reality. All she cared about was that Millie was okay, but Patsy couldn't bring herself to go see.

"Clear out, clear out!" Miss Spade said as she plowed through the swarm of students.

She bumped into Patsy, who fell back into the cold lockers, but she didn't care. The counselor, Mr. Turner, and the assistant principal, Mr. Preston, were both on Miss Spade's heels. The three of them cut an open path in the throng as they rushed toward the source of the commotion. Once inside the restroom, Miss Spade let out a frightful yip, and walked directly out again. Her face was white, and she looked like she was going to be sick, prompting some of the closer students to veer away.

The look was devastating to Patsy, whose heart jackhammered in her chest.

Then Mr. Preston was there, raising his hands, waving them to catch everyone's attention. "Cafeteria! Everyone to the cafeteria, right now!"

Numb, Patsy allowed herself to be swept up in the rush to the cafeteria. There weren't enough seats for everyone. Normally, the school took lunch in four parts so that their numbers were thinned enough to fit everyone. Block one—as they called it— would have thirty minutes, and then head back to class, and then block two would have their turn. Patsy was in block two, and so were Millie, Chelle, Yvette, and Aaron—but they were absent, leaving an icy mood about the room. With all the blocks merged, many students were left without seats. Joan and Donna found Patsy, and sat at the spot known for being the popular table. Her mind had taken her there on autopilot.

"What happened?" Joan asked.

Patsy jerked up, awakened from a state of shock. Joan didn't have her usual smoky-eyed look. Her eyes were puffy and red. Her lips weren't painted the normal pink color she favored. Something about her looked both weaker and harder, like a wall that had been torn down and then restored but not decorated yet.

"I don't know, but I heard her scream," she started crying again. "Millie. She was—in the restroom—she was screaming."

"But so?" said Donna. "I mean, nobody liked her anyway."

Patsy threw her a look that could have knocked down a building.

"Donna!" Joan said. "What a horrible thing to say!"

"Sorry, but it's true." She shrugged. "You know it. I know it. Everyone knows it. If the killer got her, I'm just saying, I'm glad it wasn't someone who mattered."

"I've never liked you," Patsy said, and Donna's mouth dropped open in shock. "But now, I think I might hate you."

Patsy got up and moved away from the popular table. Popularity didn't matter anymore. It was a stupid label assigned by people she didn't even like, with lifestyles she couldn't keep up with. She'd wasted all this time worrying about being liked by others, when her only true friend was habitually hounded by them, and it hurt. Patsy's chest ached as she wandered away from the others, out into the hallway—where she saw Millie, covered in blood but alive, being escorted to the lobby by Mr. Turner and Mr. Preston.

Thick air lifted, and Patsy's heart soared. An amazing opportunity had just been presented to her. She had another chance to make up for all the time she and Millie had missed. Millie would never have to worry about facing the bullies alone from now on, Patsy would make sure of it. All the horrible moments Millie had endured would now be replaced with moments of friendship and love and forgiveness.

"Millie," Patsy called out. "I'm so happy you're okay!"

"Not now, Patsy," Mr. Turner said. "Mildred has witnessed something terrible. Please, give her some space."

They ushered Millie down the hallway, while Patsy stared on. If Millie was okay, whose blood was that?

"Hey, anyone seen Herman?" someone in the crowd asked loudly.

Several minutes passed before the police and ambulance arrived. They passed by the cafeteria on their way to the restroom. By then, the students who had run into the restroom had joined the group in the cafeteria, and rumors were already spreading.

Herman dead.

Millie almost.

He was decapitated.

No, mauled.

No, strangled.

Millie saw it all.

Almost killed her.

Patsy sat on the floor, apart from the others, but she still heard the passing voices. It was scary to think that the thing attacking people had been inside the school among them, wandering the halls in an aimless hunt. Any one of them could have been picked off.

A loud whistle cut through the chatter of the cafeteria, and Patsy jerked toward the source. An older officer stood at the front of the room, calling order to the chaos. She remembered seeing him calling everyone to order back at Aaron's crime scene as well. Was it Detective Carter? Detective Hyde? No, Hyde was the younger one. Carter was the chubby, gray-haired man in front of them, standing next to Principal Spade. Patsy could see Miss Spade's hands shaking. The room grew quiet and Miss Spade spoke.

"Students. There was a tragedy here today. We have informed

the family, and now I can regretfully tell you that another of your fellow students has been murdered: Herman Bernstein. We hope you will keep his friends and family in your prayers."

She stopped speaking and Detective Carter started, cutting out any chatter that began to rise. "We will not be releasing anything further at this time, but anyone with information may follow us down to the station," he said.

Patsy had stood up during Spade's short speech, and she now made her way to Carter.

"Where's Millie?" she asked.

"Mildred Waco?" he asked.

"Yes."

"She will be accompanying Detective Hyde to the station for a further interview."

"What does that mean? Is she in trouble? Has she been hurt?"

"No, we just want to ask her some more questions." With that, Detective Carter gave her a final "I'm sorry," and left.

She had hoped to be there for Millie, but instead Millie was stuck with a bunch of cops, being interrogated. That's what it sounded like. Patsy could bet anything that Mr. and Mrs. Waco were out of town, as always, so she wouldn't even have the comfort of knowing a parent was nearby for her former friend. Millie was all alone after seeing something like that. Patsy hadn't even gone in there, but she'd heard about how the other bodies looked. Barbeque pulled pork had been the words used by someone. It stuck in her mind, because when she heard it, she wanted to hurl. Comparing a dead body to food had been too much.

"There you are," Seth said, startling Patsy out of her dark thoughts. "I've been looking everywhere."

The nerve, thought Patsy. *Didn't he get the hint?* She hadn't shown up this morning for a reason. She could hardly look at him after the way he'd acted last night, and she wanted to tell him as much, but Joan and Donna were next to him, and even though Donna was a callous fiend, Joan was in a terrible place right now. Patsy felt that fighting with Seth in front of them would be too selfish. Patsy's forgiveness was being stretched thin.

"You found me," Patsy said in a deadpan tone.

"Patsy," Joan said. "We just wanted you to know that Donna is really sorry about what she said earlier. She didn't mean it."

"Yeah," Donna said, with a sincere expression on her face. "I don't know why I said that. It was really stupid."

"It was mean," Patsy said.

"I know. And I'm sorry. I didn't mean—" Donna stopped and took a breath. "Millie was your friend, wasn't she? Chelle told us that you used to hang out with her."

"Yeah. She was my best friend," Patsy said.

"That's cool," Donna said, and she gave Joan a look that puzzled Patsy. A subtle lift of the brow.

"Yeah, we were thinking, Millie really isn't that bad," Joan said. "I mean, she *is* really pretty."

Pretty wasn't at the top of Patsy's list of what made a person good or bad, but she knew that Joan and Donna based a lot on looks. So did Seth, who watched the whole exchange as though he'd coached them on what they were going to say to Patsy. *Popular people always have to meet up and have their future conversations or purchases be approved by other popular people,* Patsy thought with a sigh.

"Yeah, she is pretty," Patsy said.

Joan and Donna shared another look and some creepy best-friend thing passed between them. Patsy didn't understand it, but whatever they had cooking, she wished they would come out with it.

"What are you getting at?" she asked.

"Well," Joan said. "We thought you'd maybe introduce us. The whole crew. We could welcome her in. I mean, there's not many of us now and we have to stick together. I think Millie would be a wonderful addition to our group."

Patsy's spirits lifted. "Really?"

It would be great if Millie could be accepted—even if Patsy didn't particularly care about hanging out with the popular group anymore, it would be nice to walk down the hallway at school and not be ridiculed. To not have Millie continue to be made into a punching bag whenever a popular person was feeling down.

"Yeah, totally," Donna said.

"Yeah!" Joan agreed. "And, well, I would also really like to know what she saw in there . . . because . . . well, you know."

Because of Aaron, Patsy thought. Because the thing that attacked Herman and Millie had killed Joan's brother. It was only natural that she would want to know more. Get a firsthand account, and maybe in the process Joan could gain some respect for Millie.

"You're serious, right? Just talk?" Patsy asked.

Joan and Donna nodded.

"This isn't a prank or something?" Patsy asked.

They gasped. "No way!" Joan said.

"Never!" Donna said.

"What? That's silly, Patsy," Seth said as he tossed his arm around her shoulders and gave a gentle squeeze. "Come on, you know them better than that."

She did know them, and that's why she asked. She'd heard all the rude things they'd said to and about Millie before. The way they called her lardass even though she probably weighed less than any of them. The way they called her crater face even though her skin was smooth as silk. They were nothing more than lies designed to break down Millie's self-confidence.

But people can change, Patsy thought. It would be nice to not have to look behind her back all the time. To not have to worry about other people instead of focusing on the actual monster on the loose.

"Yeah," Patsy agreed. "I'll take you to her house tonight, but you have to promise that if she doesn't feel like talking about it, you'll back off and give her space."

They readily agreed.

30

"One more time, Mildred," Detective Hyde said. "How did you come to be in the boys' room at Roanoke High?"

Sitting at a plain brown table across from him, Mildred shifted in her seat, uncomfortable with the horrible things he was asking her to replay in her memory. She thought of the two dreadful creatures she'd seen in her garage and again at the magic shop. "I saw them . . . in the hall. I-I ran in there to hide from them." Tears glistened on her long dark lashes. Cops had questioned her for hours, this same old song and dance. One cop would leave the room, time would pass, and another would come in, ask her the same set of questions in different ways. Each time she got more convincing with the haunting scene she'd spun for them. The victim act had come easily to her, being that she had spent so many years as an actual victim. They bought it hook, line, and sinker.

But Hyde was tougher to reel in than all the others, and he was currently in for his second set of questions.

The overbearing inner voice hadn't spoken since the last kill.

For that much she was thankful. Its absence allowed her to think clearly enough to defend herself. In the back of her mind, however, she began to wonder *why* it was being so quiet. She'd always heard that if someone was being too quiet, they were up to something. The saying was usually about kids or pets, but maybe it could be true for monsters as well.

Monsters.

Now that Mildred was a smarter version of herself, she didn't feel like *monster* was exactly the word for the creature tormenting her or the two she'd seen in her garage. She felt like there was a more fitting description available.

"What were *they*?" Hyde pressed.

Demons. That's precisely what they were. And she wasn't under a curse either. Things were clearer to her now. She was being possessed . . . only it was different from most possessions. She was taking on demon aspects. Rather than the demon simply wreaking havoc in her body, it had somehow blended with her and shared her body. With this revelation came new possibilities. Exorcism was an option. Magical suppressants were a possibility she could investigate.

"I don't know. I don't know what they were, maybe aliens," Mildred said, with the memory of the creatures in her garage vivid in her mind. "That sounds crazy, but I've never seen anything like them before. They were like things from horror movies. I've never seen anything like them in real life. One was large and looked like an ape of some kind, but also like something else." She made her voice unsteady, as if she was weakening at the memory of them. "It was growling and . . . and the other one . . . it was like a small person with alligator skin—you probably think I'm insane." She left out the detail about the horns on the small one, feeling that it would be too much. She didn't want to sound too crazy, just terribly rattled.

"I don't, actually. I think you were frightened so bad that your mind is telling you that's what you saw so that you can make sense of it all. Nobody wants to believe that another person could do something like this. Do they, Mildred?" Hyde stared at her like a hypnotist willing information out of her.

"No. How could anyone?"

"Right. How? Because what kind of person would it have to be, right? An evil person."

Mildred felt as if her breath had been slapped out of her.

"A coldhearted person," he went on. "Someone who maybe felt joy from the pain of others? Do you think the killer felt joy?"

She hesitated. "I-I don't know . . . maybe?"

He scribbled in his notebook, and an inward panic swept through her. Had she said the wrong thing?

"Maybe it wasn't human," she said. "Maybe it was some sort of animal."

"Two of them?"

"Uh-huh. Two animals, and maybe they were hungry." She hoped by suggesting that option, she was retracting whatever statement she'd just given.

"Maybe," he agreed. "If they were beasts, maybe it was a kind you've never seen before, and that's why they looked so strange to you."

"That could be it." It seemed to make people feel more comfortable when Mildred agreed with them, and she was eager to, if it would get him off the track of a human suspect. Even if, during the kills, she wasn't exactly human. "They were so scary—I just got a glimpse and then ran. I'm sure my mind could play tricks with that. I'm sorry I can't be more certain."

She wondered if the inner voice's silence meant it was gone or just momentarily satisfied. It couldn't be gone. Possessions didn't just end without a whole ordeal involving prayers and crucifixes and holy water and flies.

Then another thought came to her: now that she was smarter, was it possible the voice was having more trouble getting through to her? Control was more of a power struggle with smart Mildred than it had been with dim Mildred—and, oh, how dim she'd been. She'd left traces everywhere. She'd left saliva.

If they test my DNA, I'm done for . . . but wait! I was different. I wasn't me, I was a demonic being at the time, so would the DNA be mine? Would it change as I changed?

There was probably a good chance that the DNA sample she'd given the police wouldn't match up with the demonic DNA she'd left at the scenes.

She was starting to like this smarter brain.

"You can't remember anything else?" Hyde asked. "Did the things speak or make any sounds other than growls? Anything would help."

Mildred shook her messy head, her hair still splattered with bits of Herman. "The big one just growled. I'm sorry. I was so scared."

She stared at him with big innocent eyes, willing him to want to protect the damsel in distress. There was more to Detective Hyde than he realized she knew. All the time they'd left her in the interrogation room, she'd been discreetly using her phone to hack into police files and snoop. This computer skill was something she'd never known before she'd eaten Herman. Once she'd discovered she had that knowledge, she'd put it to good use.

Detective Garrett Hyde was born on October 8, 1993. He was a Libra. One sibling: a brother. Their mother was attacked and left for dead when Hyde was eleven years old. The first officer on the scene was able to revive her and keep her alive until the ambulance arrived.

That's why he became an officer, because of the officer who helped save his mother. He wanted to be a hero.

Mildred next searched his mother's name: Beulah Hyde. Mildred had to do some sidestepping through a bunch of fire-walls in the system, but she'd found an open file there as well. It appeared that they'd saved her life but they couldn't save her sanity. She ended up in a psychiatric hospital because of what had happened to her. In her records, Garrett Hyde seemed to be her only visitor. Every Tuesday and every Friday, like clockwork. A devoted son with a hero badge.

It was so touching; Mildred felt a little misty when he came back into the room and began a repeat round of questions. She was more prepared after her own form of sleuthing. Working on his sympathy was the best route to take with this one.

"I understand," he said, softening beneath Mildred's helpless stare. "So, you hid in the stall?"

Hyde the suspicious. Mildred's handy new brain had found a solution to that.

"Yes, and then I heard them come in, moving fast. They were looking for me, smacking a few stall doors in. They got so close, but then . . . then Herman came in—oh God!" Mildred cried out. "It was all my fault! If I hadn't run into the boys' room, they might've followed me into the girls', and he'd be okay."

"You couldn't have known, Mildred. They were wild beasts. Maybe only one would have come after you, and the other might've seen him."

Hyde offered her a tissue from the box on the table, and she made a big show of blubbering into it. Inside, she rejoiced that he had changed his tune. The scale had tipped, and at last he was treating her more like someone who had experienced this horrible ordeal rather than someone who could have caused it.

"The bell rang. It must have scared them, because I heard them take off. Then I tried to save him."

"I can tell that you tried. That was very brave of you," Hyde said, as he took in her gory appearance.

They hadn't allowed her to clean up yet. Herman's blood was still on her face, chest, hands, and knees. It was dry and cracked now. They seemed to believe her when she told them it was because she'd tried to perform CPR. It helped her defense, making them think she didn't know his brain was gone, that she had no clue there could have been no help for Herman Bernstein.

Despite her best efforts, she still felt that something about her story didn't sit right with Hyde. She did her best to keep the innocent look going; he was being a lot nicer now. Unfortunately, as he studied her, she could have sworn something flickered within him. Could he see that she was hiding something?

Paranoia, she told herself. No way could he still be a skeptic; she'd done what she needed to. Told the story over and over without changing anything. Sometimes she gave more details as she "recalled" scenes, pretending that she wasn't sure of some things—just as a real witness might be shaken and uncertain at times. She couldn't be a suspect.

But she wanted to get away from him. He made her limbs weak and her heart race. If they strapped her up to a polygraph test and shoved Hyde in the room, she'd fail point blank. His intuition was first rate and it frightened her.

Knuckles rapped softly on the door, then it opened. A young woman came in. Mildred noticed her hair before anything else: a long mane of light-brown hair with bright blond highlights, pulled back in a ponytail. Her ID hung from a lanyard around her neck, informing Mildred that she was Forensics, M. Hannigan.

"Sorry to interrupt, Detective, but I've got to do my job too," she said in a cheerful tone.

He nodded without showing any frustration. Earlier, when a couple of forensics people had come in to swab Mildred's nails and take samples of the blood on her face, the other detective, Carter, had been cross with them. She knew why. He felt that they were crowding her and making her feel like she'd done something wrong. He was the kind of fellow who made his mind up about someone quickly and he'd seen a victim as soon as he'd looked at Mildred. Unlike some others . . .

"I think we've covered everything for now," Hyde said as he arranged papers in the case file.

"Great!" M. Hannigan turned her attention to Mildred, sparing her a sad smile while holding out a gray sweat suit. "Sorry, sweetie, but we need you to change into these. And I've got to bag your clothes as evidence."

"Yes, please," Mildred said. "I'd love to get out of these clothes." *And away from Hyde.*

She took the clothes and followed Hannigan through the maze of hallways. The woman was fit and she walked fast. Had Mildred been her old out-of-shape self, she wouldn't have been able to keep up. As it was, she had more time to spend thinking rather than rushing. The woman's smooth ponytail swayed from side to side and Mildred found the color to be admirable. Mocha with a caramel drizzle. Wouldn't it look great—

Wait, thought Mildred. *Don't think it, don't think it, don't think it!*

But she did think it, even while she dreaded the results. Surely her envious thoughts would bring the insatiable demon to the surface once again—during the most inconvenient time—at the police station.

Hannigan led her into a small room with no furniture. It looked like a giant shower, full of tiles, with a slim mirror on one wall beside a sink. She pulled back a privacy curtain, then waved Mildred to the other side of it.

"Did it scratch you or bite you anywhere?" Hannigan asked.

"No, it didn't touch me. I hid," Mildred said, reinforcing what she'd told the officers already.

"Just checking. Sorry we gotta put you through all this. You've been through a lot already."

You couldn't even imagine, Mildred thought.

Hannigan took Mildred's soiled clothes—her new beautiful clothes from Secret Threads, Mildred thought with a pang—and shoved them into a clear bag. Mildred slipped the sweats on and soaked in her image through a wall mirror. The sweatshirt and pants fit her loosely. She pulled back the curtain and saw her new self in the small police station mirror. *RPD* stretched across her chest in black print. The words *Roanoke Police Department* were spelled out down her right leg. While Mildred looked at herself, she pondered why the demon didn't make a peep the whole time. With the others, Mildred had admired something about them, and then she took it. Mildred admired Hannigan's hair, yet the demon didn't push her to take it. She was stumped.

"They look a little baggy, but it's the smallest we had," Hannigan said.

Mildred tried not to frown as she looked at herself. She was so different; she could barely see herself anymore. This wasn't her, and as much as she'd hated herself before, she would rather go back to who she was than be right here, right now. Everything had gotten so out of control. Now here she was surrounded by dozens of cops, wearing police station clothes and the parts of other people she'd killed.

"All done. Back to Detective Hyde you go," Hannigan said.

No, I didn't kill them. The demon killed them, thought Mildred as she walked back to Hyde.

Hannigan led her back through the maze of hallways and into the interrogation room. Hyde was standing in the middle of the room, the file tucked under his arm, his little notebook, no doubt, tucked away in his pocket. It looked like the interview was over.

"Are there any other questions I can answer?" Mildred asked.

"We're all good for now. Would you like to try phoning your parents again? See if they can call someone, a friend maybe, to come get you?" Hyde asked, indicating her phone lying facedown on the table where she'd left it.

They could have looked in it, seen her map search for 6 Hollow Grove. She should have taken care of that by clearing out her history, but she wasn't smart enough to cover her tracks before. *What other idiot things have I done on that phone?* she wondered, but she didn't have time to think of anything she might've done. She was taking too long to answer Hyde, and he would pick up on that.

Mildred shook her head. "My parents never answer when they're working. They like to get lost in their work."

He gave her a sympathetic look that confused her. Usually, no one cared how absent her parents were in her life—even in emergencies. A lot of teenagers would say she was lucky to not have strict parents breathing down her neck. A lot of adults would assume she was the mature, independent type since her parents clearly trusted her home alone for long periods of time. Nobody ever seemed to react the way Hyde was now.

"It's . . . no big deal," Mildred said with a shrug, trying not to feel awkward. "I'll get them once they've finished work for the day. They'll come back."

"But they're in . . ." He consulted his notes. "Hawaii. It'll take a while."

"I suppose so."

"At least let me give you a ride home?" Hyde asked. "It's a long walk. An even longer wait for the bus, and it'll be dark soon . . . and dangerous."

Mildred paused. He had a knack for throwing her off her game. She wanted to say, "Why do you care?" or even just refuse. But it *would* be a long walk and she didn't like the idea of piling into a bus full of strangers. She'd always disliked public transportation.

"Okay. That would be great," she said, remembering to put on her distressed victim look again—it wasn't very hard, considering she'd sort of been a victim in all of this.

At least one good thing has come of this police station visit, she thought. *Not a word about the evidence stolen from the trash.* She smiled to herself as Hyde turned to open the door.

Why did the demons take it? They must have had a specific reason, she thought.

Ø

Hyde's car smelled like a stale breakfast sandwich and a faint hint of his usual alluring cologne. She saw the empty coffee cup in the console and the discarded sandwich wrapper on the passenger side floorboard. He hadn't tidied up, and it made her feel a little better to know that he wasn't perfect. He looked well organized but had a tendency to let things slide sometimes. Hopefully one of those slippery things would be her guilt. The passenger seat felt stiff, as if anyone rarely—if ever—occupied it. Mildred was with the good guy, so her main goal was to appear as if she felt safe and relaxed, even though she felt like jumping out of the car and running away. She put the seat back a bit to allow more comfort while Hyde made his way to the driver's side.

The click of the driver's door caught Mildred off guard. She blushed and looked out the passenger window, trying to ignore the waft of cologne as Hyde swiftly sat down.

Did I just think of his smell as alluring? Mildred thought.

To her dismay, she realized her sudden nervousness didn't stem from a fear of being found out; it was because someone inside her found Hyde extremely attractive. She found herself watching the muscles in his arm contract as he pulled the gearshift into reverse, then again into drive. The urge to feel his arm around her flashed in her mind and she understood.

Herman had been gay. His brain was now reacting to her situation.

Apparently, the tough, athletic type was his bread and butter. *That's why he spent so much time with the football players,* Mildred realized. She had assumed it was out of admiration before, but things seemed much clearer now. His willingness to do what they asked, his devotion to them—it all stemmed from attraction.

Having been skeptical of most people her whole life, Mildred had never been attracted to anything but a box of Debbie's Doughnuts. Now that Herman's brain had mingled with hers, it wasn't surprising that she would also feel this attraction. For the brief moment Hyde turned his mesmerizing green gaze from the road to her, Mildred's heart skipped a beat.

"Are you okay, Mildred?" he asked. "I mean, what you witnessed, it must have terrified you." He had turned off the detective voice and taken on a friendlier tone. One full of concern.

"Yeah, it was pretty scary," Mildred admitted, but she wasn't thinking of what happened back in the school restroom. She was thinking of this new thing she felt when he looked at her the way he did sometimes . . . like he cared about her as a person.

"Are you sure you're okay on your own? There isn't an aunt or uncle we could call?"

"No," Mildred blurted a little too loudly. She quickly recovered. "I really have a lot of things I can do to keep my mind busy and when my parents get the messages I left, they'll rush home."

"Will they?" he asked skeptically.

She studied his profile a moment in the darkening vehicle. Noted the smooth line of his masculine chin, the slope that was the bridge of his nose. He was so handsome and *Oh no, this can't be happening right now*. Mildred couldn't develop a crush on the detective whose job it was to catch her and throw her in jail.

"Yeah. Yeah, sure they'll come home." It was a lie, but one she could tell easily, because their presence didn't matter. Little did he know, she'd be safe either way—as safe as she could be when the thing to fear was herself.

By then, he was pulling into her driveway. The auto lights flicked on inside the house right on time—dusk—giving the illusion that someone may have been home to turn them on. After Hyde saw them, he nodded, somewhat satisfied. Still, when

Mildred started to open the passenger door, he asked her to wait. She had already pulled the latch and the dome light had come on. He pulled out a business card, flipped it over, and scribbled something on the back.

"I'm going home now, instead of the office, but if you get scared and need to go somewhere safe, here's my address," he said, handing her the card. "My number is on the front. You can call or stop by. My door is always open."

His writing was messy and curly. He'd written *anytime* on the bottom, which Mildred found charming.

"I mean that, Mildred. Anytime you need help or someone to talk to, I'll be there . . . or at the office. You don't have to be here alone and afraid," he said. "If you hear anything that doesn't sound right, you give me a call."

Wow, thought Mildred, *he's really the knight-in-shining-armor type.* She felt a lump in her throat. Would he have offered to help her had she looked like gross Mildred? *Probably not,* she told herself, but she knew that was another lie. This man seemed like he would help anyone in need, but she didn't deserve his protection and she knew it.

"Thanks," she said. She stepped out of the car and added, "Don't worry. It'll be fine."

31

Ubiti sat on the floor, his horns scraping against the bare wood as he dipped his head low. He knew what was coming.

"They caught the girl because of you!" Ruza, her evil face twisted with fury, shouted angrily in her native tongue. It was loud enough to cause Pohlepa to flee the bed, where she'd perched, and find a nice dark hiding place in the far corner.

Pohlepa whimpered as she cowered but Ubiti did not even flinch. His eyes burned in hatred of the witch. Ruza threw her hand out as if she was pitching a baseball and a cage of jasper appeared, encasing Ubiti. He crumbled to the floor, weakened by the stone, yet he refused to call out to her. Nothing could make him beg for mercy from this witch.

"Let that seep into your thick skull!" she shouted.

The door shook the walls thunderously when Ruza slammed it. Pohlepa whined, but Ubiti laughed. He had just noticed something. From his position on the floor, he could see into Pohlepa's favorite hiding spot for her treasures, only a couple of feet away from him. Wedged among some useless chewed items and covered partially with ripped papers lay the very things he needed. A hand mirror, a black candle, and a few pieces of charcoal. Ruza had made a terrible mistake allowing Pohlepa to get her greedy paws on these things. It was likely that Ruza didn't know their potential, being that she wasn't a demon herself, but they would serve as her downfall. Ubiti knew exactly what to do with them; it had been taught to him in case he was ever stuck in the human world. He slipped his arm between the bars of his cage and snatched the mirror, black candle, and a piece of charcoal.

Pohlepa immediately fretted angrily at the sight of him taking her things. "Mean Ubiti, stealing Pohlepa's things!" she barked in a demon language. Her words twisted around her huge fangs. "Put it back, put it back, put it back!" She thrashed about and banged against the wall and floor like a spoiled child.

"Shut up, you! I'm not taking your things; I'm borrowing them for a moment. Wait till it's done," he wheezed weakly. He sat the candle down in front of him. "Need fire. Give me fire."

She may not have liked him using her things, but since he said he'd give them back, Pohlepa's anger dissipated enough that she grew curious. "But what is Ubiti doing with Pohlepa's things?"

"Maybe setting us free. Maybe killing the witch."

"Killing the witch?" Pohlepa's eyes widened in surprise, then curiosity, and then she broke into a crooked grin. "Pohlepa will get fire." She rummaged beneath the bed for a moment and came back with a matchbook. "Here. Fire for Ubiti to kill the witch." She threw it at him.

A burst of light erupted and then dimmed. Ubiti lit the candle. He crumbled the charcoal in a fine dust onto the mirror. After the candle burned for a while—during which Pohlepa paced the floor worried it would burn away and she would lose it for good—he poured the wax onto the charcoal and mixed them together. The mixture dried on the mirror quickly and when it did, Ubiti bit his hand and spilled his blood over the dried wax and charcoal. Finally, he was able to shove his arm completely through the glass without harming it. He felt the underrealm on the other side. Already the weakened state he'd been put in while locked inside the jasper started to lift because of the demonic power of the underrealm, but it wasn't enough. Ubiti did not plan on staying in the jasper cage. He reached in farther and farther.

Pohlepa was amazed at what Ubiti had done, and also a little frightened. "But can't go. The witch will be mad. Punish Ubiti bad, bad, bad."

"She never said I could not visit my home, only that I must serve her for eternity. I break no direct orders. I do not leave this room in any way she's aware of," he said, then he slipped completely into the mirror.

Ubiti stepped out of a dense smoke cloud into the underrealm. The instant his clawed foot touched the soil, fresh energy jolted him. All the weakening effects of the jasper cage faded away, but he still felt the glue that bound him to Ruza, and he knew what he needed to do about it.

There were many regions of the underrealm, but the one in which he emerged resembled a rocky desert during the night. The only light came from flames that rained from the blackness above and eternal bonfires that burned on the ground. In the air, a million screams mingled into a chorus of screeches. A symphony of pain and torture. A giddy feeling blossomed in him at the sound of the continuous wailing.

Home.

Through the haze of his jubilation, the harsh stench of the underrealm hit him with fervor. Rancid garbage, human feces, and bodily fluids. Above all they lingered, accompanied by the sulfurous fumes that clung to everything. He focused on the raining flames as they dropped from above, something that Ubiti had taken for granted before. Now he marveled at how intoxicating the flickering flames looked. How their glow enhanced the beauty of everything their light touched.

Until the light of the flames fell upon the Furies.

Ubiti recoiled when he noticed the Furies near, having fun with some of their human captives.

Of all the places I could have stepped into, he thought. He would have preferred to slip away unnoticed, but the one in the center, with the most snakes crawling about her limbs and tangled in her wild hair, had already set her snakelike eyes upon him.

Damn.

She struck out, sending her black snakeskin whip flying. It wrapped around Ubiti's neck, tightening like muscle.

"You dare shhhhow your faccce?" she hissed.

Her sisters chanted, "He shhhhowssss, he shhhhowsss."

Ubiti disregarded the sisters as they bared their fangs, and spoke directly to the Fury at the end of the whip. "Tisiphone," he croaked. "I've been trapped."

"Liesssss!"

"Liessss, liesss."

Tisiphone pulled the whip, and Ubiti wrapped his claws around it and fought her efforts, keeping the pressure off his neck, so he could speak.

"I speak the truth!" he growled.

Tisiphone's bare feet dragged along the rocky ground, leaving three large gashes in the dirt from her attempt to maintain her ground with her claws. She was clearly losing, and she began to cackle.

"Oh, you ssssmell like human ssssin, but you sssstill have demon sssssstrength!"

"I reek of human because I've been born into flesh!" Ubiti declared.

At his words, the Furies gasped and shuddered. One of the ugly sisters gripped her hair, locks and snakes alike, and the other held herself as if she'd gotten very cold. Tisiphone's whip uncoiled itself from Ubiti's neck, came back to her, then slithered around her waist where it came to rest, like a belt.

"Who could have done sssssuch a thing? Nobody hassss that power, not ssssinccccce—"

"Ruza the witch!"

The three Furies stared in shock, but knew Ubiti told the truth. He'd been missing for a long time. The Furies let out screeches loud enough to awaken the dead. Screeches that ripped through the underrealm like lightning and thunder. Nearby, two one-eyed demons who'd been playing hangman by cutting into a human's back abandoned their game to watch. In the vast openness around them, other demons stopped their fun torturing the damned. The Furies called out for him: their Master.

In a blink, the Master stood before them, the only one that didn't look like a monster, but a well-groomed man. His hair was pitch black and gelled into a modern style. He wore a fancy tailored suit in red, with a red tie and a black dress shirt. He stood tallest of Ubiti's group. Demons all around, including Ubiti and the Furies, dropped to their knees to worship him. Although he looked like a human man, power radiated from him in waves that all hellish creatures could feel. It came to them like adrenaline that got stronger the longer they were in his presence. Some demons inhaled it like a drug and would seek any chance to be near him—but Ubiti had never been that sort. Whenever Ubiti encountered the Master, he always had an urgent purpose.

"Rise," the Master said.

They did so.

"Why have I been called away from my work?"

"Forgive us, Master," Tisiphone said. "Ubiti has seen the witch."

He stared. They stared, awaiting an explosion.

"Well, you'll have to be more specific. There are thousands of witches."

"There is only one who has planned to overthrow Master," Ubiti said.

Muscles tensed in the Master's smooth face as it grew a deep shade of red. When he opened his mouth, fire spread from it in a quick burst.

"No! I destroyed her!"

"It's true, Master. I saw her, I've been forced to serve her. Ruza the witch lives."

The Master paused, glaring, in deep thought. "Ruza the witch lives?"

Ubiti nodded, his neck now somewhat sore due to the weakness of his human half being snared by Tisiphone's whip.

"You serve her?"

"Against my will, I assure you."

The Master nodded. "And she doesn't know you're here?"

"Hells no."

"First of all, let's deal with this." He waved his hand before

Ubiti and Ubiti felt the metaphorical cords binding him to Ruza snap. Then the Master's face broke into a devilish grin. "She should have known she couldn't hide from me forever. While she's unsuspecting, let's give her a lovely present, shall we?"

Ubiti tingled with excitement. "*Nothing* would please me more."

32

Mildred wrapped a towel around her wet hair and slipped on a clean pair of sleepwear shorts and a tank top. Finally getting to wash all of Herman's blood away, and feeling comfortable with her appearance for once, she felt like she'd just had the best shower of her life.

But everything had a price. What had this beauty cost her? Mildred couldn't call those people her friends, so not that. She'd never had much dignity to speak of, so not that. It cost her something else, and she knew that. Something dark. Her only hope was that maybe it had ended.

She fired up her laptop and typed *how to break a curse* into the search bar. Again. With Herman's brain she was confident she'd navigate her way to an answer this time. No sooner had the results popped up than someone knocked on her front door. As Mildred made her way to the foyer, the person on her stoop continued pounding at the door for all they were worth. It was a desperate, alarming kind of knock. Mildred's heart raced. *Only cops or people being chased knock like that,* she thought. Neither of those prospects appealed to her. She considered several scenarios before she reached the door and peered through the peephole.

A pale face framed by white-blond hair looked back without seeing her. Joan Renfro. The girl's usually delicate face was marred with the same type of pain and intensity that Mildred had witnessed that very morning. A small gathering of other students were with her, including Patsy and Donna. Patsy's face was twisted with worry. It looked very guilty to Mildred.

Patsy led them here? Mildred realized that had to be the only way. Why else would the others—a gaggle of cheerleaders and a few football players—come to her house? She knew the girl was dangerous.

Joan kept knocking.

"Hello in there!" she shouted angrily.

Enough blaming, Mildred thought, *they've figured it out. I'm caught. Now here they are, like a mob from one of those old movies Patsy and I used to watch, ready to take care of the village monster. I've got to escape . . .*

She was about to run for the back door when the front door burst open. She was almost to the hallway when a hand snatched the waist of her shirt and jerked her back. The fabric ripped. Mildred's scream was cut off with Joan's words.

"What was it? If it was an animal, give me a type," she demanded as she rushed forward. "Wolf? Bear? A land shark? What?"

"We shouldn't do this!" Mildred heard Patsy pleading with the others.

Mildred, shocked and a little angry, focused on Joan. "You can't just come in here."

"I will go anywhere I need to. I will cover every lead. Those cops won't do their jobs. They're looking for an animal, but it wasn't an animal, was it, Millie?" Her words came heavily, the way she breathed them all out with determination. She seemed so sure that Mildred knew all the answers. "Why won't you tell them?"

Mildred's heart pitter-pattered and the air felt thick. Her guilty mind was making her feel directly accused. "What are you saying?"

"What did you see, Millie? Tell me now!" Joan shouted. Her voice boomed through Mildred's big house.

"I didn't see anything," Mildred said, trying to keep calm, hoping that her calm voice would bring down Joan's angry, desperate one.

"She's lying. Look at her finger! That's Tiffany's ring!" Donna said cruelly. "She definitely knows something. Tell us what you know! Where's Tiffany?"

"Yeah!" someone in the throng shouted.

Mob mentality suddenly elevated the situation. Mildred felt sure that had everyone not been behind her, Joan might've been calmer. Nicer. Instead, Joan rushed Mildred, pinning her to the wall with the help of Donna.

"No!" Patsy cried. "What the hell? You said you'd only talk to her!"

But they ignored her as they pressed and squeezed Mildred. "Tell us who it was!"

"Stop it!" Patsy screamed, tugging at Joan and Donna. "She doesn't know!"

"Yes, she does! Tell us, Millie, or we'll hurt you!" Donna shouted.

"I don't—" Mildred started, but something struck her hard across the face. Donna's tight fist.

"No!" Patsy cried.

Blood seeped from Mildred's nose and dripped on her white tank top. She felt herself being shaken and shoved, as though she were a doll some kids were fighting over. She felt the towel tugged from her head.

"She knows and she won't tell! She's just as guilty!" cried Joan.

Someone hit Mildred again and again. Her cheek and eye stung as much as her bloody nose did. Someone was pulling her hair; she could feel and hear it ripping. Screaming, she flung her arms and twisted around, somehow managing to slip behind Patsy, who stood like a rock in Mildred's defense. Mildred didn't stop. She ran through the house, even as she heard the others break past Patsy. She flung open the back door and took off into the dark night.

33

Hyde sat on his couch, obsessing over crime scene photos. There had to be something. Some sort of a clue. There was always a clue. If he could just find anything . . .

In front of him, a photo of the first boy, lying on the ground. The wall beside him was splattered and the grass around his head was stained with his dried blood. His crushed skull and his torn-out tongue still gave Hyde the heebie-jeebies, but the most disturbing thing was the fact that they had next to no trace evidence. They'd found a plain brown hair that could belong to a dozen people and could have been left there long before the murder. It wasn't terribly incriminating, but they sent it off for testing anyway. It hadn't come back yet. Then there were tire marks. At first, he was sure that they'd matched the moped that the strange girl, Mildred, drove. But now that he had gotten to know Mildred a little better while questioning her, he doubted that. She was so afraid and, more notably, she was small. She couldn't possibly have enough strength to do any of these terrible things.

Hyde slid the photo aside to reveal a horrific scene of tile and gore. He recalled the facts without looking at his notes. Two girls. Dead by very gruesome means. Punctured and ripped apart. Eaten. No one had seen anything out of the ordinary except a light-pink moped parked in an employee parking lot at the mall after hours, which they found odd. But it couldn't be the same moped Mildred drove. No way could it have anything to do with that timid girl he'd dropped off only an hour ago.

Yet, today she'd actually been there, when the latest dead boy, the boy who'd found the first victim, no less, had been savagely attacked and eaten.

Hyde's guts wrenched. He'd seen messed-up things, scenes that would make even the strongest men sick to their stomach, but these murders were the most horrific. Whatever was doing this, it was a beast. No human or tool could do that kind of damage to a body. Was it following Mildred? Was it trying to get to her? Why? And how could he stop it? He wished he could get the approval to set up surveillance on her. He'd do it on his own but taking a step in that direction without the paperwork was basically just following around a teen girl and that could look bad. That was the sort of thing they arrested civilians for. Nope. He had to stick to the books, even if he felt she was in serious danger—

A knock at his door startled him out of his deep thoughts. Leaving the photos uncovered, he went to the door with the weight of the world on his mind.

"Oh no," Hyde said when he saw a battered, bloody, and bare-foot Mildred standing at his door. He silently cursed his superiors for not getting that damn surveillance order he'd requested to keep her safe. "Mildred, are you okay?"

She sobbed. "No."

Tears streamed down her freshly bruised cheek. Blood oozed from her nose and dripped down her shirt, and it angered him. Who or what could want to hurt this girl? A girl whose parents wouldn't even come home to protect her? She looked broken and frightened. He stepped aside and motioned for her to enter.

"What happened?" he asked.

Even though his voice sounded calm, he was anything but. He fully expected that whatever was after her this morning had made another attempt. If he'd just been permitted to stay on her street in his car and watch her, had been allowed to make sure she was okay—but the system was moving too slowly for this case. Things were happening left and right but the department ran in a straight line. That line had never felt more frustrating to Hyde than it did now.

"They attacked me. Aaron's sister and her friends," Mildred sobbed. "I'm sorry it's so late, it's just . . . you said any time and I didn't know where else to go . . ."

"No, no, I'm glad you came here," he said. "This is a safe place. Everyone needs to have a safe place to go."

But it could look wrong, he thought. He needed his recorder. It was in his bedroom, shoved in his nightstand. At the same time he pondered this, he struggled for the right thing to say to let her know that everything would be okay, but he couldn't lie to her right now. Something worse than a group of teens might be after her, but he shouldn't tell her and frighten her more. Instead, he said the only other thing he could think of: "Let me get the first aid kit, then you can tell me everything."

He rushed into his small bathroom and opened his mirror cabinet to retrieve the first aid kit. From a shelf beside the claw-foot tub, he grabbed a washcloth, then he slipped into his bedroom to get his recorder from the nightstand. He checked the tape and hit the record button—that way he'd have proof he'd never said anything inappropriate to the teenage girl in his house at night. When he got to the living room, Mildred was staring down in fear at the crime scene photos. He mentally scolded himself for leaving such things lying about. He was just too used to being alone.

"Sorry about the mess," he said, steering her away lightly by the shoulder. She tore her eyes away to look at him. Her eyes softened. "Come into the kitchen, the lighting is better. Then you can tell me everything that happened while I see if I can do something about those wounds."

Her injuries were minor, so there was no need to take her to a hospital and take up space in the ER. He led her to his small dining-room table and offered her a seat. She sat, sobbing quietly while he filled a bowl with warm water to dip the washcloth in. He didn't have much experience doing these things, but he remembered his mother cleaning and treating scrapes and bumps he'd gotten from falling out of trees and wrecking bicycles as a little kid. She winced as he cleaned a cut above her eye. It wasn't deep, but it would be sore for a few days.

"You said some of the students attacked you? Who? And why would they do this to you?"

"Joan, Donna, Seth . . . some others were there. They thought I knew something about . . . you know. They thought I was hiding something."

"You should press charges for assault." He spoke softly as he dabbed alcohol on her head.

"I don't want any more trouble," she said.

"But you can't let them get away with stuff like this. They hurt you, Mildred. They could've killed you. I'd hate if something happened to you." Though true, he had blurted the words without thinking. As a detective, he shouldn't be so personal. It was his job to keep her safe, yes, but he'd just made it sound like more. Now that he could see the look in her eyes, he knew maybe he should have rephrased.

As he thought of how to follow up, Mildred crushed her lips against his and he was caught off guard. He jerked backward and held her by the shoulders at arm's length. This was going so wrong.

"I'm sorry, did I do something wrong?" Mildred asked nervously.

"Yes, Mildred," he said. He was just as flustered. "I mean, I don't want to hurt your feelings, but—"

"You don't think I'm pretty." It was a statement, not a question. She honestly thought he was turning her away because of how she looked.

"No, no, that's not it. You're a witness and you're sixteen, Mildred. I'm working your case and I'm twenty-six. It isn't right on multiple levels," he explained.

Mildred's face reddened. She stood up, and Hyde had to catch the bowl of water before it spilled. She rushed to the door.

"Mildred, wait, you don't have to go," he said, but she was already opening the door. She wouldn't even look at him. He didn't know what to do, how to get her to stay. It was just a mistake, but she was acting like she'd rather climb in a hole and disappear now. What had caused her to be so insecure? He started to speak—

"I'm sorry. You're a good man, Detective Hyde," Mildred mumbled before she ran out.

"Mildred, come back!" he shouted, and then he added rather pathetically, "You don't even have shoes on!"

34

Ruza stood at the corner of the building and watched the girl leave the cop's apartment building. Osveta showed herself quite clearly to Ruza now, though any regular human wouldn't have been able to see her at this moment. Her features seemed perfectly human for now. The girl was clearly still at the forefront of the life vessel, but Ruza's eyes weren't as easily fooled as the eyes of others may be. She saw a more pronounced Osveta looming beneath the girl's surface and it excited her.

Soon, she thought. *I'll gain another demon servant and be one step closer to ruling.*

Nothing thrilled Ruza more than the thought of coming out of hiding and taking the throne of hell, a place that she felt was rightfully hers. She smiled impishly as she followed the girl and her demon. The night was chilly and the girl wore next to nothing. She was already feeling like a demon, even in her human form. It didn't matter that she seemed terribly upset—Ruza barely noticed. The girl mattered because she was merely a shell for her demon to grow in; the girl's emotions didn't matter at all. All that mattered was that she continue to collect souls and darken her heart for Osveta to exist in her flesh.

The girl veered off the sidewalk and into the park. Ruza stopped at an old crooked oak tree and watched. Normally, Ubiti would be assigned this tedious task, but his mistakes had cost him dearly. Pohlepa was almost useless without Ubiti to guide her, so it was left to Ruza to do everything. But Ruza was prepared to clean up the next mess to ensure nothing happened to the girl before her part in the scheme was done. It would be only a matter of moments before Osveta's lust for murder would be unleashed again—Ruza could almost taste it coming.

Suddenly, the air stilled and complete silence fell. Everything froze. The girl's leg was raised in midstep. Ruza's eyes narrowed suspiciously. Very few things could stop time, even for a second. Except . . .

No! He couldn't have found me . . .

Before her, she saw a shape taking form. Minute particles floated about, fusing together to create—

Ubiti?

Ruza glared into Ubiti's triumphant face. She didn't like the look he wore, nor the power he clearly had wielded to stop time. He was supposed to be locked in a cage of jasper, weakened to the point of a heavy sleep by now. Yet he stood before her, grinning. His very presence unnerved her. Where had he suddenly gained this elite power? Fortunately, he was still her servant, and she could deal with him later. Keeping an eye on Osveta was far more important at the moment.

"How did you get out? Be gone with you, back to your room

until I need you," she demanded, fully expecting her order to take hold right away. It did not.

"I am not yours anymore, witch," he said mischievously. He practically sang the word *anymore*, giving it emphasis.

Ruza puzzled at his declaration. How could he not be? Nobody could break the bind with which she'd ensnared him.

"You are, and you'll be mine until I choose to free you, which I have not."

He ignored her pathetic words. "Master knows what you've been up to, nasty witch."

Ruza's cold heart came back to life, beating in fear, deep within her.

"Impossible! He can never lay eyes on me—I've made sure of it!"

"Not his own eyes, but Ubiti's eyes." His eyes glowed red and he cackled.

"No! How dare you!"

She began to step forward, but he raised his hands, and in them was an old wooden box, the sight of which froze her with fear.

"Master sends a gift. A gift for the witch who would steal his demons and imprison them for her own greed."

The box was dusty and big enough to fit only a ring inside. Ruza's darkened eyes widened. She knew full well what the box encased. For the first time in a long time, true fear flooded her senses.

"No. No . . ." She started to run, but Ubiti opened the box and held it toward her.

Eight long shadowy limbs darted out. Ethereal hands, still connected to the box, reached for Ruza, lifting her slim, fragile body so that she couldn't flee. Her screams were no more than gasps, lost in the icy night. She was the mouse caught by the boa constrictor. Squeezed, helpless. Her neck, each arm, each leg, and waist were held firmly. She began to weep, knowing it was her end. One of the hands plunged into her chest and came back out with her inky-black heart. It beat feebly a few more times before it stopped forever.

Ruza's wasted body was torn in different directions by the terrible, shadowy hands. Once she was in no fewer than six pieces, the hands magically pulled them all into the small box. There was nothing left of the witch except the echoes of her screams.

The box vibrated in Ubiti's hand and then popped out of existence, back to the underrealm where he'd gotten it. Night came back on around Ubiti as the Master restarted time. There would be no more orders from Ruza the witch. It was exhilarating to know the night was completely open to him. He was finally free. Pohlepa was finally free. But Osveta was still locked inside the human girl . . .

Ubiti decided to observe. Osveta had almost taken over the girl's flesh, and if she succeeded in doing so, she would need help adjusting to her human senses. He hoped to see her soon.

35

Mildred fled to the park in a state of embarrassment. What could she have been thinking? She knew zilch about romance. Even with her limited knowledge, she was pretty sure sneaking a kiss from an unsuspecting person while he was fixing your bloody face was probably not that much of a turn-on. Herman's brain was clouding her own judgment with his attraction toward Hyde.

Need more, a familiar voice hissed in her mind.

An icy sensation spread inside Mildred's chest at the sound. This was the last thing she needed at that moment.

"I hoped you'd be gone for good," she grumbled.

Not until we're done.

"Done?" She laughed mirthlessly. "I am done. Why can't you just leave me alone?"

You let me in, you invited me, the voice hissed.

"I'm done with this whole deal and I'll figure out how to break this curse." Mildred's voice rose, growing angry as she cut into the park.

Curse? The voice laughed, amused by her simple assumption.

"So I'm right. You're not a curse. Possession?" Mildred asked. Curses shouldn't be able to talk to you. This was something very different.

The thing inside her changed the subject quite abruptly. *You still need more things. That's why the detective didn't want you. You know it.* The last sentence echoed in her mind, defeating her previous train of thought.

"No," she protested. "He just didn't want to take advantage—"

Didn't you grow any smarter, human? You think he would love you with your murky brown eyes, your lifeless hair? You think he could kiss a mouth with those crooked teeth? He's just like them. He spent his whole life making fun of people like you.

"Stop it! That's not how he is!" Her eyes teared up. "Go away! I can't do it anymore! Just go away!"

I have a better idea . . .

Mildred heard new voices rising in the distance and her throat tightened. Her hands trembled. One of the people was Donna for sure—Mildred could hear her shrill laughter. Seth's deep voice joined in. There was only the two of them coming this way from the sound of it.

". . . and then when you punched her, I was like, wow! Totally unexpected," Seth said.

"I know, like, I didn't expect it, either, I was just so mad," Donna said.

"You are so cool. Patsy would never do anything like that."

Donna grinned and stared up at Seth as though he'd just asked her to prom.

You see? They're happy that they attacked you, happy to hurt you. It's time for you to hurt them! the inner voice shouted, sending vibrations of adrenaline through her body, fueling that consuming hatred within her.

The pair chortled on, coming obliviously closer to her as she stood silently in the dark. She felt the anger charging, roaring within her at their laughter. All the embarrassment from the kiss with Hyde was forgotten. Now there was only the rage she felt for these two, who found her pain comical. While she fumed, her teeth grew into grisly and sharp points. Her fingers grew longer, her nails thicker, sharper, like diamond daggers. She felt as if she could lift a car and throw it at them, and it made her realize that she was growing more demonic than she'd been previously. It was a brief, horrific thought that snuffed away in the face of the demon's blood thirst within her.

Donna was dangerously close. Mildred swiped at her, scratching her cheek with four deep lines. The scent of fresh blood filled the night. It made Mildred's corrupted heart race. The beastly side of her wanted one thing: to devour. Donna screamed angrily, then cried out in fear when she saw the creature in the moonlight. Donna backed up slowly, but Mildred followed with a menacing glare in her bright-red eyes. The fear was intoxicating to Mildred. This emotion that they'd instilled in her for so long was now being reflected back to her, and it felt great.

Donna tripped over a tree root and tumbled onto her back, bumping her head on the ground. Mildred laughed deeply, but it sounded like a growl.

Seth stepped into Mildred's path to block her access to Donna. He had produced a huge hunting knife. Where he got it from and why he had it with him, Mildred had no idea, and she didn't care. It was an obstacle, a hurdle she had to leap to get to her target. Donna's long black hair. Her straight teeth.

Seth's blue eyes caught in a streetlight, and the force in Mildred twitched.

Those eyes! You need them! Such beauties! The voice was eerily gleeful.

"Little boy blue," Mildred teased, oozing words from Aaron. "What are you going to do with that big knife?"

She took his wrist. He was so shaken, he didn't even have time to react as she twisted him around so his back was against her. His left hand was twisted at his back with hers as she also took hold of his right, still holding the knife. He fought hard to keep her from manipulating him, but the sharp point of his knife was at his eye anyway.

"These are going to look so much better on me," she said.

He screamed while she used his own hand to dig the blade into his eye socket, gouging straight through to the brain. She pulled the knife back out with his eyeball sticking on the end. Straight into her mouth it went. The same fate befell his other juicy eye. She flung him away when she was done. His body hit a tree thirty yards away.

"Mmm, not bad," she said. "But he was only an appetizer."

When Mildred turned to the foot of the tree, Donna was gone.

Fortunately for Mildred, Donna was injured and hadn't gone far. Mildred spotted her hobbling near the sidewalk. Her breaths came harsh and whiny with each limp. When Mildred came close, she spun around with her cell phone pointed at her. Bright flashes caught Mildred by surprise.

"Don't frigging come one more step!" Donna shouted, her voice terribly shaken. "I'm going to send these to everyone! Frigging murdering freak!"

In a swift movement, the cell phone was in Mildred's hand instead. She slammed it onto the sidewalk where it busted, pieces flying everywhere, then she dove for Donna.

36

Donna's shattered phone lay on the sidewalk. The cracked and broken screen was splattered with blood, and more blood pooled around it. Her blood. Beside it lay her hand, barely able to move any more than a weak twitch. Her mouth was already void of teeth, taken by the creature while Donna screamed for help and fought the metallic taste that almost drowned her. Donna could feel strands of her hair being yanked and pulled away. She whimpered. Her eyes blinked away fresh tears. The monster crouched over Donna, choking down clumps of her long, beautiful hair. *Help me, Seth,* she thought, but Seth was dead. Then she heard footsteps drawing near. *Seth?* And her vision faded. The last thing she saw was the person wandering yards away, on the street. The last thing Donna's mind registered was *Patsy*.

Ø

Patsy was searching for her boyfriend. She expected to find him with Donna—since the Pal Finder app was showing them near each other—and was looking forward to finally breaking up with him. It had taken her a while, but she had finally realized the maroon lip print on the note in his car was in Donna's favorite shade. Aside from cheating on her, Seth was rude to his parents, smoked cigarettes, and didn't have any sympathy for anyone. After the way he'd helped trick her into leading that group to Millie's tonight, she was done with him for good. No person should ever be treated the way they'd treated Millie. Patsy was just over his cruel, immature ways.

She was also searching for Millie. Patsy only hoped Millie could forgive her now. Everything that had happened back at the Waco home that night had hurt Patsy as much as it'd hurt Millie. Patsy was furious at them all because of it, and felt guilty because it wouldn't have happened if she hadn't been so gullible as to take them straight to Millie's house in the first place. Would Millie ever forgive her?

Patsy had unhooked the necklace she usually wore, where she kept Seth's class ring, fully prepared to throw it in his face when she next laid eyes on him. She'd also ridden the bus home to retrieve Millie's pearl necklace. It was going back where it belonged, with Millie, and Patsy was going to beg for her forgiveness. She'd been unable to reach Seth or Millie at their homes or on their cell phones, but the Pal Finder app was picking up Seth somewhere around the area.

As she searched the night, an eerie sound caught her ears. Her footsteps slowed. Something beside the park was snarling.

Ø

Hyde jogged down the street. By the time he had gotten out of his pajamas and put on street clothes, Mildred was well out of sight. He thought there was a good chance that Mildred would go this way to get back to her house. Relief seeped in as he turned the corner of a building and saw a girl standing near a streetlight. The feeling sank quickly, however. She was the redheaded girl he'd seen hanging out with Aaron's sister and her friends. Not only was she *not* Mildred, but a frozen look of horror was plastered on her face.

That expression got Hyde's blood pumping double time; he picked up speed. Laying a hand on his sidearm, he sprinted toward the girl while he searched the area with his sharp detective eyes. He saw the source of the girl's fear right away, heard the slurping sounds. The thing hovered over a new victim just across the street, but it was too dark to tell what kind of animal it was. Hyde unholstered his sidearm and disengaged the safety feature.

"Stay here," he whispered quietly to the redheaded girl, giving her the stay back hand gesture he used often with his colleagues.

Tears in her eyes glistened in the glow of the streetlight when she nodded, but then she stopped and gasped. The creature had heard him and raised its head. Its horns silhouetted in the moonlight.

"Oh God," the girl cried.

Ø

In a blink, Osveta was on her feet. Her movements were primal as she jumped from a crouch to a standing position. Hyde fired at her as she moved but she was too fast. *Guns,* she thought, *an odd little human gadget*—useless against a demon of her caliber.

In one instance she was standing beside the dying girl, and in the next she was standing a few feet from Hyde and Patsy. Long strands of black hair stuck out of her monstrous mouth. The hunting knife she'd taken was still in her clawed hand.

Don't hurt them, please!

Her head twitched to the side. The girl was fighting hard to take over this body. Osveta hadn't experienced this level of persistence from the girl thus far. Her body jerked. The rage was slipping. She roared.

Stop, stop, stop—

Ø

Hyde's detective instincts noticed quite a few things then. This thing was wearing Mildred's clothes. This thing was barefoot. This thing had Mildred's blue eyes . . .

"M-muh-Mildred? Wha—" Hyde struggled for words, but the horrible realization had taken away his ability to form a coherent thought. He was confused. Should he shoot? No, he couldn't shoot. He knew this . . . thing. It wasn't a thing; it was a girl . . .

Then he saw Mildred before him, all traces of the menacing creature completely gone. Only Mildred Waco. He was no longer confused, although the memory of the creature was already fading in his mind.

Ø

Patsy was scared. She didn't know how, but Donna looked dead and Millie was covered in blood. Her one-time best friend had done this somehow. Patsy was afraid for Millie. Her heart cried out for her, because surely all of the bullying had pushed her to this. All those years of abuse had caused her to finally snap and hurt someone. It never should have happened.

"I'm so sorry, Millie," Patsy said in tears. She felt just as responsible as the abusers, because she'd never actually stopped it, she'd never . . . but events were growing fuzzy. There was a creature . . . Seth was lying in a pool of blood near a tree . . . Donna was dead . . . Mildred must have seen it all. She must be so disturbed that she didn't know how to cope with it.

∅

"Mildred, it's okay now, I'll help you," Hyde said. He still had his gun pointed at her. "Just put down the knife now, it'll be okay."

The girl has a kind heart. It's the last piece. Take it, eat it. Become whole.

"No, no, I can't," Mildred sobbed.

"Yes, you can," Hyde said, completely oblivious to Osveta's coaxing.

Take it! Then, I'll be gone. It's what you want.

"Please," Mildred said. She was trying harder than ever not to give in to Osveta's will, but Osveta was even stronger and more convincing than before.

Or the cop. He is just as kind. We could use his heart, oh yes, we could.

Anger festered beneath her surface but it was different from the rage she'd felt with the others. It swirled around in her, reminding her of Patsy leading the mob to her doorstep. The stiffness in Hyde's lips as they connected with hers, the way he retreated from her as though he'd been singed.

"No!" Mildred cried out in a garbled scream. "Please, don't make me do this."

"I won't, I won't do anything. We'll just talk, okay?" Hyde said calmly, staring down the big barrel of his pistol.

Take the heart and you'll be free of me, girl! Take it!

The bad memories prodded at her and the voice resonated. The hatred tried to slip in, but it couldn't find a stronghold. Little spurts of anger flickered, and Mildred tried to remember good things about Patsy and Hyde. How Patsy always tried to stick up for her, how Hyde had been honestly concerned about her. The way they were both here for her now instead of running away.

Take the heart, or you'll be stuck with me forever!

"Just put the knife down. Let me help you, Mildred, please!" Hyde begged, sounding desperate now.

The knife, Mildred realized. She had forgotten she had it. She'd held it so long that it was warm in her hand—a hand that didn't really belong to her. A hand she'd taken from Tiffany. She looked at it now. It wasn't hers, not really. None of this body was hers. What had she done? And she'd have to kill again or the voice wouldn't stop. It had to stop. She raised her hand with the knife.

"No!" screamed Hyde.

But she brought it down anyway, plunging it straight into her own chest. The voice inside her screamed, then something wispy poured out of the wound in her chest, howling as it escaped, and the voice was gone. Mildred was lying on the pavement with a knife in her chest. Hyde and Patsy crouched beside her. She coughed; blood sputtered from her mouth.

"No, Millie, what did you do? What did you *do*?" Patsy panicked.

"Don't remove the knife, it'll make it worse. Just hold her, talk to her." The detective's words were rushed. Then there was a crackle. He rambled off some numbers and told someone that he had a female stab victim.

It burns, Mildred thought. She felt drunk. The world was swaying as if she was on a boat.

"It's okay," Patsy said, sobbing. "You'll be okay, Millie . . . Mildred! No, don't close your eyes, Mildred, don't close your eyes!"

Mildred didn't want to close her eyes, but they were so heavy and the earth wouldn't stop spinning. It would be okay, just for a while. People who cared about her were here.

She wasn't alone.

EPILOGUE

Patsy felt as if she were stepping onto an unknown planet as she walked through the wide glass doors. She was entering a building that she'd stared at from the outside for two months now. *Am I doing the right thing?* she thought. But there was no time to rethink her decision, because the doors opened into a lobby, with a reception desk front and center. The young man behind the desk had already seen her. His thick glasses and prematurely receding hairline were familiar.

"Mr. Lawrence?" Patsy said. "Wow, it's been a while since I've seen you. Needed a change of scenery?"

"Hello," Mr. Lawrence said. He straightened his thick glasses. "Yes. It's good to see you again, Patsy."

"And you."

"Who are you here to see?" he asked.

"Mildred Waco, please," Patsy said.

"Great, just sign in right here." He picked up a clipboard, fumbled it in his clumsy fingers, then handed it to her.

"Pen?"

"Oh, erm . . ." He searched his desk, lifted his keyboard, moved a potted plant—

"It's okay, I think I might have one."

Patsy smiled politely and rummaged through her purse, eventually locating the pen under a bunch of old receipts. She looked at the clipboard and signed her name, noting the words at the top: Rosewood Mental Health Institute.

Was it too soon? Mildred had been improving, they said. She'd come extremely close to dying. So close that it had affected her mind—specifically, her memory. She'd forgotten almost all her past. She knew some faces but she couldn't recall small details.

"They said she will remember, but it's best to not overwhelm her at first," Mrs. Waco had said.

Mrs. Waco had been delighted when Patsy had given the necklace back to her so she could take it to Mildred when she was ready.

Ø

"I'm so sorry! My mom means well," Patsy explained as she stood at the Wacos' front door. "She really cares about me, and sometimes she makes bad choices."

"I understand," Mrs. Waco said. She ran her thumb over the pearls in her hand, with a sad kind of smile on her face. "I have a daughter too."

"Sorry . . ."

Mrs. Waco was crying. "It's okay, Patsy. It's not your fault. I'm the one who's sorry. I never should have kept you and Mildred from each other. It was stupid—"

"No, *you* care about her, and you didn't know I wasn't the culprit."

"I wish I had known. There are a lot of things I wish I'd known, if only I'd listened. I won't make that mistake again."

"If you're going to press charges, please let me know so I can say good-bye to my mom."

"No, no. The pearls are back, there's no need to . . . I mean . . . I don't want . . . I understand how difficult it can be."

"Yes. Thank you."

Mrs. Waco shrugged. "Water under the bridge, dear. Please, go see Mildred when she's feeling up to it? You're her only real friend." She paused. "She needs you."

But did Mildred need Patsy now? It still felt like yesterday when Mildred had plunged the knife into her own chest. She had been so ill, so deeply disturbed by all the bullying and by the attacks, she hadn't been in her right mind at all. What if seeing Patsy brought too much flooding back to her at once? The thought made Patsy's nerves jitter. During all three bus rides it took her to get here, she kept pondering, but Mrs. Waco's words—*She needs you*—had pushed her this far. She might as well see it through.

Now or never.

Patsy waited until Mr. Lawrence buzzed her through another set of doors and told her what room number to find Mildred in.

The moment she stepped inside the room and saw Mildred's huge smile, she knew she'd made the right choice. Mildred was wearing a cozy dark-blue pajama set, with little yellow stars and moons on it. Mrs. Waco had said that she had bought Mildred a whole new wardrobe and thrown out all her old stuff. Something about needing a change. The pajama top completely covered the scars from the incident and the subsequent surgery. Mildred's long dark hair was brushed neatly. Her skin was clear, with a healthy glow. Her blue eyes were as bright as the sky. She didn't look sick, but Patsy knew that mental illness didn't always show on the outside.

"Patsy?" Mildred said, as if fighting through a fog. She pulled Patsy into a hug and all the doubts she had drifted away. This was all right.

"How are you feeling?" Patsy asked.

"I feel different. Like I've been given a new life," Mildred said.

She seemed different, in a good way. Happier. Her room looked like an actual bedroom, with a bed, nightstand, dresser, bookshelf, and desk. On the wall was a flat-screen TV with a DVD player built in—Mrs. Waco had told Patsy this, because she knew their favorite thing was watching movies together. The only thing that could remind Patsy that this was a hospital bedroom was the lack of windows. The wall was painted a sunny yellow to make up for the lack of sun inside.

Patsy reached into her purse and pulled out a couple of lighthearted family-friendly DVDs.

"I brought your favorites."

"Favorites?" The word seemed foreign to Mildred—*Probably because she has trouble remembering*. She took the DVDs from Patsy and glanced at the covers. "I liked these? They're for children . . ."

"Well, it *was* a long time ago."

"Do you have any others? Anything scary?" Mildred asked.

Patsy hadn't been sure if Mildred would be up for anything

scary after all she'd gone through—after all *everybody* had gone through—but old habits died hard and Patsy hadn't broken her horror film habit yet, although now she found some scenes difficult at times.

"I always come prepared."

It felt like old times, except Mildred seemed a lot braver now. The days of covering her eyes at the scary parts were long gone, and instead, it was Patsy who was a little shaken by some of the scenes. Too much blood made her think of Mildred lying in a pool of it on the ground with that hard, sharp metal jabbed through her center. Any glimpse of a creature reminded Patsy of the thing they'd seen that night, the thing that had attacked Aaron, Chelle, Yvette, Seth, Donna, and Tiffany—whose remains had been found in the woods a few weeks later. Tyler was still technically listed as a missing person, but everyone had their theories.

It turned out a bear had wandered into Roanoke and attacked everyone. Every time Patsy thought about it, it just sounded so lame. She'd told the police time after time that the thing she'd seen wasn't a bear. "You were so afraid, your mind must have been playing tricks," they'd said.

Ø

"*Detective Hyde, please back me up,*" Patsy said.

"*It was dark when we saw the thing standing over Donna,*" he told them. "*Then immediately after the thing fled, Mildred showed up, blaming herself . . . hurting herself. I don't think we're thinking clearly right now . . .*"

Ø

Hyde hadn't been much help in identifying the creature. It almost seemed like he was ashamed of what he'd seen. What they'd *both* seen. It wasn't a bear, but the only person who would listen to her was Joan Renfro. Joan's mother had returned for her son's funeral and Joan had left town to live with her. Now there was nobody who believed Patsy. Nobody she could talk to about it.

Mildred might have stuck up for her, but she would never bring up that horrific time to Mildred. Mildred was in recovery, and if she had forgotten what had gone on, then good for her.

By the time Patsy left, she was pleased with how it had all gone and eager to visit again as soon as possible. She was already making plans as she stepped out the double glass doors—

"Hey, chickadee! I thought you'd be out of here by now."

Kathy Porter was outside in a shiny yellow Camaro. Patsy's mouth dropped. Kathy was grinning from ear to ear.

"Mom?" Patsy asked skeptically. "Where did you get this?"

"I met a new friend today and he got it for me. Hop in."

Weird, Patsy thought. But switching buses three times to get home was a pain. She sat in the passenger seat and her foot touched something small. A tiny glass vial that looked familiar.

ACKNOWLEDGMENTS

A huge thanks to my editors, Jen and Rebecca, for their brilliance and hard work. Thanks to my family, who always believed in me, even during the bad times. And thanks to everyone at Wattpad who stood in my corner—both the staff and my readers.

ABOUT THE AUTHOR

Sam Schill penned her first story at age nine, after telling scary stories as a child. She's had a slew of jobs in retail, housekeeping, and even dabbled in tattooing, but writing has always been the most natural to her. When she isn't reading or writing horror, Sam enjoys art and '90s music karaoke. She lives in Southeastern Kentucky with her family.

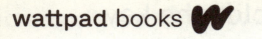

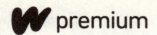 premium

Supercharge your Wattpad experience.

Go Premium and get more from the platform you already love. Enjoy uninterrupted ad-free reading, access to bonus Coins, and exclusive, customizable colors to personalize Wattpad your way.

Try Premium **free** today.